with or
without you

with or without you

BRIAN FARREY

Simon Pulse

New York London Toronto Sydney

SIMON PULSE
An imprint of Simon & Schuster Children's Publishing Division
1230 Avenue of the Americas, New York, NY 10020
First Simon Pulse paperback edition May 2011
Copyright © 2011 by Brian Farrey
All rights reserved, including the right of reproduction
in whole or in part in any form.
SIMON PULSE and colophon are registered trademarks of Simon & Schuster, Inc.
For information about special discounts for bulk purchases, please contact
Simon & Schuster Special Sales at 1-866-506-1949 or
business@simonandschuster.com.
The Simon & Schuster Speakers Bureau can bring authors to your live event. For
more information or to book an event contact the Simon & Schuster Speakers
Bureau at 1-866-248-3049 or visit our website at www.simonspeakers.com.
Designed by Cara Petrus and Karina Granda
The text of this book was set in Stone Serif.
Manufactured in the United States of America
2 4 6 8 10 9 7 5 3
Library of Congress Control Number 2010038722
ISBN 978-1-4424-0699-5
ISBN 978-1-4424-0700-8 (eBook)

Excerpts from KEITH HARING JOURNALS by Keith Haring, copyright © 1996, 2010
by The Keith Haring Foundation, Inc. Used by permission of Viking Penguin,
a division of Penguin Group (USA) Inc.

Lyrics from the song "Hard" used by permission of Gregory Douglass.
All rights reserved.

The author has been remiss in expressing his heartfelt thanks
to those teachers in his life who encouraged and nurtured him
as a writer. He'd like to make up for that now by
dedicating this book to them:

Donna Weber
Sheila Pervisky
Lois Dassow
Ann Kroll
Mike Hensgen
Mary Greenlaw-Meyer
Helen Cartwright
Priscilla Voitman
Anton Dern
Dick Cavanaugh
Ted Moskonas
Bob Slaby
J.D. Whitney
Bill Deering
Mary Jo Pehl
Deborah Keenan
Sheila O'Connor
Lawrence Sutin
David Haynes
Patricia Weaver Francisco
Mary Logue
Susan Power
Brian Malloy

Looking at the list now, it seems smaller than I imagined.
I guess it's their fondly remembered contributions that make
it all seem much, much more vast.

Pure Art exists only on the level of instant response to pure life.

—Keith Haring

rules

Hit the ground.

  Curl into a ball.

  Cover your head.

  Don't cry. Ever.

All this I know. It is instinct, as automatic as any breath, any blink, any beat of the heart. I repeat eighteen years' worth of these hard-learned lessons over and over in my head, waiting for the hail of blows to stop.

I worry it won't be enough.

Over the war cries and laughs from above, I hear a whimper. It's Davis. He's nearby and while I can't see him, I know he's gone fetal, mirroring my position on the ground. I'm still, silent. I offer no sport. But Davis just made a mistake. His groan earns him the undivided attention of our attackers. I venture one impossibly short glance out between my elbows. Four different pairs of feet launch into a vicious, steel-toed assault on my best friend.

"You got something to say, faggot?"

Pete Isaacson, of course. I dare another look and see five of them total. The usual suspects. Pete's mob from the wrestling team: the troglodytes. Pete lords over them all in his trademark bowling shoes, burnished emerald and ochre. Two glints of gun-metal silver, dog tags on a chain around his neck, shoot the sun's reflection like a laser. He's grinning. "Come on, faggot. Lemme hear you howl."

When Davis doesn't answer, Pete stomps on Davis's hip, eliciting a scream. I'm too sore to take in a breath. I can only send silent pleas to Davis: *Shut up, shut up, shut up.* Davis sobs. The savage blows pitch his short, skinny body this way and that.

Don't cry. Ever.

I've never cried during a beating. I used to think that I didn't want to give them the satisfaction of knowing they'd hurt me. The real reason? Crying solves nothing. I only do things that make a difference. Like now. When I summon the strength to cough.

The effect is instantaneous. Three of the trogs break off and renew their assault on me. One of them falls to his knees, pummeling the side of my head and my right arm with his fists. A year and a half ago, Kenny Dugan broke that arm when he slammed me into a locker. That might be him now, trying to recapture the glory. So, I do all I can do. I take a diversion.

LOCAL TEEN DEAD IN
GAY-BASHING INCIDENT

Madison, Wis.—Authorities are questioning five local wrestlers in the death of Evan Weiss, a senior at Monona High School. Just one day before all six were set to graduate, the students are facing charges of first-degree murder in what authorities are describing as a clear case of gay bashing.

Weiss and his best friend, Davis Grayson, were walking home after the last day of school when the suspects allegedly jumped the pair in a field behind the school and beat them.

Grayson remains hospitalized in critical care.

Perhaps most tragic is that Weiss died mere blocks from the state capitol, where Governor Doyle Petersen is days away from signing major hate-crime legislation into law.

When asked to comment on the incident, Governor Petersen said, "It's difficult to comment without all the facts. But once these boys are found guilty, I plan to lobby for the death penalty and see those little fuckers fry."

My self-inflicted fantasy does the trick and carries me away into unconsciousness. I don't know how much later it is when I feel someone gently prodding my chest.

I move and my body explodes. A discharge of pain from my shoulder leaves my right arm flaccid. I wail and pull it to my chest.

I look up at Davis. His left eye is swollen; it'll be completely shut by morning. His sandy blond hair juts out in every direction, decorated with grass clippings. Dark streaks crisscross his face like war paint and, with the sun disappearing behind trees and houses, shadow and blood fuse into one.

"A car drove by and they freaked." His whisper is like grinding glass. "You were out. I didn't know what to do."

He holds out his hand to help me up but I shrink away, keeping my right arm against my chest. He sees this.

"Is it broken?"

I vividly remember what it felt like when Kenny broke it—a river of knives flowing up to my shoulder—and this does not feel like that. I shake my head and, using my good arm, push off the ground. We stand facing each other for a moment, each fading into a silhouette. We limp back to my house.

octagon

From the safety of my bedroom window, I watch day retreat, leaving a scarlet-toned dusk. Colors ebb into shadows, segregating the houses on our street. Two blocks over, I hear joyous shouts from James Madison Park, heralding summer vacation for one and all on Lake Mendota. I want to enjoy this, my favorite season, but enjoying hurts.

Davis sits at the edge of my unmade bed, his feet not even reaching the floor. He's playing with the tear in his shirt. It's his favorite shirt. His mother bought it for his birthday a year ago. He's protective of things his mother buys for him. It's ruined now.

Davis smolders—corrugated brow, blue-flame glare. Everything in him focuses on a single spot on the floor. He is gone.

"So close, eh?" I ask, shaking my head. "Almost made it the whole school year. Timing couldn't be worse. I was going to make us T-shirts—'372 days without a work-place beating.'"

It should get a reaction. It doesn't. I press on.

"I heard Pete's going to Ohio State. Wrestling scholar-ship. I think they should offer a scholarship to anyone who can explain how wrestling is *not* gay."

Still nothing.

I should know better. What happened today wasn't typical. Pete and the trogs went all out. Way beyond being slammed into a locker or given a simple black eye. This wasn't just bullying. With graduation coming, this was their last hurrah. They wanted a memento: perma-nent damage. So, I shouldn't be making light of it. Why can't I stop?

Because I have to reach him. I have to reach Davis. It's what I know.

I pull our triage kit out from under my bed and kneel next to Davis. I can smell his blood. The scent overpow-ers the sharp sting of acrylic paint and turpentine in my room. I can only smell blood.

"I think Kenny Dugan is staying here in Madison but I heard he couldn't get into the UW. I wonder if the Tech offers a major in 'Duh.'"

Davis glares at the floor, avoiding my eyes. But the corner of his mouth shoots up, just for a second. Almost there. Drive it home.

I lower my voice and do my best Kenny. "Yeah, I'm here to major in 'Duh' and minor in"—I strum my lips up and down with my finger—"bebedebedbeebededebe."

Davis shouts, "Quit being such a tardmonkey! This isn't funny."

His voice shakes on "funny" and his periwinkle eyes moisten.

We don't say anything. I dab at his face with a dry sponge. He returns the favor. The routine is sad but has a strange, familiar comfort.

I stare over Davis's left shoulder at the wall by the head of my bed where half a dozen of my own paintings hang. Each one evokes the style of a different artist—O'Keefe, Seurat, Van Gogh—but the subject matters are mine.

Unlike my predecessors, I don't paint on canvas. I paint on glass. I go to auctions and pawn shops to buy old windows. Some still framed, others just sheets of glass. Oval, rectangle, I've even got a triangle. I built my own easel years ago out of an old music stand and a series of rusty vise clamps that extends out in a bunch of Shiva-like arms. Davis dubbed it THE CLAW. It's heavy and awkward, but I can position the window with the clamps and angle it toward whatever I want to capture. Then I paint the image I see through the glass, stroke by stroke, until the world beyond the window is replaced with my acrylic reality. My sister, Shan, used to tease me by calling it "poor man's paint-by-number." I miss my sister.

My favorite is an octagon-shaped window, just more than a foot across, with an oak border and slats that divide the glass into a tic-tac-toe board. I found it at an estate sale at an old farm house about twenty miles north of Madison. I lugged it around with me this past year, painting different scenes into each of the little squares within. This is what's in each box:

The perfectly toned pec of a UW volleyball player	The Orpheum movie theatre marquee with two lights burned out	The snake-like chain shackled to a bike in James Madison Park
Two chop-sticks next to a broken fortune cookie on a white plate	A stack of lead bars, as seen on the Wisconsin state flag	The antique doorknob to the Rainbow Youth Center
A street map of Madison with a large star labeled YOU ARE HERE	Three blue squiggles and two yellow circles on a white background	

Each box depicts a moment from my nine-year friendship with Davis. A moment that represented a turning point for us. A moment when everything that followed could no longer impersonate what had gone before. The last box is empty. My plan was to fill it in tonight after our last day of high school—with what, I still don't know. Of all my work, this is also Davis's favorite. He doesn't know it, but I've been planning to give it to him as a graduation gift.

I'm no longer sure that's a good idea. None of the images represents the Davis sitting in front of me. The Davis that I see in my mosaic hasn't been around for several months. Senior year was hard. I keep hoping that if I wait it out long enough, the Davis I grew up with will come back. But I don't think that's going to be tonight.

I wish Davis had a diversion, like I do. I envision my death and the repercussions for those who remain. It's not, as I've explained to Davis countless times, a wish for death. I just find a strange solace in the imagined aftermath.

Davis is logical. He has no use for imagination. He has no way of escaping. So everything rots inside him. Davis rarely chooses anger.

He chooses it now.

Like an eruption, he leaps from my bed. I fall back,

9

favoring my left side. Davis slams my bedroom door shut. He kicks the wall. My paintings—most hung from hooks by thin wire—dance in place. His face, freshly cleaned, is marred with more tears. This is not my best friend. This person is molten. Dangerous.

He falls to his knees on my lousy old carpeting and keens. I have seen Davis cry many times. High-pitched and intermittent. Not this time. His sobs are low and forceful, what I'm sure the end of the world will sound like.

"I hate this fucking city!" He pulses, beating useless fists into the floor. It's a sentiment we've both uttered over the years, neither completely believing it. But he makes me believe it now.

I kneel next to him; he sobs uncontrollably. I lay my left arm across his shoulders, easing my right arm around his front, and I hold him. These moments—where consolation seems impossible—are rare, but I've always excelled at getting us through. He continues to cry, words reduced to fevered gibberish. He shakes. I shake.

"Don't forget," I whisper, praying quietly for the words that will fix this. If they exist. "Chicago. In the fall. College."

The University of Chicago has glimmered on the horizon since last summer. No matter what happened, we told ourselves, "Next year, we'll be in Chicago." The worry that ate our lives for months—would we both get in?—vanished when our acceptance letters came in January. Done deal. Escape from trogs, from parents, from everything that held us down never felt closer than when we discussed our college plans.

"Chicago" is the magic word. Davis stops shaking. This is where, if we were boyfriends, I would kiss him. But we never went there, he and I. That's not who we are, and that's not who we can be. That was decided long ago. Maybe forever ago.

His peace evaporates. Davis gets up and paces a fiery swath across my room. "And do what? Meet another version of Pete Isaacson in college and get the shit kicked out of us all over again? No. Bullshit. I'm sick of this. We're done. Right now."

I've seen this. Heard this. For nine years. And like saying he hates Madison, I believe he means it. And it worries me.

He reaches into his pocket and pulls out a crumpled piece of paper, which he thrusts in my face. It's a lousy photocopy job of a handwritten flyer:

CHASERS
Learn what it means to be gay!
Stop being a doormat!
Join Chasers
First meeting: this Friday
7:00 p.m. RYC—Upstairs, room Four

11

"These were posted at the Rainbow Youth Center," Davis says as he continues to pace.

The Rainbow Youth Center, Madison's only hangout for GLBT teens, is always starting new social groups. But the notices are usually typed, with tacky clip art. This one pings my radar as suspect.

There's something familiar about this: the energy burning in his eyes, the apprehension building in my stomach. Probably because I've spent nine years following Davis on any number of schemes aimed at making us fit in, finding us friends besides each other. None of them has worked. But I always followed. I probably always will.

"Sure," I say, setting the paper down. "If that's what you want."

I don't argue. Davis has enough on his mind. Next week, he's moving into the shelter at the RYC. His dad, one of those "you're eighteen, you're graduated, you're no longer my responsibility" kind of guys, is kicking him out. He thinks it will build Davis's character. I think he's an asshole.

My response calms him down but his eyes are still determined. Then, a grin slides across his face.

"Besides," he says, "maybe we'll meet some hot guys. We could use a couple dates, right? First time for everything."

His laugh sounds more like a grunt. I nod, but I look to the side. My eyes would give too much away.

"C'mere." I ask him to take the octagon off the wall, which he does without question. We go downstairs and into the empty garage. I tell him to take a seat on a stool while I attach the window to THE CLAW. Every time I tighten a vise clamp to secure the octagon, my tender arm threatens mutiny.

Davis laughs nervously. "What are you doing?"

I hide the pain as I fasten the last clamp. "I'm finishing your graduation present."

His mouth drops and forms a smile for just a moment. He winces—smiling hurts—and lets his face harden again. His unswollen eye meets my gaze, saying what a smile can't. Not thanks, exactly.

I turn THE CLAW so it's facing Davis and I push it toward him, zooming in until his ravaged, discolored eye fills the last empty box in the lower right corner. I squirt paint from my wrinkled tubes onto a palette and quickly begin to mix colors.

Davis stiffens. He wants to be perfectly still while I paint. He wants me to get it right. He knows that I paint honesty. I can do sunsets and perfect pecs when the moment merits. But I can also do life when it breaks and you can't ignore it. Davis respects that about me.

I stare through the glass at my best friend's grotesque

eye, preparing to make Pete's handiwork my own. I choose to mimic Seurat with this picture. Painting hundreds of tiny dots should give Davis time to stress down. "I'm calling this: *Last Time*."

"Fuck, yeah," he whispers with that darkness I've grown to fear. The Davis I know has taken his leave again. "Last time."

His eyes, using our unspoken shorthand, tell me he's got something planned. I don't ask. I can only wait. It's what I do. He gets reckless and I fix things. That's the way it's always been.

"Hold still."

I paint hurt.

TITLE: *Perfection*

IMAGE:
The perfectly toned pec of a
UW volleyball player

INSPIRATION:
A single panel of Warhol's
Marilyn Monroe prints

PALETTE:
Flesh tone = lavender
Musculature highlights = pink
Nipple = off-white
Background = cobalt

The strokes are thick and precise. The colors are harsh, surreal, like holding a Technicolor film negative to the light. There is no doubt a lifetime of push-ups crafted the subject. From a distance, the contours resemble a child's failed attempt at drawing a circle.

A year ago, Davis and I took THE CLAW to James Madison Park. I tried to paint Lake Mendota while he sorted through

college brochures. A gaggle of shirtless UW guys were play-
ing volleyball nearby. Davis was so busy drooling over the
guys that it took no time at all to talk him into the most
convenient choice for school: the University of Chicago. I
started mixing blues on my palette, our futures decided.

When the game finished, one of the volleyball players—
not too muscley, but not exactly rail thin like I was—made to
leave the park, then turned and walked straight at us. Davis
and I shared a glance: When guys with arms that big come
our way, pain typically follows.

Not this guy. He smiled, looked THE CLAW up and
down, then asked what it was all about. I explained how
I paint on windows. Volleyball Guy smiled again, said he
loved the idea, and asked if I ever painted people. I told
him the truth: I'd never painted a person. Only still life.
Expecting him to leave, I turned back to have another go at
painting the lake.

Volleyball didn't leave. "Maybe you just need a model?"

He kept staring right into my eyes, pouty lips in a half
smile. His head, while in no way unattractive, had a slightly
atypical shape, like a square egg. It was kinda sexy.

My body tensed, still not convinced this wasn't a joke
where the punch line involved actual punching.

That's when I caught Davis's glare: Are you crazy? He's
gorgeous. Do it.

Volleyball stood there as I lined up the window, wiped

the glass clean, and painted his pec. Davis tried to make small talk but Volleyball gave only one-word answers: His eyes never left me. When I was done, Volleyball came to my side of the window to inspect my work. He laughed, clapped me on the shoulder, and said, "So you're a chest man?"

Volleyball tossed his shirt over his shoulder and dug in his pocket. He scribbled his phone number on the back of an old receipt and told me that he knew someone at an art gallery who might be interested in my work, because my medium was so unique. I thanked him and tucked the receipt in my pocket as he walked away.

All the way home, Davis talked about how cool it would be if Volleyball could hook me up with an art gallery. But we laughed it off. We didn't get beat up this time, but guys like that never helped guys like us.

Later that night, I examined the receipt and found Volleyball's name—Erik—and phone number, followed by a single word:

Dinner?

secret

When I stumble bleary-eyed into the kitchen for breakfast, Mom stops darting around the kitchen and gags into her coffee cup when she sees me. At first, I think she notices: the scrapes on the side of my head, the light purple bruises shaped like knuckles that dot my chin. My war wounds are subtle and could be the result of anything. One of those mysterious doors that I always claim to walk into. Maybe if I hadn't fed her a steady diet of stories growing up, explanations for where various black eyes and sore wrists came from, she'd take more interest. My fault, I guess. Still, given that she bought every story, she must believe painting is a full-contact sport.

Her eyes fix on the graduation gown I'm wearing, a little test-drive before the main event. I pour a bowl of Cheerios as she eyes me up and down, a slightly guilty frown crossing her lips. "Graduation's tonight. Isn't it?"

"Got it in one," I say, drowning my cereal in milk.

"Don't be smart," Mom warns. She's running late, snatching at stacks of inventory lists and spreadsheets before pulling her long green work smock from a hook on the wall. "Gina called in sick and I'm opening alone. I'm not in the mood."

We live above the small corner grocery store that she and Dad own. The store's cute, old-fashioned. We let customers run up a tab and we deliver groceries to people's homes, to give you an idea. You have to watch TV Land to even know what a grocery tab is anymore.

Mom's stress is easy to understand. Last week, Dad fell down the stairs. Broke his leg and shattered his hip bone. He's in pretty rough shape and getting him around is not easy. The burden of keeping things running is all on her, and pressure is not her friend. It doesn't help that every day since his accident, Dad's been calling down every half hour to make sure she's handling things. Right now, I can tell she's not handling the thought of more questions about handling things.

I grimace, sucking air in through my clenched teeth. My arm, which was sore yesterday, is practically unusable this morning. Time to dig out my sling.

"Shan mixed up her flight," Mom mutters, and it takes me a moment to realize she's talking to me. "She won't be at graduation tonight."

I drop my spoon into the bowl. "You're kidding, right?"

Shannon, my older sister, lives with her husband, Brett, in New York City. She's taking the summer off from grad school to come home and help around the store while Dad's laid up. She was *supposed* to be flying in this afternoon so she could make it to graduation.

"Joan!" Dad calls from the bedroom. I can hear him down the hall, grunting and gasping as he fusses to get dressed. "Joan, it's Thursday. It's Dairy Day. You need to call Land O'Lakes to—"

"—get the milk order in, I know!" Mom hollers back. "Have you taken your pills?"

My mother becomes an asylum escapee: wild green eyes, clenched fists, gritted teeth. No one can push Mom's buttons like Dad.

"Listen," I offer diplomatically, "since getting Dad around is such a pain, I'll understand if you need to skip the ceremony tonight." I measure my tone. It says *I'm only thinking of you* and not *Please, for the love of God, don't come to graduation*.

Neither message is received. She peers at her reflection in the microwave, fixes her hair, and heads to the door.

"Don't forget. Your summer hours start tomorrow. No running off with *him* until work is done." Anyone unfamiliar with a Wisconsin dialect wouldn't know that *him* is how Mom pronounces "Davis."

That's it. No "Happy graduation." No "Congratulations." An outsider would assume my parents and I don't like each other. "Like" doesn't figure into it. It's more a matter of failed comprehension on both sides. They think, *How did we raise a daughter who's outgoing and a son who's an introvert?* I think, *Who wants to run a grocery store?* Trying to be helpful, I offer, "Ceremony starts at seven. Just, you know, so you have time to get Dad down the stairs—"

Mom clenches her teeth, growls, and slams the door on her way out.

"Joan!" Dad calls. "It's Dairy Day!"

I meet Davis near the Coke machine in the commons at school. It's half an hour until graduation and we're two bruises in a sea of goldenrod robes. I've got my sore arm in an old sling, hidden under my robe. Davis is antsy, his eyes darting everywhere, his fingers flexing open and shut. I know he's looking for Pete and the trogs. If they plan to continue what they started in the field, it'll be tonight.

"Isn't Shan coming?" Davis asks. I follow his eyes to where everyone's families are filing into the gymnasium for the ceremony. I spot my folks. Where other parents dressed up a little, Mom's still wearing her clothes from work. Dad's in a wheelchair, his leg thrust out in front of him like a lance. He's wearing his red flannel shirt, the one he wears when he works the meat counter at the store. Classy.

"No," I grumble. The one person in the family I wanted at graduation and she screws up her flight home. But I can't complain. Davis's dad is, of course, absent. And his mom . . .

Davis isn't listening anymore. He's spotted Pete and the trogs across the way. They're not even looking at us. Just laughing to one another. Instead of honors cords, Pete's wearing those stupid dog tags over the top of his gown.

Out of the corner of my eye, I see Davis's arm retract into his gown. His fingers emerge a moment later, a flash of silver catching the light.

"What are you—" I gasp, snatching his wrist with my good hand and pulling his arm toward me. I nearly nick myself on the kitchen knife he's palmed.

"Pete's two spots behind me in the processional," Davis says through gnashed teeth, his eyes never leaving Pete. "He's gonna try something tonight. I know it. If he touches me, if he even comes near me . . ."

Even with his fist clenched, it's easy to pry the knife from his small hand. I toss it in a nearby garbage can.

"Are you crazy?" I say before he can protest. "Tonight, Pete's just a turbo-douche. Nothing illegal about that.

A knife"—I point to the garbage—"can land you in jail. Pete can't touch you. There're witnesses everywhere. Just relax."

His jaw stiffens but he won't stop glaring at Pete. "I'd like to shove those dog tags—"

The destination of the dog tags will forever remain a mystery because Vice Principal Hagen enters with a bull-horn and begins directing students to line up for the pro-cessional. Dutifully, we arrange ourselves alphabetically, which separates me from Davis. But from the back of the line, I keep an eye on him and hope that knife was the only thing he hid under his gown.

The orchestra plays and we enter the gymnasium. The center of the gym is filled with folding chairs for the graduates. Friends and family flank the chairs on either side, sitting on bleachers. Flashbulbs ignite the air. Look-ing around, I see people weeping through smiles. Before I take my seat, I catch sight of my folks in the front row. Mom's checking her watch. Dad shifts uncomfortably in his wheelchair.

The choir sings. Principal Andrews speaks. Our vale-dictorian drones on about the future and the friendships we've made during our "school careers." How great it was to share these years together. It's all I can do not to laugh. Ask Davis's swollen face about sharing these years.

23

There are tears. There is boredom. I want it to be over with. What feels like a year later, we're all asked to stand.

Do not applaud for the individual graduates; hold all applause until the last graduate has received their diploma.

The crowd is not deterred. They holler and whoop for their favorites. Someone from the orchestra shouts, "Hey, Boom Boom!" as Heather Carter, class slut, shakes the principal's hand. If she's embarrassed by the nickname, she doesn't show it. I stand on my toes and look toward the head of the line. Davis must be near the front by now. I've got his back, scanning the line to see if Pete's preparing.

"Davis Grayson."

Davis takes the stage with a confident strut. If I didn't know him, I might be fooled. As he shakes the principal's hand, someone in the bleachers yells, "Faggot!" There is laughter. Davis turns in the direction of the shout, glares, and flips the bird. Gasps, boos. Davis is ushered offstage by a teacher. I catch a glimpse of Pete, who's laughing. Big surprise.

Our assembly line trudges forward. As I get to the stage, I look over at my parents. Holy shit, Mom brought a camera. Ten bucks says Shan had to remind her. Now I have to worry about smiling. I almost miss hearing my name.

"Evan Weiss."

Posture perfect, stride sure. Shake hands, pause for picture. Then, from somewhere out in the crowd, comes a piercing whistle. Not derisive, but celebratory. It's certainly not my parents; they're grimacing at the noise. It's not Davis; he can't whistle. The warbling, lauding whistle continues until I finish crossing the stage and step down.

Weird.

More words. More choir. Canary cardboard hats sail into the air and then there is screaming. Lots and lots of screaming. The orchestra starts up and everyone begins filing out. I navigate my way through the mob and meet up with Davis near the front of the stage. Angry, knife-wielding Davis is gone. He smiles and my closest friend is back. We hug and cry and, with everyone else doing the same, for the first time ever, we go unnoticed.

"Next stop: Chicago!" Davis whoops.

I scan the crowd, hoping the mystery whistler will appear. No suspects emerge.

Davis glances at his watch. "Shit. I gotta get the car home."

I nod. "Yeah, my 'rents are probably waiting in the parking lot. Mom will need my help maneuvering Dad into the car."

He nods. "See you tomorrow, right? Chasers. RYC."

We separate, negotiating the current of sobbing families.

I make my way to the exit on the side of the gymnasium. A hand waving near the back of the bleachers catches my eye. I squint. Someone definitely wants me. I head over and once I'm close, the hand grabs my shoulder and pulls me into the shadowy niche below the bleachers. I flinch, squeezing my eyes shut.

Hit the ground.

Curl into a ball.

I brace for the whiff of wrestler sweat coupled with the first blow. But there is no sweat, only chai-scented breath. Instead of a fist in my stomach, soft, full lips press hard against my own. I don't need to open my eyes to know what's happening. I go back to the volleyball game at Madison Park, almost a year ago. The one that lead to my first date. My first yoga lesson. My . . .

When the lips pull away slowly and I finally open my eyes, Erik grins at me in the crosshatch of light filtering down through the bleachers. Breathing becomes something I forget how to do. My insides lurch, powered by shock and ecstasy.

His brow scrunches and I worry that he's mistaken my surprise for disappointment or fear. He asks, "What happened?"

I wipe my eyes. "This? No biggie. Tears of joy, y'know?"

Erik takes hold of my chin and tilts my head left to right, like a mother inspecting for dirt. He examines the bruises and cuts that Mom missed this morning. Thankfully, he can't see my arm.

"Did somebody hit you?"

I have seen Erik angry exactly twice since we started dating a year ago. Last fall, when he lost out on a scholarship that he should have gotten, and on Christmas, when his car was broken into and the gifts he'd gotten his family were all stolen. He's never once been angry with me. He is not angry with me now. But he is not happy.

And I see my life for what it is: a pentimento. That's what they call it when an artist changes his mind while working on a painting—choosing another perspective, varying the color palette—so they paint over what they've already done, obscuring the original work. But over time, the paint can grow thin. Aborted lines and faded images begin to show through. And something that was never meant to be seen becomes all too evident.

My life—the one before I met Erik—cowers in the background, ghostly images of a family that doesn't get me, classmates who ridicule me, and a lone friend. My life since Erik bursts in the foreground with bright images from a year of walks at sundown, holding hands at the zoo, learning yoga, and being held tightly for the first time while completely naked.

For eleven months, I've managed to keep the layers

of my life separate. No one knows I have a boyfriend. Not my parents, not my best friend, not my sister. Here, with Erik in close proximity to the life I've hidden from him, the two works smear together in a pastiche of clashing hues. I knew this would happen at some point. Obscuring the background takes more skill than I've got.

I offer a small laugh. "If someone had hit me, wouldn't I send my manly-man boyfriend out to knock him around a little?"

Royal blood surges through my veins: I am the King of Evasions. I can change a subject with the deftness of a judo master. And no one notices when I do this. Not my parents. Not Davis.

But in Erik, I've met my match. He is the first person ever to call me on my avoidance tactics. He has two looks: The first says, *I'm not buying it. Tell me what's wrong.* The second says, *I'm not buying it but I'm going to respect your privacy and hope you'll explain things to me later.* I'm glad when he chooses the latter. I'm more glad that he has two looks he's devised for these situations, two looks just for me.

I'm marking time. Trying to recover my wits without hyperventilating. Reeling from the idea of it: Erik Goodhue, the college boy I've been secretly dating for nearly a year, is standing here in my high school. Here.

I'm scrambling for something, anything, to say.

"Were you here for the whole ceremony?" I ask, trying to carefully remove my arm from the sling under my robe and slide it back into the sleeve of my gown before he notices. I must look like I'm doing the Hokey Pokey for Dummies. My sore arm emerges from the empty sleeve and I hold him around the waist.

If he notices anything, he chooses to keep quiet. Erik cups the back of my head in his hand and draws me gently forward until our foreheads touch. His burnt sienna eyes are inches from my own.

"The whole thing," he whispers. "Wouldn't miss it."

I kiss him and, even after eleven months, I'm still astonished when he kisses me back.

I poke him in the chest. "That was you. The whistle."

His eyes dart side to side with impish denial. "Who? Me?"

That earns him another kiss.

The tumult in the gym decrescendoes as more people vacate. By now, Mom's probably muttering under her breath, wondering why I'm not helping her load Dad in the car. I'm torn. I don't want Erik to have to hide into the shadows. But he has thus far accepted his role as the Secret Boyfriend. *You'll tell your folks when you're ready,* he's said dozens of times, in that patient way of his. I've always suspected that patience would be finite. So far, it isn't.

29

So far.

I want to take his hand and walk out with him. Go right up to my folks and say, *This is my boyfriend, Erik. He's a nursing student at the UW, he's graduating this summer, and we're very happy.* But I don't want this to happen more than I sometimes wish it would.

Erik, as usual, is two steps ahead of my neuroses. "Look, I know you gotta go do the family thing and all. Maybe meet up with Davis later?"

I blush. Erik has always respected my friendship with Davis. His best friend is a guy named Tyler. They grew up together in Arizona, came to the UW together. Erik understands that impossibly close bond, carving out time in your life for that person who's always been there. But Erik knows there's absolutely nothing romantic between Davis and me. If Erik has a problem with me being close to Davis, he's never voiced it. There are many things, I suspect, Erik's never voiced. His need to trust me stops him.

He slips a small cream-colored envelope into my hand, mischief tinting his eyes. "Details for Saturday night." Saturday, we celebrate my graduation privately . . . but he won't tell me what he's planning. My guess: Inside this envelope, all will be revealed.

"And if you show," he teases, raising his eyebrows, "there just might be a present in it for you."

I grin and gush playfully. "A present. For me?"

Erik bites his lower lip and nods. "Yep. Well, presents. A couple. A few."

God, he's cute when he does that lip thing.

I promise Erik I'll see him Saturday. One more kiss, then his signature farewell: "Miss me."

Like I could do anything but.

Erik slips unnoticed into the stream of exiting families and I brace myself for the walk out to the parking lot.

My parents glare as I approach. Mom wordlessly opens the passenger door and I gently scuttle Dad into his seat. Mom hands me the digital camera before climbing into the driver's seat. I browse the memory card to find she took one shot of me shaking the principal's hand. It's blurry and the top of my head is cut off. Ansel Adams, eat your heart out.

On the drive home, Mom and Dad drone on to each other about the state of the grocery store. I've heard this all my life. They might as well be reading from a script. Two topics of conversation in our house: how the store is doing (usually bad) and what Shan is working on. Tonight, they debate changing vendors to cut costs. It's like they hadn't just sat for two hours in a fluorescent tomb of a gymnasium watching me graduate.

But this is how we are, my parents and me. Shan was

the outgoing, popular kid. I am the silent enigma. Sad as it sounds, I've come to see their indifference as a kind of acceptance. They don't even care that I'm gay. When I came out, I had a fantasy that they'd get angry. Scream and shout. But they said nothing. Sometimes I wish they'd at least gotten mad. It would have meant they felt something.

Quietly, I thumb open the envelope to find a pink notecard inside. Erik's neat, slanted script commands: *7:00—Saturday—The Studio.*

"Evan!"

Looking up, I find Mom staring at me in the rearview mirror. Her tone says this is probably the third time she's said my name.

"Yeah. Sorry. Yes?"

"Shan's flight lands at six o'clock Saturday night. We need you to pick her up."

FML.

"Shan. Airport. Saturday. Done deal."

No worries. This past year with Erik has taught me I can do anything. An hour is more than enough time to span Madison's two farthest points—the airport and Erik's studio. I think.

She turns back to Dad and they resume their conversation about . . . oh, I don't care what. I stare at the pink notecard, thinking about how Davis and I have finally graduated. That we're finally rid of Pete and everyone in school. That, most importantly, I know a secret my tenth grade math teacher never knew:

Parallel lives defy the rules of geometry and find ways of intersecting.

chasers

Friday night. Davis and I walk down State Street, headed for the RYC and the Chasers meeting. State Street is Madison's carotid artery: a pedestrian mall dotted with used clothing shops, alternative music stores, thunderous bars, quirky restaurants, and consignment furniture outlets. Everything a college student could ever want, all within walking distance of the UW. You can wander off a block or two to find great clubs and entertainment. But the heart of it all starts and ends with State Street.

Bohos clot the sidewalks. This might be my favorite place in all of Madison. Here, everyone is someone and no one. People here don't care if I'm gay or an artist or a grocer's son, or anything else the dregs of my school think I should be ashamed of. Here is where I come closest to being.

Davis squints at the infant I've hastily sketched onto

the palm of my hand with a Sharpie. The baby is just an outline, crawling on all fours, with lines of radiance shooting out in all directions, like how a child draws a sun. It's actually not a bad replica of the original.

"It's . . . a baby."

"It's called *Radiant Baby*."

I started painting when I was ten. Every year, I pick an artist to study. I study how they work, how they manipulate color and light, how they frame the world and how the world frames them. I mentally catalog brushstrokes and subject matter and tints and points of view and media. And once I've absorbed it all, I paint. I pick my own subject, evoke artist's technique, and paint it as they would have done. No. I don't evoke. I perfect. Teachers have told me I'm good at imitating others. My sister has told me it's creepy.

Since January, I've been studying Keith Haring. And this is probably my four hundredth attempt to get Davis to see what I see. Davis doesn't get Haring. His brain gets math and computer programs and other things that are binary: either this or that, black or white. He's not into possibilities. Davis insults Haring's work, calling it "comic-strip art." I think Haring's brilliant. I'm amazed at how much emotion he can elicit with so little.

I trace the baby with my finger. "It's Haring's trademark. It's how people know him and his work."

"Okay, if you say so."

I rally. He *will* appreciate this. "I love it because it's so simple. It could be any baby. It's universal. But the radiance makes this child an individual. Community and individuality all at once. Perfect synthesis. With this one little image, Haring instantly made people think of him. I mean, no artist can be summed up by their work, but this comes pretty close."

Davis scoffs, puffing out his chest. "Not me. I'm complicated. You need more than a radioactive baby to sum me up."

"Radiant *Baby*," I growl. When will I learn it's useless to explain my artist obsessions to anyone?

Except Erik. He gets it.

We arrive at the Rainbow Youth Center and find Malaika Achebe sorting mail at the front desk. She's a beautiful, dark-skinned woman, wearing intricate purple and brown robes from her native Nigeria. The RYC is *her* radiant baby. She moved to Madison seven years ago with her partner, Alyssa Holt, a poet who teaches at the UW. Malaika became very vocal when she found that the city had no place for gay youth. She and Alyssa wasted no time ingratiating themselves into Madison society and raising money for a youth center. She's what Davis calls "a power lesbian."

As always, she smiles when we sign in.

36

"Good evening, gentlemen," she says warmly, then spots the crumpled flyer in Davis's hand. "I see you're here for Mr. Sable's meeting. Let me know how it goes."

We nod, no clue who Mr. Sable is. Davis peers just past Malaika. On the wall is a small row of mailboxes, one for each of the shelter's bedrooms upstairs. Next to each mailbox is a hook where the keys are kept. Only one of the six sets of keys hangs there: Room Three. Malaika follows Davis's gaze.

"Reserved in your name," she says reassuringly. "We'll be seeing you next week?"

"Yeah." Davis frowns. "Tuesday."

Malaika smiles at us again. "Mr. Sable is in Room Four. Have a good time." She turns back to sorting mail.

We walk through the pool hall and up the creaky stairs. Room Four is halfway down the hall, door propped open, muted chatter just beyond. Davis raps on the doorframe. The room is sparse, like a nun's cell. A twin bed on a rusty frame, a small trunk at the foot, a lamp and a bedside table.

Half a dozen mismatched folding chairs form a semicircle in front of the bed. Each chair is filled. I recognize most of the guys from seeing them around the RYC, but there's no one we know by name. Everyone's our age, more or less.

On the bed is a guy sitting cross-legged, swathed in

a huge black trench coat. He looks up as we peek in. A mess of thick dark hair, like the kind you see in Japanese anime, hides his eyes. Cargo pockets, most looking hand sewn, litter the coat. Army boots dart out from under. His build is hidden beneath the coat, but it's obvious he is neither thin nor a bodybuilder.

He smiles. His face is at once humorless but friendly. There's something uncanny about him, like God forgot to give him lips, and two thin black scratches were an afterthought, a compromise for a mouth.

"Here for the Chasers meeting?" Trench Coat asks, beckoning to us. His voice is scratchy. I can't get a read on his age. Twenty-one? Twenty-four? "Good to have you. You wanna catch the door? Then we can start."

I shut the door, and Davis and I go to sit on the floor when Trench Coat stands. He is *very* tall.

"Plenty of room over here."

He moves to the head of the bed and pats the mattress. Davis casually sits next to our host and leans in, no doubt hoping for an "accidental" touch. The first sign that Davis is smitten.

Trench Coat extends a huge hand, first to Davis, then to me. "I'm Sable."

When their hands meet, Davis grins. "I'm Davis. This is Evan."

I reach out to shake and, just like my dad taught me,

I meet Sable's gaze. His face is sallow, his eyes a little sunken in, but there's a hard beauty to his features, like something that just stepped out of Tim Burton's wet dream. As Sable shakes my hand, I catch a glimpse of the black T-shirt beneath his trench coat, which declares, "I'm the one your mother warned you about." Of this I've no doubt.

"Is Sable your first name or last?" I ask him.

Sable brushes it off. "Your pick." Then he gives his meaty hands a single clap and addresses everyone. "Okay, so, thanks for coming, everybody. I always hated doing this part in school, but we're not getting very far if we don't know each other. So let's just go around and say our names. You don't have to do anything retarded like say your favorite color. Just a name is cool."

A thin-faced, mousey guy named Ross starts off. He introduces the sour-looking guy next to him as Del. A small guy—about Davis's size, build, and demeanor— looks at the ground and introduces himself as Micah. Next to him is a chunky Asian kid who wheezes when it's his turn: Danny. On Danny's left, a confident-looking tanned guy slouches in his chair wearing a backward baseball cap.

"I'm Mark," he asserts, "and I think this group is gonna be fucking cool."

Sable's head goes back and he laughs like a demonic PEZ dispenser. "That it is, my friend, that it is."

The final chair is occupied by a string bean with tawny, bowl-cut hair who avoids all gazes. When he finally looks up, he's got a shiner to rival Davis's.

"Will Carter." He sighs. Sable gives him a thumbs up, though it hardly seems Sable's style. The raised eyebrows, the overly emphatic smile . . . everything about the gesture comes off as awkward. He's mocking Will's shyness, but I think I'm the only one who sees it.

Shields up.

Davis and I mutter our names again. Sable nods approvingly and surveys us all slowly, face like stone. I swear Davis beams when Sable looks at him.

Sable sniffs. "Okay, cool. So, why are we here?"

We all look around uncomfortably; we weren't warned there'd be a pop quiz.

Micah's the first to chime in. "'Cause we're all gay?"

Mark scoffs, throws his head back, and rolls his eyes. "I think we'd figured that much out." I'm not a Mark fan.

"Cut the kid some slack. He's pretty much right," Sable says, gesturing to Micah. "No matter what school you came from, what neighborhood, what family—it's the one thing you have in common. On second thought, there are two things you have in common." He sweeps the room, pointing an accusing finger at each of us. "None of you has any clue what it means to be gay."

Mark's derision continues. "Gee, last time I checked, it means I get stiff for guys and not girls."

Sable sits up straight and reminds me, just for a second, of Erik in the lotus pose when we practice yoga. But where Erik's face exudes tranquility and peace, Sable's face contains a maelstrom. I can't help but feel something bad is about to happen.

Sable fixes those eyes and that smile right at Mark and says, "Well, hell, if that's all it means, I'm just wasting your time. You wanna take off? Don't let me hold you back." He jerks his thumb at the door, never breaking eye contact with Mark. They sit there for a moment—predator and prey, but it's hard to tell which is which. Mark shifts in his chair, then looks away.

"So, what else does it mean?" Mark asks the wall above Sable.

Sable looks first to Micah, then to Davis, and says in a throaty whisper, "Power."

I almost laugh at how dramatic he sounds, but Davis is enthralled. When he's really into a movie or a TV show, his eyes glaze over and he's totally in the moment. Just like now. I swear I can see him mouth "power" in a silent echo.

Ross holds up a flyer. "So, what's this? What are Chasers?"

"Not what," Sable corrects. "Who. Everybody in this room has the potential to be a Chaser."

Ross looks baffled. "Yeah, but I don't get it. What does 'Chaser' mean?"

Sable shrugs. "We're all chasing after something, right? Respect. Friends. Love, maybe. A place to belong. Chasers can give you all that, if you're willing to listen and put in the work."

Micah leans in. Mark's posture improves. Even Will manages to tilt his head up and keep his eyes parallel to the ground. I'm listening too.

Del's sour look softens. "So, it's like a club."

Sable slaps the mattress and grins. Why do I get sick to my stomach whenever he smiles?

"It's better than a club. It's like a fraternity. It's a ticket to a past you never knew you had and a passport to places you never thought you could go. It's not gonna be easy. This isn't the fucking Girl Scouts where you sell cookies and sew shit. You gotta prove yourself, show that you've got what it takes to be a Chaser. And I promise you, if you listen to me and follow my lead, your lives will change.

"You'll be with people who understand you. You'll be able to go anywhere with anyone and not worry about getting messed with. No more disrespect. No more"— Sable grabs Davis's head and turns Davis's face sharply for all to see his eye—"getting the shit kicked out of you. You'll have respect . . . and you'll have power."

When Sable releases Davis's face, my friend's eyes lower. If Sable's words weren't enough to get Davis's attention, physical contact did the trick. Davis doesn't get much of that. Rough as Sable was, it wouldn't take much for Davis to imagine it as a lover's caress. Which I'm sure he's doing now.

"Okay, boys, show me what you got." Sable gets up and starts pacing, weaving in and out of the arc of chairs. "When did the Stonewall riots occur? A date, I need a date."

Seven sets of eyes hit the floor. Davis continues to watch Sable with rapt attention.

"No one?" Sable frowns. "Okay, something easier. What *were* the Stonewall riots?"

We're all quiet until Ross ventures an answer. "Wasn't that, like, a bunch of gays who got beat up or something? In New York?"

Sable slaps his hand down on Ross's shoulder and squeezes it. "So close, man, so close. See, guys, that's the problem. You don't know anything about your own heritage. You ever feel like you don't belong? Any idea why? It's not because you're gay. It's not because you get picked on or shit like that. It's because you can't connect. You have no idea where you came from."

Sable jumps up on the bed, looming over us like a stone soldier from a war memorial, preparing for battle.

He speaks faster, an occasional fist into his palm punctuating his fervor. "You might be proud to be an American because you spent years studying American history and you know what a bunch of dead guys did to make the country great. But you can't take pride in being gay because you don't know jack shit about what your gay forefathers did."

Sable steps down and turns slowly, making eye contact with each of us as he speaks. "The best way to understand what it is to be a Chaser is to wrap your head around gay history. It all started with Stonewall: June 27, 1969. That was the night—"

"Hang on," Mark interrupts, adjusting his baseball cap. "1969? So, what, nothing important happened before then?"

"Sure, stuff happened." Sable dismisses the question with a wave of his hand. "A lot of shitty stuff. But Stonewall is what turned all that around. So that's where we start."

"But . . . ," Danny, the Asian kid, speaks up, looking very confused. "History is all about context, right? I mean, don't we need to understand what went on *before* Stonewall to appreciate why it was important? I mean, c'mon, there were nightclub raids and blacklists and—"

Sable lumps his fists on his hips, his face strikingly neutral. He takes a step toward Danny, who looks up at him. "You know a little something about history, Danny?"

Danny manages a small grin and shoots a look to the group before returning Sable's gaze. "Well, yeah. It's sort of what I'm going to major in next fall."

Sable leans in. "So . . . when I asked if anyone knew about Stonewall, why didn't you speak up?"

Danny laughs nervously. "Habit, I guess. Showing off at school attracts attention, y'know? I mean, you're totally right that it's really the start of the gay rights movement. I just think it loses its significance if we don't understand everything that led up to it. You know what I mean?"

Sable nods with an eerily familiar expression. Something that reminds me of Pete. Bloodlust? "Yeah, Danny, I know what you mean." Sable doesn't break eye contact but asks, "Okay. Everybody wanna know what life was like before Stonewall?"

No one moves. Sable continues to glower at Danny and I feel the need to break the tension, so I nod. Then Davis shrugs and says, "Sure." Halfhearted agreements all around.

I never see it. There's a twist, a blur, and a gasp from Danny. Sable, his mammoth hand clamped around Danny's neck, lifts the kid up, spins him around, and throws him to the bed. Danny's right arm is pinned under his own body. Sable's free hand fastens Danny's other wrist to the mattress. Sable plants his knee just below Danny's chin, the length of his shin pressing down on Danny's ample torso. Sable's dark hair falls forward, shrouding his face like a murder of crows in flight.

"Here you go, Danny," Sable spits, his ferocity thick as blood. "This was gay life before Stonewall."

lesson

In a second, we're all on our feet, shouting.

"Hey, wait—"

"Dude, that's not cool—"

"Sable, c'mon—"

Our protests overlap, saying something and nothing. Danny's pleas are limited to raspy gurgles. His nostrils flare and his eyes bulge. He's afraid for his life.

Sable's grip closes tighter. "Did your books tell you all about this, Danny? Huh?"

The rest of us look from Sable to one another, not sure what to do. Even Mark is alarmed, pulling his baseball cap off, looking at the door like he wants to bolt. Ross, the mousey one, takes a surprising step forward.

"Sable, let him go."

Danny sinks deeper into the mattress as Sable applies more weight. A sickening mix of air and spit shoots from Danny's mouth. Sable swoops in so he's face to face with his victim. "Why bother reading about oppression when you can live it? Better than the History Channel, eh, Danny?"

I look around, ashamed of the recognition I see. Each of us has been through this before; our eyes say that much. Everybody here has had a Pete or Kenny to contend with, and now we just let it happen, like we've always done. I look at Davis who, finally, looks uneasy about all this. Like when I drew the trogs away from Davis, I decide to make a difference. I charge at Sable, trying to pry his fingers from Danny's throat.

"Let him up!" I grunt, but Sable's fingers aren't going anywhere. I swear I hear him chuckle.

Then Mark is working on Sable's other hand, trying to free Danny's wrist. We shout more. Davis and Micah, the smallest of us, throw their arms around Sable's waist and pull him backward with all their meager girth. When it looks like Sable might be losing balance, Ross and the sour-looking Del join the fray, yanking until Sable tumbles back, banging his head on a folding chair. Bean-pole Will pulls Danny from the bed and into a corner where Danny falls to all fours, wheezing for air. Thick red welts zebra his wrist and neck.

Once Sable's off, we all take a step backward, not sure what's going to happen next. Sable starts laughing. He leaps onto the bed and starts jumping up and down gleefully.

"You did it!" he bellows. "I never thought you guys would do it. But you did!"

He hops down off the bed. Bewildered, we all clear a path as he bounds toward Danny. Will feebly puts his arm around Danny's shoulder to protect him and Danny cowers, but Sable merely ruffles Danny's hair.

"You did good, Danny, real good. Hope I didn't scare you too bad. But you understand now, right? You get gay life before Stonewall."

He turns now and addresses everyone. "Gays were beaten. Ridiculed. Told who we could have sex with, who we couldn't. We lived in constant fear, under the knee of society. I thought it was going to take you guys forever to figure out Stonewall and what it made us into, what it forced us to do as a community. But you got it on the first try."

Nobody moves, all eyes on Sable. The crooked smile I've come to fear in just fifteen minutes is having the reverse effect on everyone else: They're beguiled. One by one, the guys return to their seats. Even Danny, still rubbing his claret-colored throat, takes his chair, although he no longer meets Sable's gaze. Ross and I exchange glances, and I'm glad I'm not the only one still wary.

Sable goes on to explain a bit about Stonewall. I catch bits and pieces of the discussion—random raids at gay bars in New York, finally the patrons of the Stonewall Inn in

New York fought back against the police and turned the tide—but I'm watching Danny, who looks like he's reliving his worst nightmare. And I'm watching Sable, who is now gentle and nurturing. And I'm watching Davis, who is listening with fascination, obedience, and awe. It's only in Ross's crestfallen face that I find shared fear.

"Now," Sable says, cradling the back of his head in his folded hands, "Stonewall wasn't like a light switch. It wasn't a couple days of rioting and suddenly gays were respected and admired. But it was a turning point. It was a statement. It was a community, banding together and saying, 'Enough of this shit. Let's throw down.'"

"Like now." The words croak from Danny's lips.

We all turn. Danny should be angry, but it's like he's hit upon some brilliant idea. "It took everyone here to stop you. To get together and stand up to you."

Sable makes a gun with his thumb and forefinger and shoots Danny. He then points with both index fingers and sweeps the room like spotlights crisscrossing. "You guys . . . ," he says proudly, "when you stand together, when you say you're not gonna take any more bullshit . . . *You* are Stonewall."

Dawn sparks like twinkling lights and cascades, first into Davis's eyes, then Mark's, and Del's, Micah's, and Will's. Some even smile. They get it now. Ross and I, still the lone skeptics, look only at each other—better this than betray our doubt and become part of Sable's next lesson.

"Okay, I'm in."

I almost don't recognize Davis's voice. It's confident and strong. He nods at Sable and continues. "I want to be a Chaser."

Ross says what I'm thinking. "You don't even know what that means."

Sable sits on the edge of the mattress again. "It means . . . connecting. Learning about the past. Seizing the future. It doesn't happen overnight. You've all got a lot to learn. But when you finally get there . . . When you finally can call yourself a Chaser, the possibilities are endless."

He slides his left sleeve back, exposing the underside of his wrist. Tattooed on his forearm is a bug with an obsidian body and saffron wings. Ross grimaces. But Mark looks at it and grins.

"Awesome," he whispers.

"Back home in New York," Sable says, "the Chasers call me Cicada. Everyone who progresses gets a new name for their new identity."

For a few minutes now, I've noticed that Will is breathing heavily, and I'm unsure if it's excitement or an anxiety attack. Probably a little of both. "How do we do that?" he asks.

Sable slides his sleeve back into place. "Show me what you're made of. We'll meet regularly and I'll teach you.

Show me that you're listening. Show me that you under-stand what it means to be gay. You'll progress. You'll be a Chaser."

As Sable declares an end to the first meeting, the energy in the room practically crackles. Sable sends around a sheet of paper to collect everyone's contact info, saying we'll get an e-mail telling us when to expect the next meeting. Davis is last to sign up. He starts writing, then scratches out what he wrote for his home address. He then writes, *RYC. Room Three.*

Sable looms over Davis's shoulder, reading with that lacerated smirk. "Hey, stud, you live across the hall?"

"As of Tuesday." Davis exhales, handing the sheet back to Sable. "That's moving day."

Sable looks Davis up and down. He might be checking Davis out, but I can't shake the feeling he's sizing up his next prey. "Need some help?"

I glance at Davis. Outwardly, he's playing it cool. But I know my best friend. Inside, he just went liquid. He blushes.

I'm about to say "We got it covered" when Davis pipes in. "Sure. We're starting at nine. Thanks a lot."

"Don't sweat it. You're part of a family now. We watch out for each other." Sable pokes the address Davis scratched out on the paper and nods. "I'll be there."

By the time Davis and I spill out onto State Street, you could power all of Madison with his enthusiasm.

"What?" Davis asks, noting my reserve.

"Wasn't that . . . a little extreme?" What I'm not saying is, *This guy is clearly nuts.* I can tell from Davis's behavior that this would be a bad move.

"It had to be," Davis explains, and there's something slightly condescending there. "Made the lesson memorable. Will you ever forget it?"

No. I have no problem remembering these kinds of lessons.

"Besides," Davis reasons, "if anyone should be mad, it's that Danny guy. And he said he'd be back for the next meeting."

Point to Davis.

"C'mon, Ev," he whispers urgently, "don't blow this."

The fire in Davis's belly is something I can't deny him. And even if this doesn't turn out to be like all the other things he's gotten excited about—then abandoned once they got hard—I reassure myself that it's only for the summer. In the fall, we'll be in Chicago and he'll forget about all this.

Until then, it's safest to stick with Davis. How can it hurt to learn a little about gay history?

TITLE: *Midnight Feature*

IMAGE:
The Orpheum Theater Marquee with
two lights burned out

INSPIRATION:
Van Gogh's *Starry Night*

PALETTE:
Marquee lights = saffron
Marquee frame = carmine
Marquee sign = eggshell
Lettering on the sign = maroon

The strokes begin and end in a point. The
marquee, the lights, the lettering are all
comprised of sharp polygons that curve in
upon themselves.

*I have two distinct memories of the marquee lights at the
Orpheum Theater. The first involves what I call Boing.*

*Boing is this energy that churns and burns inside Davis.
When he gets a thought into his head—we should join the
drama club, we should run for student council, we should
get jobs as lifeguards so we can gawk at hot guys—the Boing*

engulfs him like a wildfire and I brace myself for the ride ahead. More often than not, I wait it out until it's time to pick up the pieces.

When we were thirteen, the Boing told us we should sneak out to see the weekly midnight showing of Rocky Horror at the Orpheum Theater. We had no idea what it was about, only it was something really great to do because it involved sneaking out at midnight. So we met up outside Davis's bedroom window and made our way to State Street.

This was right around the time I'd worked out that I was gay. It only took months of staring at pictures of naked girls with zero reaction before reality set in. I liked looking at guys. And I was pretty sure Davis did too. And because I didn't know any other gay guys, I'd come to the conclusion that Davis and I should be boyfriends.

It made perfect sense at the time.

So as we stood there in line for the movie, I waited until I was sure no one was looking and then I kissed Davis. One quick peck on the lips.

Swallowing a gallon of paint thinner and letting it eat me from the inside out would have been preferable to seeing the look on his face. He wasn't angry. He wasn't disgusted. But he was certainly surprised.

"What the hell did you do that for?"

I almost ran away. I almost threw up. I almost did a lot of things, including kissing him again, just assuming I'd gotten it wrong the first time. Instead, I said, "I'm gay."

Davis rolled his eyes. "Uh, yeah, I guessed that."

"Aren't you gay?"

Davis put a gun made of his fingers to his head and pretended to blow his brains out. "Duh. Of course."

The tightness that had locked my shoulders disappeared and I exhaled gratefully. We could be boyfriends. I leaned in for another kiss but he pulled back.

"Evan, do you love me?"

Love hadn't entered my mind. I wanted to be with someone who was the same as me. When he confronted me with the word, I knew what I felt for Davis wasn't love. It was deep and strong, but it was brotherly and nothing like romance. It took Davis saying the word, it took almost making another mistake, before I understood not what love was but what it wasn't. Love wasn't desperation. Heavy shit when you're thirteen.

I muttered something like, "Man, I'm stupid."

"Pretty much," he agreed, elbowing me in the ribs. I laughed and slugged him back. There it was: my first rejection. And I survived it with most of my dignity intact. More or less.

We made it to the front of the line, where Davis bickered with the stoner in the ticket booth, who was so zoned it didn't take much to convince him that we were seventeen. Now that's stoned.

I thought the movie was kind of funny. Davis hated that everyone in the audience was saying the lines and singing the

songs and tossing toilet paper in the air. To him, it was just one
more joke he wasn't in on, one more clique he didn't belong to.
I tried to convince him we should keep coming back until we
knew the songs and lines. I even suggested we could get cos-
tumes. But by then, the Boing was gone.

Second memory—my second date with Erik, last summer.

For our first date, we met at State Street Brats on a Sunday
afternoon for brats, fries, and Cokes. We talked about art and
Madison and college and a hundred other things that all took
backseat to one simple fact: We were talking. After a couple
hours, we did that awkward "do we kiss on a first date?" dance,
talking about dumb stuff and praying the other guy would
make a move. We ended up shaking hands, and we went our
separate ways. I assumed I'd never see him again.

Ring, ring. Hot College Guy, line one. Something
about a second date . . . ?

Erik had friends in a choir that was singing with the Madi-
son Symphony at Monona Terrace—did I want to go? I almost
said no. Things had gone so perfectly the first time around,
why give him another chance to run away screaming? But I
made it work once. Making it work twice would be a cinch.
Maybe.

My dates with Erik became a doctoral dissertation on
building the ultimate relationship. One minute I was the class
punching bag, the next I was strolling along Monona Terrace

with a gorgeous guy. It took some getting used to. Every bit of stimuli introduced a new reaction from my body. My breath caught in my lungs when he slipped his hand into mine. My brain found religion. Ohmygodohmygodohmygod.

My heart was the next bit of anatomy to rebel when, later that night, we walked down State Street and ran into some of Erik's friends from school. They invited us back to somebody's apartment to watch a movie.

"Whatcha watching?" Erik asked.

"Brazil."

Then, at the same time, Erik and I said, "Where the nuts come from."

We looked at each other. We didn't giggle. We didn't say, "Jinx!" We just smiled a knowing smile. And Erik said to his friends, "Maybe some other time." And then, with his friends right there, under the Orpheum Theater sign, he kissed me.

Cue heart attack.

Boing.

big

As the King of Evasions, I've become adept at the story.

Inventing plausible mishaps to explain away the physical evidence of a troglodyte encounter. Playing Artful Dodger between the time I figured out I was gay and when I actually told my family. I always had a story ready for any situation, doling out explanations with the guile of a blackjack dealer. I don't enjoy lying, not to my family or to anyone else. But while I don't enjoy lying, I happen to be very, very good at it.

I have, in my mind, very good reasons for not telling anyone about Erik. Bitter as it sounds, I just don't think my parents deserve to know. I'm pretty sure the only reason they've never said much about my sexuality is because they don't think it's something I'd actively pursue. If I told them I was dating, if there was even a hint that I might be *being* gay, I don't know what they'd do. Kick me out? Send me to therapy? I don't worry about that. I won't tell them about Erik because they haven't earned the right to know that I'm happy.

Davis. Davis is complicated. I sometimes think that my dating someone would be like abandoning him. Or at least, that's how Davis would see it. I never said a word, even when things got serious with Erik and I wanted—needed—someone to talk to about all the incredible and horrifying feelings of having a first boyfriend. Part of me wants to think Davis'd be happy for me. But I'm afraid of how it might change our friendship. So, until I can figure out how to do this, Erik remains mine and mine alone.

So far, my stories have gotten me out of every scrape. Davis believed I couldn't make it to the RYC's latest rave because Mom and Dad were making me work, when actually I was doing yoga with Erik. Mom and Dad bought that I couldn't work Sundays in March because I needed more study time at the library, when I was really helping Erik cram for his anatomy midterm.

But a story won't allow me to drive to the airport, pick up Shan, take her home, then race across town in time for my date with Erik. And now that it's Saturday, that's exactly the story I need.

Here's the master plan: I work at the grocery store from open to five. Ditch the arm sling, shower quick, change, and I'm on the road to pick up Shan at the Dane County

Airport by six. Take her home. Scarf down a light dinner with the fam. Make an excuse (Davis needs help?) and leave at six forty. Hop the six forty-five bus to Thompson Boulevard and arrive at Erik's Studio in time for our date at seven. No problem.

Problem. The universe counters with a series of cataclysms aimed at undermining my Perfect Plan. Mrs. Nash calls at three forty-five with her weekly grocery order. She's close to ninety, so it takes a while for her to go through the list of everything she needs.

Then Jason, one of the college kids my folks hired to help at the store, shows up twenty minutes late for his five o'clock shift. It's five thirty before I'm on the road. I smell up the car; I worked behind the meat counter all day and I stink of dead. I stop by Mrs. Nash's and then I'm off to the airport. I arrive at five to six. No problem.

Problem. Shan's plane is late. It won't be in until quarter after six. I recalculate. We can be home by six thirty, I'll skip dinner, take a quickie shower, and still meet Erik on time. He's been dropping hints for weeks about tonight. I'm not good with anticipation. Erik's not good at making anticipation easy on me.

Near the baggage claim, I mentally scroll through the Ten Commandments. "Thou shalt not strand thy sister at the airport" is nowhere in sight. But another mental calculation tells me I have more to fear from Shan's wrath than anyone waiting for me in the Great Beyond. Erik has never been angry with me. Shan is another story. I opt for the lesser of two headlocks and continue to sit in the airport waiting area.

Text Erik to say you'll be late, my brain says. I tell my brain to shut up because texting Erik means explaining that I'm picking up Shan, when originally he just knew she'd be in town. Which means he'll tell me to bring her over so he can meet her. Which means full-on DEFCON 1 panic alert. No texting. Erik will be cool if I'm late. He gets me.

Shan arrives. Her usually long cocoa hair is shorter than I'm used to, falling just under her chin. We share our father's nose—short without being pug—and our mother's high cheekbones.

"Spud!" she yells, throwing open her arms to greet me, but I grab her carry-on, snatch her suitcase from the baggage belt, and lead her, running, back to the car. Under normal circumstances, shouting that nickname in public is grounds for a Wet Willy. But I want to see my boyfriend, which makes me benevolent. Then we're in the car and on the road.

"Some brothers get all happy when their sisters come home." She sulks, fastening her seat belt. She's four years my senior but has an uncanny ability to devolve into our mother with just the right acid-laced tone in her voice.

"Some sisters make it to their brothers' graduations," I counter, matching her acid with a base. She looks away and I win.

I can tell you exactly when Shan and I first started to act like a real brother and sister. Growing up, we hated each other. She was older and favored; I was the boy so I did all the work around the house and in the store. She was the outgoing cheerleader and popular kid; I was the quiet, sensitive one. Every room we occupied together became a battleground.

But when I came out to my family, that all changed. It was like every piece of my personal puzzle finally fell into place for her. I wasn't weird. I was trapped. She appreciated that and we became allies.

"Hail Mary, full of *slowthefuckdown*!" she screeches, reaching for the Jesus Bar above her door as I charge another yellow light.

"Sorry. M and D are anxious to see you."

"Bet it's been rough with D laid up."

"'Joan! Joan, I can't reach my feet. Did you buy me navy blue socks?'"

She laughs and we finish my dad's terminal lament together. "'Jesus fricking Christ, woman, you don't buy a color-blind man *navy blue socks*!'"

Shan casts a few surreptitious hairy eyeballs my way. My face still speaks of my close encounter of the trog kind. She's probably been itching to ask since she first saw me at the airport. But years of conditioning prohibit her from inquiring. She knows she'd only get a story.

She gets very quiet and then says, "Look, Spud, I have something very Big to tell and I don't want to clue in M and D just yet. But I have to tell someone. To tell you."

I look over and her face is this odd gradient of terror and joy. I don't know what that means.

"No," she insists, "I mean this is really Big. So Big that I need a ransom."

"What?"

"You have to tell me something Big too. I need a Big that I can use as leverage."

I've never had a Big that could match any news Shan ever had. Things like, "Well, I went to my first Chasers meeting for lessons in gay history and watched some Asian kid get the crap choked out of him" don't exactly qualify as Big.

Then I realize: For the first time, I have one. I have the biggest Big. I don't know what she wants to tell me, but I'm pretty sure news of my first relationship trumps it. But I'm not ready to give up my secret yet. I like having Erik right here, inside, where he's still just mine.

I sigh. "I don't have any news. You know that."

She scowls and narrows her eyes. Launch Serious Sis Mode. Her eyes glisten, the look she gets when she's out doing her photography, and her face flushes.

"I'm pregnant."

The car nearly swerves off the road as I slam on the brakes. Shan screams, clutching the dashboard. Horns blare around me as I meekly pull off to the gravel shoulder and slip the car into park.

I grin. "Oh my God, that's totally Big!"

We hug and she starts to cry. It's not long before I'm sobbing too. So we sit with the car running on the side of the road, blubbering at each other.

"Why is it a secret?" I ask. "You have to tell M and D."

She grimaces. "You just graduated. This is *your* time. I'll tell them before I go home." Shan used to eat up all of our parents' fussing. She lost her appetite when I came out. Now she prefers to stay out of the spotlight, hoping a little will spill on me. It's a nice gesture, but it hasn't worked yet.

I take the biggest breath I've ever taken. She trusts me. And if I'm going to pull things off tonight, I have to trust her. I must be fucking crazy.

"Okay. Listen. I've got a Big too."

Shan wipes her eyes. "You little turd, holding out on me—"

"You know, if you don't want to hear—"

"Okay, cry havoc and let slip the Big."

It sticks in my throat. It's like coming out all over

again, only that was something I had to say so I could go on with my life. I'm afraid that if I reveal this, my life won't go on. Everything will come to an end. But she's trusted me with something huge (okay, something that time and an expanding belly will betray) and I feel obligated to respond in kind.

When I hesitate, she ups the ante with, "I mean, it's not like you could top my Big but, hey, take yer best shot and we'll—"

"I have a boyfriend."

I have only ever whispered this to myself in bed at night.

I have a boyfriend.

I have a boyfriend.

I, Evan Daniel Weiss, have a boyfriend named Erik James Goodhue. And he rocks.

Here, now, in full voice, the sentence detonates and resonates. The car fills with noise, like the brakes squealing again. But it's Shan shrieking, hands flailing. She reaches out and gathers me in close for another hug, this one spine-threatening. My stomach does a samba—she's happy for me. I don't know what I was expecting, but I'm glad this is what I got. Then she pulls back with a skeptical look.

"Um, Spud . . . we're not talking COD, are we?" Cauldron Of Desperation. That's her code name for Davis. It's not that she doesn't like him. Even during the years she and I were fighting, I think she'd always been grateful that I had a friend. But she's said that she doesn't like the effect Davis has on me. I don't know what that means.

I roll my eyes and we sit on the roadside for another ten minutes as I tell her about meeting Erik and his square-egg-shaped head and getting his phone number and calling him and going on that awkward first date and the less awkward date when he kissed me outside the Orpheum Theater and I skip over the dates in between and I tell her that he bought me flowers every Friday during the month of my birthday and about the stupid stories I told M and D about where the flowers came from and I share the silly list I've made in my head, alphabetizing his best features (Awesome kisser, Beautiful smile, Considerate, Dimples . . .) and how his friends all like me and the reason I've been driving like a nutjob is because we're getting together tonight.

"I wanna meet him!"

For just a moment, I can't hear the cars rushing by outside. I can't hear the radio, which has been playing softly the entire ride home. I can only see the flashing red light on the dash, reminding me the hazards are on. It takes me roughly an hour to swallow and I gulp like I'm in a Tom and Jerry cartoon.

"Yeah." I laugh nervously. "I'm gonna vote that idea off the island."

Her eyes narrow. "Why?"

Trouble is, I don't have a reason. But I can't tell her that. "I dunno . . ." Once again, I see the pentimento. My home life seeping through the life I've forged with Erik. I can't explain that I'm still not ready to make Erik real to anyone else. "Erik's busy with school and stuff and . . . We'll see."

We stare at each other.

The last fifteen minutes of pent-up joy, everything I wanted—needed—to share fades. It's like we've both woken from a dream, neither of us sure what just happened. I hate the consequences of happiness.

I lick my lips, slip the car back into gear, and merge into traffic. We're six blocks from home before she speaks again.

"Evan, I understand why you haven't mentioned Erik to M and D. I know you've got your own life to live, but I also hope you know you can trust me. I'd really like to meet this guy. I won't snitch."

"I know," I whisper. I want to leap back in time and take it all back. Keep Erik to myself. Now he's not just mine. Now he's Shan's, too. "We'll see."

We're home and Mom is fawning over Shan. Mom tells Shan she's lost weight. Shan stomps on my foot when I choke on a laugh. Dad rolls out to the living room and the three begin talking about New York and grad school and Mom says she's made Shan's favorite—shepherd's pie. I slip into the shower, then fresh clothes. On my way out, I say, "Don't wait up. Davis and I are going to a late-night show."

Shan smiles and mouths, *Have fun*. Mom and Dad don't even notice. They continue to talk to Shan. I leave without a sound.

I always have a story. The only thing worse than needing one is when I don't.

gift

I've changed since Erik came along. I know it. The single most draining effort during the last year has been trying not to let all the changes show. I used to be a sloucher. Since Erik introduced me to yoga, I have great posture— back straight, shoulders square, head up. Mom noticed but couldn't articulate it.

"We need to get you checked," she said one day at the store, frowning and eyeing my perfectly straight spine, "for scoliosis." I wanted to correct her, explain what scoliosis was, but she was showing concern and I didn't want to spoil the moment.

Dad had a whole different take. "Are you giving me attitude?" I was helping him unload a delivery truck when he noticed. Instead of always looking down, I kept my head up. Between that and the posture, Dad thought I was looking cocky. Couldn't help but smile. I was going for confident, but whatever. In a weird way, I think he started giving me more respect. I'm always more conscious of my posture now when he's around. Not necessarily because I want that respect, but because I think it freaks him out a little.

Davis was the only one who could really pinpoint the change, even if he didn't know where it came from.

"You're different," he said. "It's like you're up to something." Leave it to your best friend to know stuff he doesn't even know. So I try to slouch and cast my eyes down whenever I'm around Mom or Davis. Let them see the old Evan. Somehow, I think my life works better when I'm less real to them.

I've also seen a change in my gait. Now, as I bound toward Gorham Street, my stride is sure and strong. If the trogs saw me now, I don't think they'd recognize me. On the other hand, I worry that seeing a trog would bring out the other Evan, the one I banish when Erik's around: meek, shy, acquiescent. This straight-backed, bouncy-gaited Evan is the only Evan Erik knows. I want to keep it that way.

I break into a run and hammer on the back of the Number 14 as it tries to pull away from the bus stop without me. It squeals and jerks to a stop. I slip my bus pass into the reader and take a seat. Twenty minutes later, I'm south of town, two short blocks from the Studio. I run the rest of the way.

Erik's Studio is a self-storage unit he rents off the Beltway. On the outside it's just another sky blue garage door set in a wall of chalky concrete blocks. But throw open that door and it's like you've raised a periscope up into his brain. This is where he stores all the stuff he finds at rummage sales, estate auctions, and flea markets: a trove of spigots and toasters and blenders and mixers and rusty egg whisks, fused in combinations of two, three, four items. His creations hang from the ceiling by piano wire, jut up from the floor, and cling to the walls like postmodern tarantulas.

Erik, my beautiful boy, my nurse, is also a sculptor.

My favorite sculpture is in his friend's gallery (it wasn't just a pickup line; he really knows someone with an art gallery) in Milwaukee. He took two antique iceboxes and turned them into robots. One has mixer beaters for eyes, toilet plungers for arms, and mops for legs. The other is meant to look incomplete. It has no eyes but a spiral mouth—a discarded burner from an electric stove—rolling pins for arms, and one leg made from a tower of fused pork-and-beans cans. Two strategically placed potato mashers assure you each is male. They're holding each other. And you get the idea that the one with the beaters wants to look into the eyes of the other robot—eyes that aren't there. Erik calls it *Some Assembly Requited*. It's the first image that pops into my mind whenever I think about us as a couple.

It's a toasty night. I navigate through the labyrinth of cloned garages toward the sounds of Gregory Douglass singing "Hard." Erik's choice of music on any given day acts like a road map, guiding me to his mood.

> I'll miss you hard enough to hide it,
> I need you hard enough to try,
> I love you hard enough to move on . . .

"Hard," in Erik's world, means caution. *Curves ahead, slow down.* It tells me he's been brooding today and he's working his way out of a funk. It tells me he's remembering past boyfriends, bad relationships. But that's about to change. Because I am here to negate all funks. The caring boyfriend has arrived.

I turn the corner to Unit 481. As expected, he's standing in just his favorite pair of paint-spattered, ripped jeans. I have seen the man in a business suit, in swim trunks, and totally naked, but nothing gets me revved like seeing him in those jeans, shirtless and barefoot. He even makes the colossal welding mask that swallows his head look sexy.

The space reeks with industrial backwash; singed metal and pungent magnesium. The familiar hiss of the welder blends seamlessly with the music's synthesizer as the squeal of two chunks of steel fusing together threatens to drown out both.

I lean on the entryway and gape at the work in progress. This is one of the biggest things he's ever done. It's unlike any of his other sculptures; very literal, not at all abstract. He's created a skeleton of pipes, around which he's wrapping long strips of steel sheeting that he's first run over with a buffer so they're coated in circular grooves, giving them a tarnished, scratched look. This sculpture is of two angels holding spears overhead in their outstretched arms, one foot off the ground as though they're leaping into the sky together. Their wings, like mirrors, shoot out with a width twice the statue's height. He calls it *Fierce Angels.*

"Why 'fierce'?" I asked when he first showed it to me.

"Angels have to be fierce nowadays," he reasoned. "We've come up with a thousand new ways to be crappy to one another since Biblical times when angels roamed freely. You've heard about people going 'where angels fear to tread'? Not these two. Nothing scares them. They'll go anywhere to help somebody out of a jam."

Erik calls this his hobby. His heart, he assures me, is in medicine. He's the top of his class in nursing school and he puts in more hours than any other intern at University Hospital. But even though he doesn't call himself a "serious" artist, I know Erik is pouring everything he's got into this piece. It's his first commission. At the end of the summer, the city is going to unveil it down at Reid Park as the celebration of their "clean up the neighborhood" project for that area.

Last year, two gay kids got the crap beat out of them at that park. One of them, a guy named Cory Tanner, was only just released from the hospital this spring, but he's still something of a vegetable. Malaika led the charge to get the city to start patrolling that area more often and rallied a group of volunteers to clean up the park and start a neighborhood watch group. Once things turned around, the mayor agreed to a "victory" celebration and the city council commissioned a statue to commemorate the event. Guess who hooked Malaika up with the sculptor?

The blinding dagger of light from the welder vanishes, the machine's hum dies down, and Erik lifts off the mask to find me in the doorway. I grin like a moron. I only have to wait the time it takes for him to discard the welder and helmet before he's pulled me into his arms. His exposed skin glistens with fresh sweat that smells like sweet pickles.

"Hey," he whispers, leaning his forehead in to touch mine. I love it when he does this. "Glad you could make it. Did Shan get in okay?"

I smile, but inside I flinch. Again, that weird feeling in my stomach: *Shan knows about Erik.*

"Piece of cake," I report.

Erik takes my chin between his thumb and forefinger. "Listen, I wanted to apologize. For just showing up at graduation. I should have checked with you first."

He cups my cheek in his hand and tows me in for a kiss. How is this happening? How has this happened for nearly a year? I silently intone my kiss prayer: *Please let this tell him that I love him and let things continue just as they have been when we go home at night.* It's childish but it's what I think whenever we kiss. It's worked so far.

When we break, I whisper, "You are always welcome in my life."

He tilts his head and I consult my mental book, where I've cataloged everything there is to know about him: I call it the DictionErik. Tilted head. Noun. What Erik does when he's not so sure about something. Add a sharp, quick intake of air and the meaning changes: *Yeah, let's talk about that.* But instead, his shoulders slump.

Slump. Verb. *Everything's cool.*

When he's this close, I can see the cracks in the armor he wears around everyone else. Not even Super Boyfriend is impervious to stress. We haven't seen much of each other lately, between our mutual race to finish school and his hospital job and extracurricular work on *Fierce Angels.* He's tired.

"How was work?" I ask softly.

As a nursing intern, Erik often jokes that he's so low on the totem pole, he's not even above ground. As a result, he gets shit on a lot, figuratively and literally. He gets all the jobs that the registered nurses don't want to do. But he takes it all in stride because he digs his work. He spends a lot of time working with AIDS patients, which alternately sends him home elated or ready to collapse. Today was a collapse day.

Worry and concern drain from his body as he announces, "Mr. Benton was discharged yesterday."

"Erik, that's great! No small thanks to your TLC, I'm sure."

Sometimes I meet Erik at the hospital, and I've gotten to know Mr. Benton over the last few months. He's an older guy, really funny, but with a lot of health problems. He's in and out of the hospital frequently, largely because he forgets to take his meds. Erik went so far as to use his own money to buy this guy a watch that went off whenever it was time to take his pills. But he still forgets. Erik loves Benton and I love that he's happy Benton's home again.

We talk about little things. Movies we want to see, new restaurants we want to try. We're swaying, not necessarily to what the boom box dictates but to what we want to hear. When we're like this, I forget that I lead two lives. I don't care.

I close my eyes and dismiss any conflicting sensations. The total commitment to joy when I'm with him versus the stifling tundra that is my other life. Happy/Sad. Hot/Cold. Somewhere in the middle lies the exact synthesis of how I feel about Erik. Rapture at absolute zero.

I know that if I keep us here, our foreheads touching and dancing to internal syncopation, there will be more brooding and reflection. "When I'm like that," he told me once, "don't let me go there." So I reach over and tap the pause button on the boom box.

Then I poke him in the ribs. "So, uh, you know, not to be rude, because I'm all about the slow dancing with my topless boyfriend, but didn't someone mention something about presents? Evan needs presents."

Brooding Boyfriend evaporates. Erik slaps his forehead. "Presents! I forgot about the presents! Yes, we must have presents!"

He takes my hand and yanks. We exaggerate giant steps over mounds of broken pails and make contorted turns around dilapidated wagon wheels toward the back of the garage. A tall something, hidden beneath a rumpled blue tarpaulin, waits in the corner, the end of our trek. He positions me in front of the mystery object, stands to one side like a magician's assistant, and snaps off the tarp with a flourish.

I'm facing a tall, U-shaped frame made of dark fin-

ished oak. I'm reminded of this antique standing mirror I saw in a second-hand shop over on Monroe Street,
only here the mirror is missing. The thick poles on the
sides are hand-carved, with grooves that spiral down. Up
and down the vertical poles, reaching out into the empty
space where the mirror should be, is a series of polished
steel clamps in various sizes. The poles connect near my
feet to a thin horizontal base that anchors the whole con-
traption firmly to the ground.

Erik throws his forearm over my shoulder and leans in
to me. "Now, I haven't taken this for a spin yet—I thought
I'd leave that up to you—but I'm hoping this will be less
cumbersome than THE CLAW."

And then I recognize it. I once sketched something
very similar to this for him, on a napkin. I had been
agonizing over how clumsy, heavy, and awkward THE
CLAW is and told him about my dream to build something more versatile. That same day, we'd passed that
second-hand shop on Monroe Street and I held the napkin design up to the display window, comparing it to the
antique mirror, asking him to imagine the frame without
the mirror. Only Erik did more than that. He made it for
me. It's beautiful and thoughtful and I don't know how
to tell him that it looks even more awkward than THE
CLAW.

"And you haven't seen the best part!" he exclaims as

he points out a series of hinges that he's installed strategically around the frame. Like Houdini, he begins to twist and pivot the frame so it folds into itself until it's a thick beam nearly as tall as I am. Small knobs are at the top and bottom of the beam. Erik takes a leather strap, loops each end to a knob, and slings it over his shoulder.

"Totally portable!" he proclaims, beaming. "I've tried the clamps on windows of all shapes and sizes and I think you'll find it pretty flexible. It might take some getting used to—"

"It's perfect." I cut him off, transferring the new easel onto my own shoulder.

A cream-colored envelope dangles from my gift. I squint at him and he looks away, whistling innocently as he tosses on a T-shirt and flip-flops. I open the envelope and find another pink notecard. I read aloud:

"Go to State Street Brats."

Erik smiles. "Well, if you insist!"

He snatches my hand and we're out of the garage. He quickly locks up and, hand in hand, we run back to his Jeep. A second later, we're driving back toward State Street.

"I always sucked at scavenger hunts," I warn him.

"No worries," he assures me. "You got da master scavenger hunter on your team."

A team. We're a team. Damn straight.

We park in an alley off State and make our way to the

site of our first date. Jimmy, our favorite server, greets us at the door. We get a patio table, down a couple red and white brats each, and when the bill comes, Jimmy brandishes another cream-colored envelope, this one with a misshapen bulge in the middle.

Something inside jingles as I open the envelope. A key ring tumbles out. Attached are two keys, one shiny silver key and one shiny gold key.

"That one will get you through the security door downstairs," he says, pointing to the gold key. "And this one"—he points to the silver—"is for the apartment. To quote a wise man: You are always welcome in my life."

Keys to his apartment. It must be love. Or massive head trauma.

My brain percolates with visions: After work, I walk down to State and let myself in the security door with MY key and on the second floor, I let myself into Erik's apartment with MY OTHER key. Good-bye, calling to be let in. Adios, buzz and click as the door unlocks itself. I'll miss you.

Not.

"Thank you." I kiss him, clutching the keys so tightly I create pink impressions in my palm.

He coughs in that oh-so-conspicuous way and nods at the envelope. Inside, another pink note. "Back to my apartment," I read aloud.

He rolls his eyes. "You're so demanding."

We pay the bill and make the short walk down State, stopping in front of the Bookworm, the coolest used bookstore in Madison. It's not cool because it has the best selection or because the employees really know their stuff. It's the coolest because Erik lives in the apartment above it. Coolness by proxy. I make a big deal of opening the security door with MY KEY and we enter.

We climb the stairs of the second floor, where we find Cece, Erik's neighbor from across the hall, exiting Erik's apartment. Cece is a self-designated nouveau Goth. Each nostril, plus her lower lip, sports a small safety pin, and her ears house so many sparkling studs they look like runway lights. But instead of dousing herself in black like other Goths, she chose to rebel against the rebels and dress herself in hot pink, from her tinted hair to her specially dyed Doc Martens. She wears a large black bow tie around her neck, in the center of which is a small button that reads, "I'm so dark I fart bats."

She and Erik each check their watches and speak at the same time.

"You're early!" says she.

"You're late!" says he.

Stalemate. She points at me—"You never saw me!"— tosses a book of matches at Erik, and disappears into her abode.

I squint at Erik. "What was she doing in your—?"

Erik sighs and opens the door for me.

His space is what you'd expect from a college student's apartment. It's microscopic. A combination living/dining room. A kitchen that was very probably once a closet. A bedroom and Lilliputian bathroom. Furniture is a bean-bag love seat and a papasan chair, pointed at each other to form a conversation area. He has a couple of his small sculptures in the corners and some of the paintings I've done on the walls.

And tonight, he's challenging fire codes: More than two dozen flickering candles tickle the darkness. I'm staring in amazement at this, my own personal constellation, but he's leading me into the bedroom where one last envelope—this one quite a bit bigger—sits in the middle of his bed, tied with a violet ribbon. He nods at it. I sit on the edge of the bed as he squats nearby.

"Happy graduation." From the DictionErik: Rubbing forefinger under the nose—*I'm nervous*. I don't see him nervous much.

I open the envelope and I find a plane ticket inside. One-way flight to San Diego. My name is printed on it.

"San Diego?" I smile at him. His eyes say he's clearly worried. "What's up?"

He sits down next to me. "Evan, I'm in. I got the phone call last week."

Two months ago, Erik flew out to California to interview for a graduate program at an HIV research hospital in San Diego. It's a very prestigious facility, and it's all he's talked about since I met him. Every double shift he's ever worked, every sleepless night of studying has all been aimed at getting a position in this program. This is his dream.

I throw my arm around his neck. "Erik . . . that's . . . God, I'm so happy for you!"

His confidence remains elusive but he's all grins now. "I can't believe it. This is exactly what I want to do. They made me a really good offer—no, an incredible offer. I'll be going to school at night, working with some of the most brilliant HIV researchers in the world during the day . . ."

I glance again at the ticket and can actually feel my brain click. The departure date is August 12. The choice of date is no accident. That's the day we decided was our anniversary. Though we'd been dating since June last year, we officially became a couple on August 12. That was when we talked and agreed:

- we were seeing each other exclusively;
- we were working toward a committed relationship;
- if Guy A so much as looked at another man, Guy B had the right to gut Guy A with a spork.

When he first told me that he was going for the interview, he must have seen I was worried, because he assured me that he probably didn't have a chance in hell of getting in and he was really only going for the interview experience. He made it sound like an impossible possibility, so we never discussed a future that involved California. But he knew what I was thinking before he got on that plane: What happens to *us* if you get in?

I'm holding the answer in my hand.

reckoning

"Come with me, Evan."

Four words. I can't even reply with one.

He talks faster than I ever thought he was capable. "Here's how I figure it: We pack a moving truck on the eleventh. Tyler's agreed to drive it out to California for us. We fly out on the twelfth. Meet up with Tyler on the thirteenth. He flies home and . . ."

Erik stops. My eyes haven't left the ticket and anyone who knows me knows that stunned silence does not bode well. He starts over, slower. "School's over. You're eighteen. You can do whatever you want. You were planning on leaving Madison anyway, right? Just make a small course correction."

Absolute zero begins to overcome the rapture and I try not to panic.

"I . . . There's Chicago. I was going . . . Chicago. School." I hate it when language leaves me.

Erik places his strong hands firmly on my shoulders and squeezes. "Evan, I might be way off base here. But I always got the impression that Chicago was never really . . . your heart's desire. It was just something you felt you had to do after high school. You were going there because that's where Davis was going."

I can count on one hand the number of times Erik has mentioned Davis in the year we've been together. Now, Davis has come up twice in as many days. Something I've been dreading is coming. A reckoning.

I shrug. "No. Well, yes, Davis is going too. But they have a really great art school."

Erik squeezes my shoulders again, playfully. "But is it a school you've got your heart set on?" He takes the envelope and pulls out more papers—college brochures. "I did a bit of research while I was in California, picked up a little information. There are some really great art schools in San Diego. Some of them, that's all they teach. All art, all the time."

I glance at the brochures. When Davis and I talked college, I only knew that my heart wanted out. Something new, beyond Madison. Chicago became the most convenient route to take. But without realizing it, the last eleven months created an alternate course. I'd give anything for a compass right now.

Erik misreads my hesitation. He tosses the brochures

aside and holds my head in his hands, lining up our eyes so all I see is deep, penetrating brown. "Or you can say 'screw school.' No one is forcing you to do that. You can get a job. You can paint. God, there's so much you can do. Right now, I don't even care what that is as long as it's something you feel strongly about. Just . . . please do it with me."

Crying will give him all the wrong messages. Crying will say, *Don't you understand? I've been laughed at my entire life and when you express this much confidence in me, it chokes me and I'd run but there's nowhere to go because you're the only place I've come to know.*

I don't cry. I will later.

It's an odd sensation to get what you want and still feel terrified. Inside, aspiration accelerates, blurring everything I know. Outside, my face slackens, resolve masquerades as rejection. Erik sees the battle behind my eyes, the uncertainty in my posture. I watch as his shoulders slowly deflate.

I set the ticket down on the bed. He's still holding my face, his thumbs pressing gently just under my eyes. I slide my hands up to his shoulders and knead the muscles softly.

"I love you, Erik."

We kiss. When he draws back, he's crying.

"I am such a jerk."

And the brooding resurfaces. I can see the ghosts of disastrous relationships hover over his head. His Kryptonite: insecurity over past failures.

"This has always been my problem. I throw too much too fast at people." He stands and wipes his eyes.

I should feel completely smothered by everything Erik is suggesting. But in the presence of this mostly confident, slightly wacky, completely caring guy, I am strangely calm. Eye-of-the-storm calm.

"Hey there, Self Pity, party of one." I try to sound reassuring in my joke. "I love that you've put so much thought into this."

Erik half laughs, half sobs. "Yeah. Too much thought."

I want to say something to reassure him, but before I can think of what that is, he sinks to his knees.

"Okay, Evan, look. I can't take back anything I said tonight. Largely because I meant it all. But I don't expect an answer right now. I don't even want one. I want you to go home and just . . . think. It's a lot to consider, I know. Take your time. We've worked too hard at this for you to make a decision at the speed of stupid."

I laugh. This was how Erik's dad taught him to take his time when making decisions. He claimed that the fastest speed in the universe wasn't the speed of light but the speed of stupid. Intelligence is slow, measured. Stupidity is lightning-quick, impulsive. Every decision

Erik makes glides along at the speed of smart.

He takes my hand and gets that very, very serious look on his face. "Don't rush this. You've got all summer to come up with an answer. You've got, in fact, until August eleventh."

I ruffle his hair and he snorts. I've never done that. It's usually vice versa. It feels good to turn the tables. To be the vice versa.

"Okay," I agree. "I'll think about it." The salmon-colored ticket is neither hot nor cold in my fingers. It's barely there. I don't need to think about it. I don't want to think about it. But for him, I will.

We're both quiet. Erik stands, shifting his weight between his feet—back and forth—and nibbling the corner of his lower lip. My gut tells me this is a new entry for the DictionErik: *Yeah, let's talk about that* is about to happen. He takes a deep breath.

"There's one thing, though. And it's kind of important."

I nod. I know exactly where this is going and there's nothing I can do.

Erik smiles. No. Not exactly a smile. He tries to smile but it comes off looking more pained. "Evan, I've . . . I've been a good boyfriend, right?"

I shake and laugh nervously. "Are you kidding? The best." Does that mean anything from someone who has nothing to compare it to? I can only hope.

"I mean, I don't think I've put a lot of pressure on you. Well, not before tonight, I mean."

No pressure. I feel no pressure.

He continues. "I've tried to be there when you needed to talk and I've let you have space when you weren't ready. I've tried to be supportive without butting in."

It's all true. Erik has been close when I needed him and retreated when the time was right. And I've allowed this. In many ways, I've encouraged it.

Erik has infinite patience and trust. Given what I know about his past relationships, he should be a paranoid recluse fighting off anyone who tries to get close to his heart with a torch and a pitchfork.

But he let me in. He saw something in me that could be trusted.

And I almost interrupt with the need to confess: I've taken advantage of his trust. I can see when he wants to question me and then backs off, worried that questions will mean he's letting his fear rule his life. He refuses to let scars from his past relationships influence how he treats me. And instead of just coming clean and answering his questions, I keep quiet. It's how I've kept who I am a secret.

It's how I make this work.

But I can see in his eyes: That all changes—here, now.

I nod vigorously. "Yes. You've done all that."

Erik sighs, nervous words earthquaking from his lips as

he looks me right in the eye. "I need to meet your family."

When you put white light through a glass prism, it separates and you see it for what it really is: a spectrum. For the first time, Erik's holding me up to a prism. I'm about to be what I really am. Ready or not.

"Evan, you've met anyone who means anything to me. But I don't know anyone in your life. I know *about* your sister, the silly but serious photographer. *About* your parents, the button-down grocers. *About* Davis, the goofy best friend. I don't *know* them. And I get the idea that none of them even knows I exist. I don't know if you're ashamed of me—"

"Of course not, " I say, drawing him in close, my hands meeting on the small of his back, fingers locking to prevent escape.

I've brought us here and I should put an end to it and explain everything. Being loved by Erik has given me courage.

But not as much as I'd need to have this conversation. I squeeze. "No, it's nothing like that."

Erik shrugs. "If you were still in the closet, I'd understand. But you've been out to everyone for years. You've had several chances this past year to introduce me. Yet you never have. I've always made excuses for you. Now . . . I'm out of excuses. I need to know that I'm part of your life. Your whole life."

Please don't make me do this. Don't make me show you who I really, really am.

I owe him honesty. I opt for spinelessness. "Erik, it's not that easy."

He steps away from me, nose wrinkled, head shaking. "No, Evan. It's never that easy. But I'm tired of feeling like a dirty little secret. I think I've earned more than that."

There's an edge to his tone that apes fury but is diluted by uncertainty. We've never fought, never raised our voices to each other. I feel like all of the confidence I get around Erik is being leeched away. I might as well be back in school with Pete towering over me, laughing and pointing.

"You have." I reach out and touch his arm. He doesn't recoil, so I step up to him again. "I'm sorry. You're right. This is stupid. I love you so much I should be telling complete strangers on the street."

Erik looks at his feet. "No. You should tell your family."

I nod. "Yes. And . . ."

I can't fucking believe I'm saying this.

". . . and how's this to start? With Dad laid up, the 'rents are crazy. But . . . dinner with Shan. How about Tuesday? Tuesday night?"

He scans my face, looking for something to collar his fears. I smile a meek promise: *This is just the beginning. I swear.*

Then he rolls his eyes. "If you weren't so damned cute . . ."

I fake a jab to his chin. "But here's the deal. You're cooking. I want your famous chicken cashew. And there shall be no broccoli. Thus spake Evan."

I'm pushing it—you don't tell a nurse/fitness guru to hold the broccoli. But he squints with a threat that carries all the potency of a casual breeze.

"You drive a hard bargain. Okay. Tuesday. Six. Here. Chicken cashew."

I raise an eyebrow and he slumps exaggeratedly.

"No broccoli," he whimpers.

The storm has passed and I'm able to breathe again as we hug. Erik's back muscles are taut beneath my fingers. He's still on guard, afraid I won't go through with this. I don't know how to fix things *except* to go through with it . . . so I know what I have to do.

I glance at my watch. "I should get going. I have to open the store tomorrow."

Usually when it's time for me to leave, he asks, "Can you spend the night?" When I don't have to open the store the next morning, the answer is always yes. But even when he knows I have to work, he asks, knowing I can't. He likes to ask. And I like that he does. I wait for the question, if only because it forces me to take a moment to remember how it feels to lie under his battered quilt, spooning until sleep takes me. Tonight, he doesn't ask.

Tonight, he takes my hand and leads me back into the living room. I notice, for the first time, the tall silver mirror framed in antique oak leaning against the wall near the windows, discarded to create my new easel. I bet it cost him a fortune.

Erik opens the door and as I step over the threshold, he slips the plane ticket and brochures into my hand. My other fist is closed tightly around the key ring. We stand on opposite sides of the door, painted two mismatched shades of blue, and I can't help but feel that my smile is warmer than his.

"Thanks," I whisper, not because it's late and people might be sleeping, but because that's what you do when you're reverent. "I love all my presents."

"You're welcome." He leans on the door and finally some of the old familiarity of BF (before fight—does this qualify as a fight?) returns. Neither of us wants me to go. "Want a ride home?"

"Nah. Great night for a walk. And a nice, slow think."

He laughs. We stare into each other's eyes, waiting for one of us to be the killjoy.

I volunteer. "Love you. See you soon?" I take a step back.

He nods. "We'll check on Mr. Benton." As he slowly closes the door, I catch a whisper: "Miss me."

The door clicks shut.

Every minute I'm not with you.

I swing by his Jeep and retrieve my new easel: the perfect gift. In my free hand, I grip the plane ticket.

My plane ticket.

I start the long, long walk home.

TITLE: *Doorways*

IMAGE:
The antique doorknob on the front door
of the Rainbow Youth Center

INSPIRATION:
Grant Wood's *Return from Bohemia*
(1939)

PALETTE:
Door = heliotrope
Doorknob = chrome
Shadows = olive drab

Wood started painting rural scenes as a
reaction to Europe's abstract art. Basically,
he gave Europe the finger and kept his art
simple. The doorknob itself is a large letter *S* on its side, with decorative curls at
each end.

*Almost a year after we came out to each other while waiting
in line for* Rocky Horror, *Davis decided it was time we came
out to our families.*

"*If they kick us out,*" *he reasoned,* "*we can sue them for child endangerment or something like that." I didn't think that was quite how it worked, but the Boing was in full force, so who was I to argue?*

The RYC had just opened, so we swung by there, looking for advice on how to tell our parents. That's where we met Malaika. She took us under her wing, introduced us to counselors who offered advice on what and what not to do when coming out to your family.

Don't come out on a holiday. Have a support network. Be sure you're emotionally prepared.

We spent an afternoon in May psyching ourselves up before we each went home, determined to tell our folks.

Although my parents and I danced around each other, I knew this might actually prompt an emotional reaction. I hoped for anger, which I could deal with. I had no idea what to do if they chose hate.

I cried in my room for fifteen minutes before I told them. I took about a thousand diversions, with headlines ranging from LOCAL TEEN SWALLOWS OWN TONGUE TRYING TO COME OUT *to* PARENTS ARRESTED FOR AX MURDERING NEWLY OUT TEEN. *I prepared for every reaction.*

Except the one history told me to expect.

Mom and Dad sat at the kitchen table with a deck of cards, working on their bridge strategy. Shan was in the living room, reading one of her photography books. I planned to start slowly, ease into the story, make it a discussion of feelings and experiences rather than politics or religion. Instead, I just blurted out, "I'm gay."

The implosion, the lightning strike, the tsunami—whatever I expected—failed to arrive. They looked at me as though I hadn't spoken.

"I . . . thought you should know."

And when the silence—not even stunned silence, just run-of-the-mill, everyday, boring-family-life silence—continued, I got mad. I wanted outrage. Just this once, I wanted a reaction other than disinterest.

Mom frowned, turning her focus back to her cards. "This isn't the time to try to get attention, Evan."

"This isn't about attention," I insisted. "I'm telling you this because you need to know."

"You can't be gay." Dad grunted, shaking his head. "You're too damn young to even know what that means. Where did you hear that word? Is that something Davis has been telling you?"

Where did I hear the word? Were they living in the Fifties?

"No . . ." The voice, barely a whisper, was Shan's. "No, it makes sense."

That's when fourteen years of enmity shattered. She understood everything I'd gone through to figure out who I was. She had gay friends who'd done what I was doing now. Friends she'd celebrated with when it was over . . . or comforted when things went wrong. She was on my side.

I tried for another ten minutes to get my parents to talk to me about it. Even Shan meekly tried to suggest they hear me out. But they kept insisting it was a bid for attention. So I went to my room and slammed the door. I crawled out my window and spent the night sleeping on the roof, spitting "Fuck!" at the stars until I fell asleep.

The next day at three o'clock, I went to the RYC to meet Davis. He arrived two hours late, tossing his bike aside before sinking down next to me on the front step, back against the door.

"C'mon," I prompted, "how'd it go?"

He reached up over his head, fiddled with the antique doorknob, and mumbled.

"What?" I asked.

"I didn't tell them."

In that instant, I relived all the anxiety and hysterics from the night before. All because of Davis. This had been his idea. We'd made a pact to tell. Together.

"You . . . ASSHOLE!" I screamed. I jumped up. I kicked the sidewalk and stomped. "You fucking asshole! You asshole! Do you have any idea what I went through last night? You son of a bitch!"

Davis ignored my rant completely. His eyes fixed into space, his arm over his head, absently twisting the locked doorknob up and down.

"My mom tried to kill herself last night."

My breath arrested. When I imagined Davis telling his parents, I only ever pictured him telling his dad. I'd forgot-

ten about his mom. She'd always been this wispy nonentity in his life, fading in and out of reality. She was a shadow of a woman, taking antidepressants the way most kids ate SweeTarts. It never occurred to me how she might react to the news.

"I never got a chance to say anything." Davis shook his head. "I got home and found an ambulance outside. We spent the night in the emergency room. This morning, the bastard took her to Mendota."

Madison sits on an isthmus between two big lakes: Monona and Mendota. But everyone in Wisconsin knows that when you're "taken" to Mendota, it means one thing: Mendota Mental Health Institute. Davis's mom had been committed.

Davis's twisting of the doorknob became more agitated; it clanked loudly with each sudden jerk of his wrist.

His dirty hair had fallen so far down his face that it took me a moment to notice his cheeks were shining with tears. Snot caked on his upper lip.

I sat next to him and put my hand on his knee, squeezed it gently to remind him that I was there. His entire body shook. This was the first time I lost Davis. The first time he became unreachable. I had no idea what it would take to get him back.

"Hey," I whispered. His jaw trembled, emitting a machine gun of faltering sobs. His shaking became so violent, I thought he was having a seizure. I panicked, not sure what to do.

"Can anyone help?" I asked as people walked by. But they wouldn't even look at us. No one wanted to get involved. It was all on me.

I knelt directly in front of him, put my hands on his cheeks, and forced him to stare at me.

"Davis," I said, trying to sound stern, but my voice cracked. "Davis, listen to me. This isn't your fault. You know that, right? What your mom did. What your dad did. You couldn't stop it. Okay? Davis?"

I held his face, refusing to let him look away.

"She's gone," he whispered. "Totally gone now . . . totally gone . . ."

I was practically in tears myself but I stayed strong and tried to turn his focus back to me. "I'm so, so sorry. But I'm not going anywhere. Okay? Like it or not, you tardmonkey, you got me. Okay? Please, Davis? Okay?"

I reached up and pried his hand from the doorknob. His fingers, so colorless I could almost make out bone through his skin, were locked in a withered claw. I folded his arms across his chest and hugged him. We must have sat there just like that for an hour. The tears stopped; the snot stopped; he went limp and let me be there for him.

"Don't," he rasped finally. "Really, Evan, don't. Go, I mean."

I flashed back a year to that night at Rocky Horror. I still didn't feel that kind of love for Davis, but I wished I did more than anything. If only to give him what he wanted. Or needed.

I didn't know if my friendship would ever be enough to fulfill any of his wants or needs.

"Right," I guffawed, "like you'd last five minutes without me, tardmonkey. Hell, I give you three minutes before total system failure."

He hiccupped a laugh and threw a halfhearted punch at my shoulder. "Tardmonkey I may be, but you'll always be Lord Emperor of All Tardmonkeys."

opening

The alarm bleats and Sunday begins with a fusillade of Huge Thoughts:

HUGE THOUGHT #1: *I hate opening Sunday mornings.*

My feet meet cold hardwood floor.

HUGE THOUGHT #2: *I get to work with Shan.*

I shut the bathroom door and quietly beat my head against the wall.

HUGE THOUGHT #3: *Why the hell didn't you just say, "Yes, please take me to California," Weiss, you complete and total loser?*

But now's not the time to worry about what I should or shouldn't have said to Erik. Now's the time to face the dread of Sunday: M and D's one completely non-working day of the week, when I'm left in charge. Today the store is mine.

Bwah-hah-hah.

In reality, running the store on my own is a colossal pain in the ass. But Shan's home to help, so today is destined to rock. I get to hide out in the freezer and do the cold-case inventory while she helps people out on the floor. And, of course, there's the Game.

When Shan and I are in charge, we pick a code word and, as we help customers, we get points every time we can get them to say the word. I am the reigning champ, having made Mr. Blazejewski, one of our regular customers, say "walrus" over seven times in one fifteen-minute visit. This is a grocery store. Working "walrus" into a conversation about fresh kohlrabi is murder.

I throw on work clothes, scarf down a piece of dry toast, and meet Shan downstairs. We go through the familiar opening ritual: switching on lights, counting the cash drawer, sweeping the floors, sweeping the sidewalk, hauling out the "Specials Today!" sandwich board, rolling out the awning, and a hundred other mind-numbing tasks. We finish with the most important task of all.

"The code word," Shan says, searching over her shoulders for imagined prying ears, "is 'daffodil.'"

"Ouch." I wince. "Game on."

At nine sharp, we open.

"Okay, I'm gonna hit inventory," I announce, grabbing my coat and wool gloves.

"Did you have a good time last night?" Shan asks.

I smile. "Yeah. It was great. Remind me later and I'll show you what Erik got me for graduation."

"Are you guys serious?" She's going for casual. She manages suspicious.

Condition: Red. Our childhood flashes before me. Shan knows about Erik. Something that no one else knows. History says that I'm in trouble. Emotional black-mail is a Weiss family tradition.

But Shan's no longer the ten-year-old who tattles. And I'm not a hopeless, boyfriendless lost cause any-more. I'm Erik Goodhue's boyfriend and I say, "Yeah, we are. He's the best."

I yank hard to release the near-vacuum seal on the freezer door; its frosty breath slithers out and pools at my feet.

"'Cause you've been together a year, right?"

I try to smile in a way that says, *You know you're mak-ing me very uncomfortable, right?* If she gets the message, she doesn't care. "Almost a year. Why all the questions?"

Shan moves from the counter, takes a carton of Oreos, and begins stocking the shelf near the freezer door, bisect-ing her attention between me and the cookies. "I just, you know, thought about it last night. After I went to bed, it hit me: My brother is dating a guy. My brother is dating a college guy. My brother is . . . I must have said it a hun-dred different ways and no one way made me feel any better."

I close the freezer door. This might take a while.

"I, uh . . . I thought you were cool with the whole gay thing."

The thought of losing Shan as the one person in my family who accepts me is devastating. Right up until the day she moved out, and even after she went to New York City, she was always telling me to get out, to meet and date people. I really believe she wanted that for me. I'm not sure what to believe now.

Reading my thoughts, she sets down the Oreos, and joins me at the freezer door. "I am. I'm totally cool with the whole gay thing. I guess . . . I just feel protective. I'd feel that way if you were dating a girl. Or anyone I hadn't met . . ."

I exhale deeply; cancel Condition Red. Now, at least, I know what she's fishing for. "You got any plans Tuesday night?"

She looks up, consulting her mental calendar. "Jenny and I were going for a girls' night out. Hit the old haunts. Why?"

"That's too bad. Erik really wants to meet you and he's invited us over for dinner on Tuesday. He was gonna cook, too. He makes the best chicken cashew—"

Shan claps and bounces up and down in excitement. "Screw Jenny! I got me a date with two hot gay boys! Waitaminute. Didn't you say his head is shaped like a square egg? Um . . . he is hot, isn't he?"

I grin. "Thermonuclear."

We make a quick plan for Tuesday. I'm borrowing the store's delivery truck so I can help Davis move, but Dad wants the truck back by three so I'll be home well before the end of her shift. Soon, she's darting around the store with renewed vigor. Satisfied we're okay again, I slip into the freezer.

It takes me half an hour to do inventory. It's been pretty slow, even for a Sunday. I'm dusting the shelves behind the register when the bell over the door tinkles.

Shan leans close and whispers, "Delivery for you, Spud. COD."

I turn to see Davis holding the door open for a frail woman in a pale yellow dress, like something from a Fifties fashion magazine. Her steps are measured, as though she thinks she might crack open the earth. Davis takes her arm and leads her through the door. She scans the room blankly, the familiarity of it not registering.

Shan walks over and smiles warmly. "Mrs. Grayson! You're looking well."

On the second Sunday of every month, Mrs. Grayson gets a special pass to come home for the day. And every second Sunday for the past four years, Davis has picked her up from the hospital, taken her home, and spent the day with her. The doctors say she can't be left alone, although she's pumped so full of many meds, I doubt suicide even crosses her mind anymore. Of course, Davis's dad always finds an excuse to work, leaving her in Davis's custody. Davis has never complained, not once.

While my family hasn't exactly embraced my friendship with Davis, it's never affected how they treat Mrs. Grayson. She's the one person we can all rally around and treat kindly. Every visit, we have to remind her who we are. Mrs. Grayson's vacant, dreamlike eyes search Shan's face for recognition but come up empty. Shan pats her shoulder reassuringly.

"I'm Shannon. My parents own this store. Can I help you with your shopping?"

Mrs. Grayson's face softens. "Thank you. That would be very nice. You know, my Davis just graduated. I want to make him a cake."

Shan nods at Davis, who transfers his mother's arm to Shan, and the two begin their search for cake ingredients. Davis joins me at the checkout counter.

"Aw, man," I whisper, "I forgot your mom was home today. What does she think about your old man kicking you out on Tuesday?"

Davis shakes his head. "I told her it was my idea to leave. That I needed my own space. She got upset, but I think she's coming around."

Even when we first met, Davis was the one who cared for his mother. He can be a total spaz in social situations, but watching him as a caregiver tells me that, given the right circumstances, he can be the somebody he wants to be.

Davis traces the wavy grain in the countertop with his finger. "So . . ."

Davis has never mastered the nonchalant segue.

"Yeah?"

"Are we still cool for the move and everything?"

"Yeah, we're set. I can have the truck at nine but I gotta have it back by three. Is that enough time?"

Davis nods. "Yeah, I'm almost done packing. Can I snag a few empty boxes from the storeroom? Need 'em to pack some books and stuff. The whole move shouldn't take very long. The octagon . . ."

He stops and bites his lip.

I poke him in the shoulder. "The octagon, what?"

He won't look at me. "I just . . . You know, I've been so busy getting ready to move and making sure I would have money . . . I didn't get you a graduation present."

Davis has never missed a gift-giving occasion in the nine years we've been friends. Gifts were never a priority in the Grayson house. I think that when we exchange gifts, it's Davis's way of making up for that. I've still got the Spiderman comic book he gave me for Christmas a few months after we met. It must be killing him that he can't give me a graduation gift.

I blow it off. "It's just delayed, that's all. Wait until you're settled."

He meets my eyes again and I see that familiar gratitude. "Hey, how about I take you out for our first meal in the big city, once we move to Chicago."

We. Chicago.

San Diego.

As stupid as it sounds, this is the first time it really sets in that I'm expected to be in two different places at once this fall. In different parts of the country. With different people.

My brain tries to reconcile this. For a moment, San Diego takes over and I'm on a beach with Erik's easel, painting the waves as they desecrate a sand castle. Erik is nearby with his new friends from his new school, playing volleyball. I initially decline to join in, insisting that I have to paint. But Erik begs and I can't say no, so I take point and serve.

But something's not right. The sky, the clouds, the shoreline . . . The colors are distorted. Close to the world I know but different, like a bad forgery. On the horizon, there's a man-shaped, colorless void.

Davis.

I've never imagined a scenario that didn't involve Davis. I watch everything I know, think, and feel detach from who I am. I should feel incomplete, having so much

111

removed. But I don't. Because the colorless void is over-shadowed by an embodiment of all color.

Erik.

What happens to Davis if I go to California? What happens to me if I don't?

"You okay?"

I blink. Davis stands before me in baggy orange shorts and a faded Superman T-shirt.

"Yeah, just . . . thinking."

"Hey," Davis says, casting a glance over his shoulder at his mother, "we should ask Sable about the next Chasers meeting when we see him. I thought we'd have heard something by now."

"When we see him?"

"Yeah. He's helping me move, remember?"

Right. Guess I hadn't really expected that to happen.

But his mention of Chasers makes me realize that all is not lost. I can't imagine moving to California and leaving Davis alone. He needs someone for when the Boing overwhelms him. But what if Chasers works out? What if he makes new friends? I'm not sure I trust Sable, but the other guys don't seem so bad. It may be worth checking out just to see where the whole thing goes. For Davis's sake.

Shan and Mrs. Grayson, their small basket filled to the brim, head to the counter. I snag Davis some extra boxes for his packing as Shan rings up Mrs. Grayson's groceries. Before they leave, I whisper to Davis, who nods and grins wickedly, then I say louder, "Okay. Catch you later."

Davis gives me the thumbs-up. "You got it." He grabs the groceries, winks at Shan (who kindly waits until his back is turned to grimace), and just before he and his mother hit the door, he turns back into the store and calls out, "Daffodil! Daffodil!"

Mrs. Grayson laughs, unsure what's happening, but she also cries out, "Daffodil!"

I make three hash marks on our scorecard behind the register. Shan tugs roughly at my apron strings and growls, "Because, you know, I would have killed you if you told me you were dating *him*."

resurrection

Poets would have us believe children strike out on their own so they can "spread their wings and soar." These poets never worked for their parents' grocery stores. Otherwise, they'd know the urge to leave home is less about flying and more about dodging the need for a patricide/matricide trial.

My job's just a job, but Erik loves what he does. He throws himself into his studies because it makes him a better nurse. He brings his patients something that no anatomy textbook can teach: actual feelings. This is not to say that all nurses are cold; they just seem like it in comparison to my boyfriend, who takes a lot of time to get to know his patients.

Case in point: Today, we're checking in on Mr. Benton at his home. No one told Erik to do this. It's all on his time. His coworkers have told him he'll burn out if he takes a personal interest in each of his patients. But he just blows them off. His personal motto? Sometimes, the toughest thing to do in the world is give a shit.

After my shift ends, I meet Erik at his place. We take off in his Jeep, and a few minutes later, pull up in front of the gray stone duplex on West Johnson. Erik rings the doorbell to the lower unit and Mr. Benton comes to the door. Erik was right: He looks a hell of a lot better than the last time I saw him. His cheeks are fuller, rosy with color. I forget how old he is—late forties, maybe?—but he still looks a lot older. That's because he's hunched over a bit and his face is baggy.

Benton smiles widely as he opens the door, but Erik stands spread-legged, like a gunfighter ready to draw at high noon, all business.

"You," Erik charges, leveling a dangerous index finger at Mr. Benton's chest, "missed your checkup with Dr. Friese."

Benton holds up a few sheets of stationery. "Well, excuse me, Mr. Pretty Nurse Man, but I felt inspired and got a little writing done. I thought you'd be proud." He steps aside to welcome us in. Erik shakes his head.

Benton's place might be huge, but it's hard to tell. There are books everywhere. *Everywhere*. Each wall is lined with bookcases, some thick and sturdy, others made from flimsy particle board. Most of the shelves on the bookcases are bowed, one paperback away from snapping under the weight. Teetering stalagmites of books sprout up in clusters from the thinning carpet, forming a narrow path to the sofa.

"Shirt off," Erik says, plugging his stethoscope into his ears.

Benton bats his eyes. "I bet you say that to all the boys."

"Careful," I warn, covering my ears, "children are present."

Erik starts his examination, listening to Benton's concave chest and asking him to breathe in and out. Having accompanied Erik on similar trips, I prep the blood pressure cuff in the medical bag, knowing he'll need it next. From inside the bag, I take out a small picture frame and hand it to Benton. On the glass, I've painted the Madison state capitol building at night, in the Cubist style of Picasso. Benton grins.

"You've really got a talent, Evan," he says, holding the picture at arm's length.

"It's to celebrate," I tell him. "Erik says your T-cell count is high."

"Go T cells!" Benton yells, making a fist with his free hand.

I don't really understand what that means. I know it has something to do with HIV and AIDS and low T cells means bad and high T cells means good. Sometimes, Erik launches into deep discussions about his work and what he wants to do at the research facility in San Diego. I've never had the heart to tell him it's all going over my head. I imagine it's how Davis feels whenever I start talking about art.

"So, as I was saying," Benton says with faux haughtiness, "before Nurse Ratched showed up and broke my concentration, I was doing a bit of writing."

"Good for you," Erik says, tightening the Velcro strap on the blood pressure cuff around Benton's upper arm. "You gonna try to get it published?"

Benton cocks his head, his gray eyes dancing. "Actually, I've been thinking. If my health keeps up, I might just try resurrecting White Satyr."

Erik's raised eyebrows tell me he's impressed. "Pretty ambitious. Not to rain on your parade, but I'd be more confident in your ability to stay healthy if you did things like, oh, kept your appointments with Dr. Friese."

"Nag, nag, nag," Benton mutters as Erik continues to poke and prod.

"What's 'White Satyr'?" I ask.

"My pride and joy." Benton beams, pointing to a nearby bookcase. Every book on the shelves—easily more than two hundred—bears a bright white spine with thin red lettering. At the bottom of each spine is a horned black triangle and the words "White Satyr Press."

"Mr. Benton founded the Midwest's first gay literary press back in the Seventies," Erik reports.

Benton steps away from Erik's exam and plucks a small, tattered scrapbook from his desk. He hands it to me. I've seen this before, at Mr. Benton's bedside the few times I've visited him in the hospital. He always has it with him. The first page has a black-and-white photo of eight smiling men with their arms around one another, sitting on the lawn at Bascom Hill on the UW campus. They're wearing bell bottoms and big glasses and everyone's got wild, long hair. I laugh when I spot Mr. Benton on the end, sporting a bushy mustache, his shirt unbuttoned halfway down his hairy chest.

"These were my friends back then. Artists, poets, playwrights, actors. We called ourselves the White Satyr Collective. Things were changing for gays across the country and we wanted to be a part of that. We were all struggling to get our work recognized in venues that weren't comfortable with gay themes. One day, I said if no one else will publish the work of these brilliant people, I'd do it myself. So the Collective became White Satyr Press. We published poetry chap books, literary novels, plays, and photography books. We made gay history."

Gay history. It makes me think of Sable. But not in a creepy way. When Mr. Benton says it, it sounds noble.

Benton takes the scrapbook back as Erik continues the

examination. I take one of the White Satyr books off the shelf, a poetry collection called *Red, Crimson, Carmine*. The author is Joseph Benton.

"I didn't know you were a poet." I smile, paging through the brittle, yellowing pages.

"There's a poet in all of us," Benton waxes.

"Not me." I sigh. "Can't write to save my life."

"Different vocabularies," Benton argues. "I use words, you use color."

Color as vocabulary. I like it. I've always tried to give my colors meaning within the context of a specific work. Now, through Mr. Benton, I see them as nouns, adverbs, adjectives. Awesome.

Benton glances at the cover of the book in my hands. He sighs. "That was the last thing I published before White Satyr folded."

"Why'd you shut down?" I ask.

Benton looks wistful. "My heart really wasn't in it after I lost Arthur in '89. By then, most of the Collective was gone. By the late Eighties, with things as they were, I wasn't sure how much longer I'd be around."

I'm not sure what he means but I'm afraid to ask. I've only heard Mr. Benton mention Arthur, his former partner, a few times before. I feel bad that I've dredged this up.

Erik zips shut his medical bag and claps me on the back. "I'll make you a deal, Mr. Benton. You stay on your meds, keep up with the yoga, and stop missing appointments and I know two local artists who'll let you photograph their work so you can publish it."

Benton shakes both of our hands. "You got a deal, boys. Wait and see."

"Remember," Erik tells Benton as we step out of the apartment, "this doesn't take the place of an exam with Dr. Friese. I only did this 'cause I worry about you. Make a new appointment and get your blood work done by the end of the week or you're in big, big trouble, mister."

Benton crosses his heart and raises his hand, palm out. "Promise."

Erik and I speed away in the Jeep. Now that it's just the two of us, I can ask.

"What did Mr. Benton mean when he said 'Things like they were back in the late Eighties'?"

Erik places his hand on my knee and gives it a reassuring squeeze. "The epidemic was going strong back then and there still weren't a lot of advances in HIV treatment. Mr. Benton watched his friends die, then Arthur. Mr. Benton found out he was positive the day after Arthur's funeral. I'm sure the future looked pretty bleak for him back then."

Epidemic. Treatment. I've been dating a nurse for a year and I'm only just now starting to figure out what he does. And what Mr. Benton went through. Learning some gay history might not be so bad. Even if it is from Sable.

"We all set for dinner on Tuesday with Shan?"

Erik's trying hard to make it sound like a casual question. Why do I feel like it's a test?

If it is, I pass. "Yeppers. She can't wait to meet you."

His shoulders relax. He was expecting an excuse. For once, I'm glad to disappoint him. But one test wasn't enough.

"Aren't you moving Davis to the RYC on Tuesday?"

I'd forgotten I mentioned that. "Uh . . . yeah."

"Need an extra pair of hands?"

"Thanks," I say, waving my hand like it's nothing. "But Davis doesn't own much. It won't take long."

I stay cool. I sound breezy. He nods. Mission accomplished. A Davis and Erik meeting has been averted. For now.

The King of Evasions changes the subject with finesse. "So you think Mr. Benton might really publish a book with our work in it?"

Erik's face is noncommittal, distant. "Resurrecting White Satyr would be good for him. He needs something to focus on, to be happy about. But I wouldn't hold your breath. He doesn't take care of himself like he should. I worry about him."

I reach over and squeeze his knee. That's another reason I love Erik: He's figured out exactly what he's supposed to be doing and it's not just a life-sucking nine-to-five. I really don't know if I can make a career in art. I haven't thought much about how I can apply what I do to some sort of job that will earn a living. But Erik has and he'll take on anything, no matter how tough.

He gives a shit.

moving

I'm alone when I ring the bell to Davis's house at nine sharp. It's a big three-story house here on Mansion Hill, overlooking Lake Mendota. You'd think the Graysons have money but the truth is that Mr. Grayson just likes to appear successful. Davis told me once that his dad barely breaks even every month and that a lot of his money goes to the huge mortgage and taxes. All in the name of *looking* wealthy. No wonder Mr. Grayson wants Davis to move out. Now he gets all the frozen dinners to himself.

Mr. Grayson answers the door. He's a small, nearly invisible slice of milquetoast.

"Good morning, Evan," he says in a listless voice. "Davis is upstairs. Thank you for helping him."

I was hoping Mr. Grayson would be at his office. He must be working from home today so he can make sure Davis is out on time. What a guy.

I nod, step past him, bound up the stairs and down the hall to the second room on the right. I knock on the closed door.

When there's no response, I open it slowly. His room looks like Tetris threw up inside. There are boxes—cubes, rhomboids—piled everywhere. Half of his stuff isn't even packed. A mound of dirty laundry stinks up the middle of the room. Davis is sprawled on his twin bed, facedown, wearing only a pair of tighty-whiteys.

"Up and at 'em, soldier!" I bark, tossing a shirt at him. He moans and stirs, then shoots me a look of hot, flaming death. "Did Sable call?"

"Mmpgh," Davis gargles, crawling to the pile of clothes on the floor. He throws on some pants and resumes packing while I begin lugging boxes downstairs to the truck. Mr. Grayson makes a show of glancing up at us and then over at the grandfather clock each time we pass by his study. We're very aware of our deadline: Davis must be out by noon.

At ten thirty, when I see that Sable isn't going to show, I pick up the pace. Davis makes an excuse for him; Sable's new to town and is probably having trouble finding the house. Every time I look at the clock, Davis has another excuse. He'll be here soon, Davis promises, but he starts moving more quickly.

It's eleven fifty-eight when we shove the last box in

the truck. Davis climbs in the passenger seat. I glance back at the house. "Aren't you going to say good-bye?" I'm stupid to ask.

"Just drive."

We park on the side street next to the RYC. Malaika is there to greet us. She hugs Davis and we go into her office to do paperwork. The rules of the house: It's temporary housing; he can stay a maximum of ninety days. After two weeks, he needs to pay thirty bucks a week for rent. If he can't afford that, he'll be given odd jobs to do around the Center and must complete them in order to stay. No overnight guests; all non-residents must be out of the building by eleven p.m. As Davis begins signing his life away on a dozen forms, I snag the room keys so I can start hauling boxes.

I'm dropping off the first load to Davis's stark room when the door across the hall opens. Sable, hand shielding his eyes, leans on the door frame and smiles.

"Hey, guy."

He looks like he slept in his clothes. His big toe sticks out from a formerly white sock. His voice is light and airy and his head sways slightly. His other hand holds a clear plastic bag containing a dozen translucent-brown prescription bottles. He sees me glance at the bag and shakes it like a baby's rattle. "I loves me some vitamins."

A sweet, earthy odor—carried on a thin sheen of

125

smoke—filters from his room into the hall. He's high.

I'm pissed but I make a joke. "Morning, sunshine. We been waiting on you. Party can't start without you."

Sable squints that way people do when they struggle to remember. Then he chuckles and nods. "Yeah, right. You and Little Dude."

"Little Dude" appears at the top of the stairs, loaded down with boxes. Sable tosses the pill bag back into his room, then launches over and takes the boxes off Davis's hands. "Let me get that for you, stud. Sorry I missed the excitement this morning. I totally spaced."

Yeah. Getting stoned will do that.

"No biggie. You're here now, right?" Davis says.

Sable winks at Davis and Davis melts.

With Sable's help, it only takes us a little more than an hour to unload the truck. I'll give him this; as he sobers up, Sable becomes a workhorse, often making two trips for every one Davis and I make. Of course, we've already done this once today so we're tired.

It's just after two when we finish and sprawl out on Davis's floor, exhausted. Davis orders pizza to thank us for our help, and two larges with the works are devoured within ten minutes of their arrival. I'm cleaning up the pizza boxes when Davis produces the octagon window from a box and looks around for the right place to hang it. Sable takes it from him, having spotted a nail on the wall over the bed. He hangs it, gives it a good look, and mutters, "Cool." I almost forgive him for leaving us in the lurch.

I glance at my watch and realize I only have five minutes to get the truck home before Dad does his Chernobyl impression.

"Sorry, I'd stay and help you unpack but—"

"No worries," Sable says, gripping Davis's shoulder. "We got it covered."

I look to Davis, who grins at Sable, then nods at me. I don't have time to be annoyed; I take the stairs down two at a time, burst through the door, and race to get the truck home.

I'm only two minutes late. I walk through the store. Dad is planted in his wheelchair at the register, ringing someone up. Mom is in the back room, rifling through a pile of job applications, scowling at each one. Even though I promised to work until I leave in August, she has to start looking for my replacement now so I can train them.

"Thanks," I say, dropping the truck keys on Mom's desk. She doesn't respond. "Hey, I know replacing me will be hard but, wow . . . I can actually see mercury rising in your eyes. Like a cartoon."

She selects three applications that have somehow managed not to offend her. "Shan says the two of you have plans tonight."

I freeze. What else has Shan said?

I suck all the air out of the room through a tiny gap between my lips. It figures that the one time I need a story, I don't have one. "Yup. Some brother-sister bonding."

But as usual, it doesn't matter.

"Don't stay out too late. You open tomorrow morning." She's not suspicious; it's business as usual. She likes when I spend time with Shan. She wants Shan to rub off on me. The air slowly returns to the room.

"No problem," I promise.

"You got a letter from Chicago. I put it on your nightstand."

The hair on the back of my neck shoots up. There are two things that are very strange about what Mom just did. One: She hasn't looked at me once. When she wants me to obey a direct order—*don't stay out too late*—she always looks me in the eye. Always. Two: Weiss family modus operandi dictates that all mail, regardless of recipient, gets piled on the kitchen table. You scrounge for what's yours. A personalized delivery to my room is weird.

I bound upstairs to my room, shedding my clothes for a shower. T-minus three hours until dinner with Erik. And Shan. Erik and Shan. What have I done?

I catch sight of the Chicago letter. Right next to my plane ticket. The one I left out in the open. The one-way ticket to San Diego dated August 12.

The one I thought only I knew about.

deluge

The walk to Erik's is painful. Shan and I avoid each other's eyes. In the silence, I worry about stupid things. That I'll break out in zits because I'm worried Mom saw the ticket. That Shan didn't do her hair, which probably means she's not taking this seriously. That our outfits clash and we look like Couture of the Damned on Parade. Our only conversation consists of a warning: "If you call me 'Spud' in front of Erik, I'll put Nair in your shampoo."

As we turn onto State Street, I close my eyes and draw strength from the thought of Erik. *This will be a great night. I am totally at ease.* And then . . . I really am.

We arrive at the Bookworm and I make a small presentation of using MY key to open the locked door at the base of the stairs. As we climb to the second floor, I can already smell the powerful spices I associate with Erik making Chinese food. I'm tempted to show off again and let myself in with MY OTHER key, but I play it safe and knock.

Erik opens the door. He's wearing a russet-colored dress shirt, a striped tan tie, and bister slacks. Gel spikes his hair in that way that turns me into Captain Libido.

Down, boy.

Erik smiles and steps aside, welcoming us in.

"Shan," I start, "this is Erik Goodhue. Erik, this is my sister, Shan Reynolds."

I know them both well. Her smile: tight to the face, corners of the mouth just barely up, no teeth showing = *I'm playing it cool and withholding judgment.* The DictionErik translation of his handshake: firm, two quick shakes = *I was beginning to think he'd never let me meet anyone in his life; it's a pleasure.*

Shan squints at Erik's head, then turns around to me and says, "Totally. Square-shaped egg."

Erik, who is positioned just behind Shan, narrows his eyes at me in a mock threat. He is not a fan of my square-shaped-egg analogy when it comes to describing his head.

"What does that even mean?" he demands from me. "Eggs aren't square."

"Trust me," Shan assures him. "It fits."

He holds up his index finger, smirks, and mouths, "That's one." I have no idea what it means but I'm already plotting to make it to two.

"Make yourself at home," Erik says, sweeping his arm at the living room. Even though his place is normally immaculate, a chemical-pine sting to the air tells me he's worked extra hard today. "Dinner will be just a couple minutes." He plants a kiss on my cheek and retreats into the kitchen.

I lead Shan into the living room, trying to gauge how she handled the kiss. I don't know why it felt conspicuous. That's what boyfriends do, right? They kiss. Still, it leaves me feeling naked. If she's shocked/offended/intrigued, she does nothing to show it. I show her Erik's sculptures and she nods, impressed. I give her the quick tour—kitchen, bathroom, bedroom—and we end up back at the kitchen just as Erik is hauling two huge bowls filled with food to the table.

He's gone way out. Three place settings—a small ivory bowl atop a shiny obsidian salad plate over a matching main-course plate. Champagne flutes filled with grape juice sit near a small centerpiece of orchids. Ivory cloth napkins folded to look like swans sit atop the silverware to the right of each place setting. To the left, everyone has a set of redwood chopsticks. It's all way over the top but that's Erik. I didn't even know he owned this stuff. Then it hits me—he went out and bought it all for tonight's dinner.

I try to picture a way to love him more. I fail.

Erik begins ladling fresh egg drop soup into each of our bowls.

"Smells delicious," Shan says, dipping her spoon in. I still can't get a read on her and that worries me. I'm the one who's supposed to be unreadable. When did we swap?

We follow with a small salad covered in mandarin orange slices and then the main course: chicken cashew. Erik, the master navigator of conversation, keeps things flowing all night. He asks me how the move went with Davis. He asks Shan about living in New York. He asks us both what it was like growing up in the Midwest. Now and then, he responds with a little information about himself.

In short, he demonstrates to Shan—in one hour—everything that made me fall in love with him over the course of an entire year. I feel like I won; she got the fifty-cent version and I got the grand tour.

As the evening progresses, Shan loosens up. She's mesmerized as Erik describes his *Angels* sculpture and says she can't wait for the unveiling. She laughs at all the right places and trots out embarrassing stories from my childhood, including how I once emptied every box of Jell-O from the store into our bathtub to make the world's biggest dessert. But I know my sister. She's holding back. I hear something false in her laugh. See the surreptitious glances at the door.

When we're done eating, Erik tries to usher us into the living room while he cleans up, but we insist on helping. Shan commandeers the plastic wrap, covering bowls and slipping them in the fridge. Erik and I stand shoulder to shoulder at the sink. He sings "Bohemian Rhapsody" and we trade off on the "Bismillah!" line.

Shan rolls her eyes.

When everything is dried and put away, Erik and I sidle up to each other on the love seat while Shan sinks into the papasan. The back of the chair gathers around her shoulders like a cobra's hood.

"So," Shan says, adjusting her dress, "are you sleeping together?"

Colors usually only explode in my head during a beating from Pete and his cronies. Now I'm bombarded by mushroom clouds of vermillion, beryl, and jade, like the immediate aftermath of a head injury. My mouth goes Sahara.

Erik sits up, a pleasant smile on his face. He lets his arm drift across the back of my shoulders. "Are you asking if we've ever shared a bed or if we're having sex?"

"Either," she says.

"Both," he returns.

When did my sex life end up on the conversation menu?

Shan is, obviously, not prepared for something this direct and I catch her nibbling her bottom lip for just a moment. "He's only just turned eighteen—"

"I know." Erik nods. "If you're worried, though, we did wait until he was legal."

Coin toss—how do I feel: invigorated that Erik is standing up to Shan's wacko, totally-out-of-left-field line of questioning by refusing to feel shame about our relationship or embarrassed because my sister now knows I'm having sex? It's a tough one. I choose the former, with caution.

Shan clears her throat. "I hope you told him about all the guys you've slept with before you two did anything. The last thing Evan needs is to catch an STD from his first sexual experience."

"Why would you assume that I'm Evan's first?"

"So!" I say. "How 'bout them Brewers?" No one bites. Apparently, my sex life trumps baseball.

I'm silently begging Erik to steer the conversation elsewhere. Erik doesn't break eye contact with Shan, whose face grows darker by the second. I know she's storing up for a major fuel burn.

"But, yes," Erik continues, "before Evan and I did anything, I told him about every guy I've ever been with. I even showed him a recent STD screening. I'm clean. I'd tell you about my former lovers and show you the test results but it's, frankly, none of your business."

Shan purses her lips, looks from me to Erik to me to Erik, and says, "Please tell me you're using condoms."

MADISON TEEN DIES OF
EMBARRASSMENT

Madison, Wis.—Doctors at the University of Wisconsin Hospital are reporting the first actual death by embarrassment. Dr. Elias Schroeder, head of the hospital's trauma unit, told journalists that 18-year-old Evan Weiss was having an uncomfortable conversation with his sister and boyfriend when he keeled over.

Attempts by Erik Goodhue, Weiss's boyfriend, to use CPR to revive Weiss were thwarted by Shannon Reynolds, Weiss's sister, who reportedly pulled Goodhue off the inert Weiss screaming, "You'll give him herpes! You'll give him herpes!"

My diversion is interrupted by a pounding at the door. Erik opens it and Cece from across the hall bounds in.

"Fucking A, I can't believe this—" She glances over and spots Shan and me. "Sorry, I didn't know . . ."

We all smile at Cece. *Nothing to see here.*

"Erik, I'm sorry but I can't get Ratfuck on the phone." Ratfuck is Mr. Teske, the building's super, who has yet to be available at his twenty-four-hour emergency number. She holds up a faucet nozzle. "I went to turn the water off in my sink and this broke. The water won't stop, the drain's clogged, the sink's getting full, I'm late for work, and . . ."

Before she goes into full panic mode, Erik is in his kitchen, where he grabs the small toolbox under the sink and announces, "Lead the way."

I smirk. "I'll get Noah on the phone and have him start work on that boat he's been talking about." Sculptor, yogi, nurse—but a plumber, my boyfriend is not. Having witnessed past excursions with that tool box, I know we're in for an Abbott and Costello routine.

Erik holds his fingers up in a V and mouths, "That's two." He takes a monkey wrench from the box and waves it at me threateningly as he snarls, "Miss me," before disappearing with Cece.

I whirl on Shan and come out swinging. I've got no other choice.

"What the *hell*?"

Shan's on her feet, clutching her head and walking in circles. "Ohmygod, ohmygod, ohmygod, it happened . . . *I've turned into Mom!*" Her hands shake as she takes a deep breath. Tears form in her eyes as she looks right at me. "Ev, I'm so sorry. I panicked. I don't know where this is coming from. I'm just . . . All the stories I hear about AIDS and gay bashing and . . . I was scared and I panicked."

I exhale. "Okay. Fine. Just . . . lay off the interrogation."

She nods. Then bites her lip. "But . . . I mean . . . Look, I don't mean to sound like a crazy woman but I do think you should think things through. Don't get mad. I'm trying to look out for you. This is your first time out of the gate—"

Telling me not to get mad has the opposite effect. "That's right. And I did better than you. Your first boyfriend got another girl pregnant while you were dating. You sure can pick 'em." It's been years since Shan and I have fought but slip effortlessly back into the old pattern.

But instead of fighting back, Shan looks hurt. "Enough with the low blows. We're past that." I'm almost embarrassed as she kneels at my side. "Look, Erik seems like a nice guy. He's gorgeous and talented; I can see why you'd fall for him. But he's four years older than you and he's got a lot more . . . experience."

I laugh. "Dad's seven years older than Mom. And if you say 'that's different,' this conversation is over."

She takes a deep breath. "Ev, let's face it. You haven't had a lot of choice here in Madison. You've been limiting yourself. Wisconsin isn't the most gay-friendly state."

I want so much to think that Shan is doing this for my own good, that she's concerned for me. Because thinking that my only ally in the family has turned might just push me over the edge.

In fact, it does.

"Erik got into a really great grad school in California and wants me to move with him." I say it so fast, I'm not even sure she hears me. In my mind, the words felt like justification. Now they sound like desperation.

Shan blinks, trying to process this. "And . . . do what?"

Somehow words keep spilling from my lips. "Go to art school. Be with him."

Shan slowly gets to her feet, turns, and walks away from me. "And you said yes?"

I lick my lips but they remain parched. "I'm thinking about it. I'm supposed to go to Chicago in the fall. With Davis."

Shan turns again and joins me on the couch. She puts her hand on my shoulder and looks me in the eyes. "So that's what it comes down to? Either Chicago with Davis or California with Erik? You've got so much potential. I don't want you to jump into either situation. I just don't think you're being practical about this."

"I *am* being practical, Shan. So is Erik. He doesn't want me to rush the decision. I know I have a lot to think about. But I love Erik. I know that much."

I know that much.

The apartment door flies open and Erik saunters in—chest broad, tie wrapped around his forehead like a bandanna, sleeves rolled up, and soaking wet. He slings the monkey wrench over his shoulder and raises a fist in the air. "There is no problem Big Gay Handyman cannot solve!"

I translate. "You made it worse and Cece called the plumber?"

He nods. "Well, duh. Grab the buckets. Let's bail water until he gets here."

I'm on my feet and we're both digging under the sink for buckets we've used during Cece's past water-centric problems.

"It's getting late."

As she speaks, Shan moves to the door, hitching her purse over her shoulder. Her voice warbles.

"This won't take long," Erik says, waving his hand at the papasan. "Have a seat. And we can continue our . . . earlier conversation."

My sister's smile is an apology. "Evan and I have to open the store in the morning. Thanks for dinner. Food was great."

She steps over the threshold and into the hall, where she expects me to join her. I stand next to Erik so our shoulders touch.

"Go on," I instruct quietly. "I'll be home in time for my shift in the morning."

Her eyes dart from me to Erik and back. Why is she acting this way? I know she wants to rip into both of us and tell us what a mistake we're making. And I want her to, so we can argue and get to the bottom of it. But she's not going to do that. Shan nods and makes her way downstairs.

"You should go," Erik whispers. "She's your sister."

"C'mon." I tug him into the hall. "I think I hear Cece putting on her scuba gear."

We haul ten buckets from the sink to the bathtub before the plumber shows. He chortles at Erik's attempts to control the situation and puts an end to the problem in just under twenty seconds. Erik lays a not-a-word stare at everyone in the room who's not a plumber. Erik and I say goodnight to Cece, who runs off to work. We retire to his place. Before the door is shut, he has me pinned against it for a long kiss.

"If that's punishment for the Noah's Ark comment, I'll be a smart ass more often." I smile, slipping my arms around his waist.

"So." He sighs. "That was your sister."

I nod, eyebrows raised. "Yup. I guess that could have gone better."

He shakes his head. "Nah. It could have gone worse."

As always, he's right. "Bet you're glad I waited this long to spring her on you."

He pulls me in for a tight hug. "Nope. You just don't get it, knucklehead. I don't want to love just Evan the Mysterious Artist. I want to love Evan the Brother, Evan the Son, Evan the Best Friend. I'm here for the full package. Thanks for bringing her over."

I search his face. For now, he's content. He won't be

asking to meet my parents for a while. But I don't know how much longer I can keep these parts of my life from him. How long before he sees the pentimento with the real me, standing in the background like a giant loser.

"No problem," I say, squeezing him tighter. "And maybe, if you're lucky, you'll learn to love Evan Who Knows When It's Time To Call The Plumber."

Erik sighs. "And that's three."

In a blink, he bends over and scoops me up, throwing me over his shoulder in a fireman's carry and twirling me around the room. I squeal and laugh. When I'm sufficiently dizzy, he marches me into the bedroom.

Yep. Tonight could have been much worse.

TITLE: *Good Fortune*

IMAGE:
Two chopsticks next to a broken fortune
cookie on a white plate

INSPIRATION:
Munch's *Scream*

PALETTE:
Chopsticks = sandstone
Plate = eggshell
Cookie = desert sand
Tablecloth = maroon

Long, thin lines of swirling color make
up each item. As Munch used his art to
express a state of mind, the cookie is broken unevenly with pieces scattered across
the plate and table.

One of the first things that Davis and I bonded over was a
love of Chinese food. I'll never be able to sniff moo goo gai
pan without thinking about the nights we spent in my room,
stuffing our faces from white take-out boxes and talking
until sunup. Futures were forged during the wee hours when

we ate ourselves into an MSG-induced stupor.

Every meal ended with fortune cookies. Given Davis's life, no one could have blamed him for being cynical. But he believed in fortune cookies. Believed that every message foretold his destiny. He saved every fortune in a jar. And if it didn't seem like one would come true, he would go out of his way to make sure it did. This was how Davis kept hope alive.

It seemed like fate when Davis got a job bussing tables at China Palace, this little place off Gorham Street. Whenever Davis worked a closing shift, Mr. Lee, the owner, let him take home as much leftover food as he wanted. I swear we both put on five pounds during our junior year.

But so much changed senior year. We didn't meet for late-night talks as much. Under the guise of working more hours at the store, I spent more time with Erik. Thankfully, I never had to worry about Davis finding out I was lying because he was working mega hours, trying to save up for Chicago. Our deep discussions moved to China Palace on nights Davis worked. I ate, he bussed.

The biggest change senior year was that Davis stopped believing in fortunes. He says it's because they stopped being fortunes—"You will meet a tall, dark stranger"—and started being random observations—"You have keen insight." We still ate and chatted, but he stopped collecting the little slips of paper. He wasn't interested in anyone else telling him what his future would be.

China Palace was dead one night last August, so I went there to hang out. I got the big circular corner booth so I could spread out my Seurat books and nurse an order of General Tso's chicken for the night. I didn't see much of Davis; Mr. Lee had him in back doing inventory. I sat staring at a photo of A Sunday Afternoon on the Island of La Grande Jatte *when I heard two familiar voices at the booth next to me:*

"I heard the food is great here."

"Hope so. I'm starved."

I froze. Tilting my head slightly, I peered up at the mirror that ran the length of the wall behind me. Sure enough, Erik and his best friend, Tyler, sat in the next booth, poring over their menus.

I slunk down and tried to keep from yarking my General Tso's all over the floor. At that point in our relationship, Erik hadn't given me my first yoga lesson. We'd only done a handful any of the scores of life-changing mini-adventures that carved out who we were as a couple. We'd been on several dates and were letting things slowly build. And I was crafting ways to keep anyone from finding out about him. The three of us—Erik, Davis, and me—in this enclosed space threatened all that. I wanted to disappear, but there was no way I could bolt for the door without being spotted.

Plus, the desire to eavesdrop won out over the fear of discovery.

They ordered, then Tyler launched in with, "So, are you still hanging around that kid?"

Tyler was known in Erik's circle of friends as Mr. Tact.

"I'm guessing you mean my boyfriend, Evan?" The words slid glacially from Erik's mouth.

I sank down under the table, far enough not to be seen, not so far that I couldn't hear. Tyler snorted. "Okay, yeah, your 'boyfriend.' Don't you think he's a little weird? He's kind of quiet."

I felt dizzy. All the effort to hide what a dork I was and Erik's friend could see right through me.

Erik laughed. "You barely know him. Evan's a little shy and takes time to warm up to people. And, hey, if he's not warming up to the big lovable briar patch that is you, I can hardly blame him."

Tyler grunted. "Okay, fine. I just don't want to see you go through another Colin thing, you know?" Colin, Erik's ex, had really messed Erik up.

The waitress brought spring rolls and they dug in.

Between chews, Erik said, "Trust me. Evan is nothing like Colin. He's smart, observant, he listens to me . . ."

"Dude . . . you talk like you're in love with this guy."

Erik lowered his voice. "And if I am?"

I sat up quick, trying to hear more, and slammed my head on the underside of my table. I almost missed Tyler laughing and saying, "Dawg!" He sounded happy for Erik. I was happy for Erik. I was happy for me. My head hurt like hell.

The waitress arrived with their main courses, then swung

by my table with my fortune cookie and bill. She raised an eyebrow when she saw me hiding under the table but just shrugged and walked away.

After that, the conversation in the next booth became less interesting—school, graduation, work. I couldn't have paid attention if I wanted to. Erik had said he loved me. Not to me. And not exactly. But it counted.

I crawled back onto my seat once they were gone. A few minutes later, Davis, in his messy apron, plopped down next to me, setting his bussing tray down with a thud.

"I'm beat," he exhaled. "Lee's got me rearranging all the stock so it's in alphabetical order. Huge boxes. Do I look like a body builder?"

I nodded, too numb to speak. I reached for my fortune cookie and cracked it open. "You are loved."

Davis snatched it and snorted. "See? It's not even a real fortune. That's got to be the lamest one yet."

I slipped it into my shirt pocket and thought, Only if it's not yours.

volume

Today, there are no code words in the grocery store.

It's nearly impossible to wake up next to Erik and peel myself away to go to work. But I do. At home, I sneak up the back stairs, throw some water on my face, then jog down the front stairs to the store, where I find Mom preparing to open. She doesn't notice I'm still dressed in yesterday's clothes and doesn't seem to know that I've been gone all night.

"Where's Shan?" I ask. I spent the walk home preparing to continue our conversation from the night before. I was ready for a melee.

"Not feeling well," Mom says. "I'll help with pre-opening. Then you're on your own while I do interviews."

I can't tell from her tone if Shan said anything to her or not. But Mom's never been one to hold back. If she knew anything about Erik, she'd have laid into me right away. I'm hopeful; Shan hasn't completely turned on me. Yet.

"Got it." I start sweeping. Something inside me roils. The courage that I built up, expecting to have it out with Shan, shouldn't go to waste. "Oh, thanks for putting that letter from Chicago in my room."

I search her face for a reaction. *This is your opening, Mom. If you saw the plane ticket, speak up.*

She points to the "Specials Today!" board. "Change that to 'Asparagus, one seventy-five a pound.'"

Mom disappears to start interviews as soon as we open. The morning flies by.

Gina, a coworker, arrives at half-past noon to relieve me, and I head upstairs to change. Walking into the kitchen, I stop dead when I see Ross, one of the guys from the Chasers meeting, sitting at the table. He's wearing a thin white shirt, purple dotted tie, and faded dress slacks. It's a little surreal, him all dressed up and in my house. I haven't seen him since we quietly bonded over our skepticism at the meeting. He's just as surprised to see me.

"Uh . . . hey." I offer a little wave.

He swallows and smiles. "You interviewing for the job too?"

I hold up my apron. "I've *got* the job. All yours if you want it." When his face crinkles, I explain. "My parents own the store."

He nods and I think I just made him more uncom-fortable. At least, I assume he was uncomfortable before my arrival. He *was* just interviewing with Mom.

I grab a glass of water from the fridge. "Anything to drink?"

His face twists. "No thanks. Too nervous. She grilled me for twenty minutes, then just walked away. Is that a good sign?"

"Very good," I say, leaning on the counter. "If she hated you, she'd list your faults before saying you didn't get the job. For Mom, silence is a high compliment."

I nurse my water and we just stare at each other. I can hear Mom down the hallway, fussing in her bedroom. If she's true to form, she's looking for the W-4s she's con-stantly misplacing. Why they'd be in the bedroom is any-one's guess.

Ross shoots a glance at the hall, then lowers his voice. "Hey. Can we—? What did you think? About the other night?"

"Truthfully?"

"Yeah."

"I'm not so sure about it."

Ross's shoulders sag as he relaxes. "So I'm not the only one who thinks Sable was way out of line."

I take a seat next to him at the table. "I think we're the only ones. I mean, I guess some of what Sable said made sense. You know, about gay history and Stonewall. But what he did to Danny . . ."

Ross grimaces. "I know. That's exactly what I tried to tell Del. But he was all, 'We just have to trust him,' and, 'This guy really knows what he's talking about,' and I was saying, 'Yeah, what happens when he demonstrates on you?'"

Wow. He and Del sound like me and Davis.

"So . . . ," Ross says, a little quieter, "did you catch the drugs on Sable's nightstand?"

I think back but I wasn't paying attention. I smelled pot the day we moved Davis in. And there was the bag of bottles Sable had in his hand . . . "Pills or something, right?"

Ross nods, his eyes narrowing. "Lexiva, Norvir, Truvada . . ."

The names are familiar. I'm sure I've heard Erik mention them. When I stare back blankly, he adds, "They treat HIV." Ross leans in. "Do you . . . think Sable's positive?"

I shrug. "I dunno. Is it a problem if he is?"

"I'm not passing judgment, but . . . Sable's been around. I guess that's all I'm saying." He looks away, frustrated. His point is clear: What do we know about this guy?

I glance over my shoulder for signs of Mom. When she doesn't emerge, I continue. "So . . . I haven't heard

anything about the next meeting but . . . are you going
to it?"

He looks down. "Are you?"

Chicken shit. I don't know if I mean him or me but it
applies either way.

I say, "Until I get a better read on Sable, I should
go. Keep an eye on Davis. He has a tendency to get . . .
involved."

Ross shakes his head and says, "I'm not going back.
I'm taking a year off before I go to school, and I wanna
work as many hours as I can and save money. I don't have
time for . . . that."

I nod. "But Del . . . He's going to keep going."

Ross fidgets with his tie. "We grew up across the street
from each other. We've been best friends for, like, ever.
We never fight. But we went balls to the wall over this."

Mom comes back into the kitchen, triumphantly
holding a wrinkled W-4. She looks surprised to see Ross
and me talking. "You two know each other?"

I stand, letting Mom sit at the table. "Sort of."

Mom hands Ross a pen and points out where he needs
to start writing. "Well, good. You'll be training Ross. He
starts next week."

I salute, give Ross a nod, and head to my bedroom. As
I peel off my work clothes, my computer chimes. I have a
new e-mail. From Davis:

Been talking with Sable. He's awesome!!
Living here at the RYC is great. Big things
happening with Chasers. This is gonna be
so cool.

I should be happy. Wasn't that the plan? Help Davis
fit in and make friends with the Chasers so I don't feel
like a shit for moving to California.

Then why does it sting to hear he doesn't need my
help? He's already in.

Days pass and, quite conveniently, Shan and I continue
to miss each other. She's become a master of avoiding me,
even when I'm deliberately trying to track her down. I'm
tempted to confront her while she's working, but I don't
think anything we have to say can be said at a regular
decibel level. So I bide my time.

Late afternoon on Friday. I decide to quit moping.
I grab my new easel, a small circular window, and my
paints and head over to Bascom Hill on the UW campus.
I lock up my bike near the Mosse Humanities Building.
It looks like a concrete sugar cube with massive columns
around the perimeter and a waterfall of short, wide stairs
leading down from the doors. I make my way about halfway up the stairs and stop.

I unfurl Erik's easel (which I now realize needs a

name equally as cool as THE CLAW) and position my window to face the building. That's when I hear a click and a pop from behind me. I turn and Sable's at the bottom of the stairs, smiling up at me. His trench coat hangs loosely on his tall frame. He's holding an old camera. It's cumbersome, with a big silver dish on top, from which Sable ejects a flashbulb. As he climbs the stairs, Sable smacks his lips and yanks on a blue tab on the camera's side. He draws out the picture he just took and hands it to me.

"Hey, guy," he says with a sanguine smile. "Weird running into you here."

He peels back a thin paper that covers the photo. There I am in black and white in the lower left corner of the picture. Taking up the majority of the shot is the Humanities Building behind me. There's something about the angle and how the shadows fall that make the building look like a giant mouth: the pillars smooth, rounded fangs; the staircase a colossal, crenellated tongue. It's about to eat me.

"Awesome shot," I say, handing back the photo, but he waves at me: *Keep it.* I'm not sure if he's a good guy or a bad guy, but he's a hell of a photographer. "Kind of an old camera."

He holds it proudly, smacking his lips again. His voice cracks; he's parched. "Who needs this digital shit? Give me film any day. And the older the camera, the better. I like the effect it has on the image."

The pic in my hand is slightly distorted and grainy. There's a dark halo around the outer rim, framing the picture as if seen through a monster's eye.

"Well, you've really got a talent for this sort of thing."

"Thanks. I won some awards," he says. "I like to use lots of negative volume." He points out the gaping empty space that dominates the photo. "That means the emptiness is your main target and all the objects around just give it shape."

"Yeah, my sister's a photographer." I nod. "She says she likes to define what's there by what isn't."

Sable nods, pulls a liter bottle of water from his pocket, and starts power-chugging. It's a cool day but I notice for the first time that he's sweating. And pale. Then Sable says, "So, we're cool, right?"

"Huh?"

He takes out a cigarette and lights up. I don't know why, but when he reached into his trench coat for the cigarette, I flashed back to my talk with Ross and half expected Sable to pull out a bottle of HIV meds.

"I was really proud of you the other night at the meeting," he says, taking a deep drag. "You were the first one to step up to bat and try to get me to stop. You got guts, guy. I admire that. But I just wanna make sure you weren't all wigged out. You know I was just doing that to make a point, right? Hell, even Chinky Chinaman shook my hand."

Great. Creepy *and* a racist.

"Little Dude thought you mighta freaked a bit." Sable pinches the cigarette between his lips as he loads a new film cartridge. I don't like the idea of Davis talking to Sable about me. I especially don't like that he's reporting on my mood.

I grab my palette and start to mix some color. I think about the e-mail from Davis. "Is that why I haven't been invited to any meetings?"

Sable laughs. "We haven't had any meetings yet, guy. I promise. Yeah, some of us just kinda got together. I'm new in town; guys were showing me around. As long as you say you're still in, I'll be sure you know about the next meeting. In fact, expect an e-mail soon."

"Hey, there you are."

We both turn to see Davis jogging up the stairs toward us. He holds out a small bag. "They didn't have the flashbulbs you need at Walgreens. I had to get them from a specialty photo shop. They're damned expensive. Hey, Ev."

Hey, Ev? Hasn't seen me for days and all I rate is "Hey, Ev."

Sable tears into the package of flashbulbs. "They're

classics, my friend. Sometimes you pay for the classics."

Davis's voice is all Boing. "Cicada's teaching me about photography."

And he's calling him Cicada now? I was hoping the nicknames were a joke.

Davis continues. "Did you know that if you were to mix all your paints, you would get black? But if you mix all the colors of light, you get white?"

"Yeah, I think I heard that somewhere." Like fifth-grade science. Or maybe it was the time I tried to teach Davis to paint years ago. It's hard to hear my own words taken seriously for a change, simply because they were spoken by Sable. Like somehow, when I said them, they didn't matter.

As Sable fusses with the flashbulb package, Davis pulls me aside. "Ev, Cicada is so cool. If he'd been around when we were in school, nobody would have messed with us. He doesn't take shit. He used to pound guys who called him 'fag.' I wish we'd been more like that."

Yeah. "Cicada" doesn't take shit. Being six foot four probably didn't hurt either.

Davis studies the new easel. "Hey, what happened to THE CLAW?"

"Traded up," I say, turning back to the pool of dark gray paint I've just mixed.

Sable jams a new flashbulb into his camera and squishes

Davis and me together. He hops back two steps and takes aim. Davis throws his arm across my shoulders and I try to smile as the bulb goes *pop!*

Sometimes belonging sucks.

retreat

Negative volume consumes my life and I'm defined by what's no longer there.

No Erik—he loads up on double shifts at the hospital to pay for the big move in August. Between his schedule and mine, our relationship is reduced to e-mail and quick phone calls.

No Shan—she trades shifts with Gina so we never work together. She even seems to know when I'm sitting at home waiting for her, and she makes herself scarce.

No Davis—our work schedules keep conflicting, and on those rare occasions when they don't, I go to the RYC and Malaika informs me he's out somewhere with Sable. The "regular" Chasers meetings Sable promised have yet to happen but the "unofficial" ones continue. I start to resent Davis. Has he even once said, *Hey, let's invite Evan*? Doubtful.

With nothing else to do, I throw myself into Haring.

I trace the outlines of the paintings in library books with my fingers, trying to get a feel for what it's like to be him. Try to see how he saw things.

Distillation. Reducing detailed images to outlines, the barest components needed to render it. Fusing individuality and community, creating a symbiosis so that each requires the other to survive. My dreams at night fill with recurring themes from his work: babies, couples, UFOs, people within people.

I'm almost ready to paint my Haring.

Just when I think I'll really go crazy, Fourth of July weekend sneaks up and I get a call from Erik: *Clear your schedule, pack a bag, we're going out of town.* I don't ask any questions. I just get on the phone and start giving away my shifts at the store until the entire weekend is free. I tell Mom that Davis and I are going for a "presemester retreat" to the University of Chicago. She's just glad I found someone to cover my shifts. I practically run with my duffel bag all the way to Erik's apartment, where he's waiting with the top down on his Jeep and soon we're cruising east down I-94.

We step over each other, trying to catch up. He tells me about every drunk, pervert, and pregnant woman he's treated at the hospital. I tell him that Keith Haring is officially the coolest person on the planet who isn't my boyfriend. He talks about how close he is to finishing the

Angels sculpture. I talk about how Shan has been avoiding me. It's a rapport that's taken a year to master, but it's all so natural now as we fall into a cadence, both of us relaying all the vital information, both of us listening intently, both of us just eager for a weekend away.

"So," I finally ask when we hit the Lake Mills city limit, "where are we going?"

He teases. "I'm not sure I want to tell you."

"It's a surprise?"

"Sort of."

"Can I have a hint?"

"We're going to Milwaukee to see Nolan and Anna. Grill some burgers. See some fireworks."

We've spent time with Erik's friends at their house on Lake Michigan before. But the fact that he's being so secretive tells me there's more.

"And?" I ask.

"And that's all I'm saying."

I shoot a gaze at the back of the Jeep. A big furry blanket tied down with bungee cords hides mystery cargo. Earlier, when I went to load my duffel bag into the back, Erik jumped to block me, took my bag, and gently tucked it behind the passenger seat. Mystery cargo is apparently not for my eyes. Yet.

"Does this have anything to do with the buried treasure?" I ask, thumbing toward the rear.

"By Jove!" He shouts, posher than posh. "The boy's a genius!"

I've been to Milwaukee with Erik twice before, both times to visit his friends. Today, we're nowhere we've been before. The streets are choked with cars and pedestrians, the buildings loom higher the deeper into the city we go. The smell of hops permeates the air.

"Okay," I concede, "we're in Milwaukee. What's the secret?"

"Learn, you will," his voice burbles in his Yoda impression. "Patience, young Jedi."

A turn here, down a street, then down an alley. Five minutes later, we pull up to the curb and stop. The streets are nearly deserted here. The architecture of the dilapidated buildings feels old. But in the middle of all this, a small, very modern building of marble and glass and sinewy brass demands attention. The front has a half-moon steel awning around which, in long, thin letters, are the words FEDOROV ART GALLERY.

I start to unbuckle. Erik crawls over me and out my door, blocking my exit. He holds a single finger up and presses gently on the tip of my nose, as though he's training a schnauzer. "Evan. Stay. Stay, Evan. Stay."

I chomp playfully at the finger and he darts into the gallery. He returns a minute later with a small cart, nods at the back, and commands, "Help me."

He removes the blanket and I freeze. Wrapped in foam and cushioned with bath towels and old coats are six small windows. *My* windows. These are the gifts I've given Erik over the past year. Birthday. Christmas. Valentine's Day. "Just because" presents. Every one accounted for. Erik gently loads them on the cart.

"Erik, why are—"

"We need to work on your definition of 'help me.'" He winces, loading a heavy oak-framed window on to the cart, completing the job himself. He pushes the cart toward the building, pausing only to call over his shoulder. "This'll work a lot better if you actually come with me."

Zap. I'm at his side, holding the door as he proceeds into the gallery. The reception area is small and very, very beige. The floor is mottled, the walls are two-tone, the desk is boxy and speckled, but it's all beige. Against the far wall, I see Erik's robot sculpture—*Some Assembly Requited*. A young woman, not much older than me, hangs up the phone and grins at Erik.

"Oxana's on her way down," she informs us.

Here's where Evan goes berserk.

I should have recognized the name from the front. Oxana Fedorov is Erik's friend who owns an art gallery. *This* art gallery. The one I'm standing in right now. "Friend" isn't even right; she's actually his godmother, an old college friend of Erik's father.

And she's a world-renowned art expert. Not Wisconsin renowned. Not United States renowned. I mean, people in places like Barcelona and Zurich pay her a bajillion dollars to fly to them and appraise work and give lectures and teach master classes. USDA Grade-A Prime renown. In short, someone I do *not* want looking at my work.

My breathing grows shallow and my extremities go numb. I want to claw at Erik's arm and beg him to turn around and load the paintings back up into the Jeep. I don't want my last thought to be, *So this is what a stroke feels like.*

But a somber chime announces the opening of the nearby elevator and Oxana Fedorov, Art Goddess, emerges. She's wearing a sleeveless ebony top with billowing milk-colored slacks that ripple as she moves toward us. Her dowel-like arms are folded in a self hug. Bright red-framed glasses hang from a sterling chain around her wrinkled neck.

Her pink lemonade lips part in a smile as she kisses Erik once on each cheek. I've only ever seen that in movies. Davis and I used to make fun of it, but suddenly it's very, very cool.

"Oxana." Erik beams, his hand sliding around to the small of my back. "This is Evan."

Everything about her seems formidable. I can picture her reducing artists to tears with just the slightest arch of her pointed eyebrows. Still, as she regards me, she is warm, and her Russian accent is the shit.

She offers her hand, which I shake (after discreetly drying off my clammy palm). "Evan, it's a pleasure." She turns back to Erik. "Shall we?"

Erik pushes the cart toward the waiting elevator. I find myself unable to move. Oxana weaves her arm into mine and we follow Erik.

"Erik tells me you're a fan of Keith Haring," she says, pausing to poke the 2 button in the elevator. The doors chime, close in obedience, and we're off.

I nod. I realize that I haven't actually used, you know, words for a long time now. I don't imagine that changing soon.

"When we are through"—everything about her voice is like Willy Wonka's chocolate river—"you must go to the third floor. I have a small exhibition, on loan from his estate. It doesn't open to the public until Monday, but I know the curator."

I laugh, a little too loudly, but I welcome the knowledge that, yes, I can still make sound. The doors open on the second floor. We go down a long hallway, and at the very end is an office door bearing Oxana's name. Her office is huge and white. The walls are surprisingly stark, with only a few paintings. Six marble pedestals sit in a row down the middle of the room, right in front of her desk, which is near a giant window with a view of downtown. Erik begins setting up my paintings, laying the broadside of each frame on a separate pedestal. The phone on her desk rings and Oxana answers it. I close in on Erik.

"What. The. Hell?"

"Ah," Erik mutters, turning a painting of our favorite bench overlooking Lake Monona so that it faces Oxana's desk. "Evan go talkies again?"

"Erik, I'm totally serious. Stop this. Please. I'm begging you. Don't make me go through this." In eighteen years, my voice has never sounded this desperate. I've never been this desperate.

"You are a very talented artist. Oxana has an eye for talent. I've been promising to introduce you and now I'm following through with that promise. What's the big deal?"

I sense Oxana is wrapping up the phone call so I pull him in close and hiss, "Oxana does not have an eye for talent. She has two eyes for art. She has many, many eyes. She is a big eyeball monster when it comes to art. She can spot an amateur at ten paces. I'm not ready for this."

He stares at me and says firmly, "Evan, you need to trust me." There's something in how he says this. His emphasis, ever so slight, on "need" and "trust." Embedded meaning: It won't be long before he asks to meet Davis. And my folks.

I hear a click as Oxana hangs up the phone. Erik tips his head toward the door. "I've got a couple quick errands to run. I'll leave you two to talk. Be back soon."

ARTIST'S HEAD SPONTANEOUSLY COMBUSTS, KILLING FOUR

Madison, Wis.—The Fedorov Art Gallery, located in the warehouse district, burned to the ground yesterday. Investigators have determined the blaze was caused when the head of artist Evan Weiss, 18, exploded at the prospect of having his work inspected by Art Goddess Oxana Fedorov.

Before I can say a word, Erik's gone. I'm alone. With the eyeball monster.

unnecessary

I glare at the door and, behind me, I can hear the clicking of Oxana's heels as she makes her way to the first pedestal. I close my eyes and focus on my breathing, like yoga. Deep in through the nose, then out. I try to clear my mind but that's hard when my boyfriend has just abandoned me. *He means well . . . He means well . . .* I repeat the mantra, wanting to trust Erik but needing to run away.

Oxana walks a full circle around each painting, the cherry-framed glasses now poised at the tip of her nose. I'm not sure what's expected of me. I feel I should explain each work. Or maybe tell her what they're called. Or maybe just stand aloof like a tortured artist who doesn't give a damn what anybody thinks. I settle for giving her space, slouching awkwardly near the giant window and dividing my gaze between Milwaukee and her casual stroll around my paintings.

Twenty minutes pass. That averages out to three minutes per painting. I wonder how much this woman makes in three minutes. I wonder how much other artists would pay to have her spend three minutes on just one of their works, to say nothing of the twenty she's granting me.

With a flick of her finger, the glasses now dangle by their silver chain and she wraps her emaciated arms in another self hug.

"You're very good."

Ice blue floods my vision. I can breathe again.

"Thank you," I say almost silently.

Oxana turns her back to regard a small square window on which I've painted a replica of Cézanne's *The Abduction*. A graduation gift for Erik, who mentioned he admired the work when we saw it at a touring Cézanne exhibit. I faked sick for a week, missing school just so I could have it ready in time for his graduation.

"Your attention to detail is astonishing," Oxana whispers, wiggling her finger at the painting as though trying to recreate the brush strokes herself. "You're dangerous. You could be a master forger."

I don't know what to do with this, other than file "swindler" away as a fallback career.

My mouth is dry but I manage a small smile and say, "I like to use my powers for good."

She leans in to examine a picture of State Street at night, done in the style of Georgia O'Keefe. O'Keefe was one of the easiest to grasp. Abstraction adores me. Oxana continues to stare and, again, I'm not sure what to say.

"Will you be showing my work?"

I'll always maintain that the biggest problem with becoming an adult is our firm adherence to the concept of "no takebacks." There's no way I can withdraw the question, a bastard child of stupidity and eagerness. She turns and her face says it all. If I were anyone else—not Erik's boyfriend, not some dumb kid just out of high school—she would have laughed at me. Instead, she chooses compassion with a small smile.

"You're very talented, Mr. Weiss. I see a lot of very talented people here. I work with very, very few. What you've done is certainly good. But, ultimately, it's little more than mimicry."

My fingertips go cold and the edges of my vision go blurry. I shoot a glance at the frame of a nearby picture. She sees this and reads my mind.

"Yes, your medium is unique. Interesting. But I'm sure you know there's more to art than the medium you choose."

She stands behind me, places her thin fingers on my shoulders, and turns me to face my version of *The Abduction*. "Every detail," she breathes into my ear, "exact and perfect. Too exact. Too perfect. If people believe Cézanne did this, where does that put you? You become a nonentity. It's not your work. Where are you, Mr. Weiss? Where are *you*?"

I open my mouth to protest. Am I allowed to protest genius? Yes, I copied Cézanne, but what about the others? The subjects were of my choosing, from my perspective. And if I used someone else's methods to convey that, doesn't that also reflect on the artist? How am I missing from my own work? I don't say any of this. I'm humiliated.

She guides me to my picture of a pawnshop on State Street, reminiscent of Picasso's *The Old Guitarist*, featuring a guitar bathed in the pale blue light of a display window, sans guitarist. "Were you sad when you painted this?" she asks.

I hesitate. "No. It was a great day."

"I suspected as much," she admits. She reaches out, her fingers gliding just above the thin lines in the painting, careful not to touch. "Do you know about Picasso's blue period? He painted while in a state of depression. He chose varying shades of blues and blue-greens to show his feelings. You chose these colors because they resembled Picasso's. Inform your pieces with your life, your thoughts, your perceptions. Just as Picasso and Degas and all who came before. Let your colors be *your* emotions and combine them with *your* technique to give us *your* message."

These are all things I thought I knew. I was wrong. I think of Mr. Benton, calling my colors my vocabulary. Here I've been using the right language but the wrong words. I stare at this piece that I created, labored over, and suddenly I don't recognize it anymore. I see it as she sees it: lifeless, wan. "I only study artists' techniques. I don't know anything about Picasso's life."

A chill of shame runs across my shoulders as I hear her *tsk*. "To appreciate a work of art does not require intimate knowledge of an artist's background. Anyone can survey and react to art. But to create, it is often wise to understand where an artist has come from. What inspired them? What in their life prompted them to speak out through their art? Everyone is influenced somehow."

She opens a desk drawer and removes a weathered book. The dust jacket is missing but as she pages through it, I catch the title on the spine: *Keith Haring—Journals*. She licks her fingertips, flips through the pages, then passes the book to me, pointing out an underlined passage on the jaundiced page:

Matisse had a pure vision and painted beautiful pictures. Nobody ever has or ever

will paint like him again. His was an indi-
vidual statement. No artists are parts of a
movement. Unless they are followers. And
then they are unnecessary and doing unnec-
essary art.

Even Haring thinks I'm crap. A follower. Unnecessary.

"Think about what I said, Mr. Weiss." She fixes me with a look that's two parts empathy, one part pity. "You've done your homework. Your technique is impeccable. Now it's time to figure out what you have to contribute."

She gives my shoulder a short squeeze, then hands me a thin ivory card from a sleek silver box on the desktop. Her name, the gallery, and her private phone number are embossed in lusterless copper.

"Erik says you're thinking about art school. I know the deans of many fine institutions. San Francisco, New York, London, Florence . . . Most will have closed their fall admissions by now, but if you find a school where you'd like to study and need a reference, give them my number." A tiny smile crosses her pert lips. "You're almost there, you know. Almost."

I go to hand the book back but she shakes her head. "Let it be your first lesson on the life of an artist. Get it back to me when you're done."

I slip the card into my shirt pocket and guess that I

must look undead because she broadens her smile, hoping to resurrect me. "I'll be very interested to see where you are in a few years. I suspect I'll see great things from you. Maybe then we can talk about a showing."

She glances at the tiny clock dangling from a chain at her waist, excuses herself, and leaves the room. Numb, I begin to pack my work back into Erik's makeshift traveling cases.

All this time, I thought I was good. I thought I was a painter. Turns out I'm just a huge copycat.

I load the last window onto the cart and as I'm about to leave, I notice a silk screen on the wall opposite Oxana's desk. It's an original Keith Haring, one I've only seen in books. It's square with a black background. In the middle of it all is a huge pink triangle. Superimposed over all this is a jigsaw of many silver human figures with the thick, rounded outlines that made Haring famous.

The figures are shown only from the waist up, each overlapping another, alternating positions—some have round hands covering their mouths, others cover their ears, the rest, the eyes. See/Speak/Hear no evil. Very few of Haring's works have titles but I know this one: *Silence = Death.*

I'm drawn in, marveling at the simplicity. Here it is, cartoonlike and yet brilliant. Haring carved a name for himself. It didn't look like anything anyone else had done.

I'm sure he didn't waste his high school years replicating Cézanne and Van Gogh and da Vinci. He had vision. He is there, in the painting, staring back at me. When I look at my work, I'm not staring back.

I don't know how long I stand, gaping at the silk screen, before I realize Oxana is standing shoulder to shoulder with me.

"It was one of Haring's many responses to the AIDS crisis of the Eighties." Her whisper echoes the reverence I feel. "Part of the exhibit. I'm putting it in the gallery on Monday. I just wanted it in here for a few days so I can pretend it's mine."

"My next painting was going to be . . . you know . . ." I feel sick so I don't finish this sentence. Right now, I never want to paint again.

Oxana's tiny fingers grip my shoulder. "So do it. Paint your own Haring. Do your own *Radiant Baby*. Get it out of your system. Let it stand as a testament that it's time to move on and find out what Evan Weiss has to say. You've spent too long delivering someone else's message."

She escorts me and the dolly to the third floor where Erik is waiting. He smiles at me but I make a point of looking away. The gallery is a massive white box, almost the size of a football field. And it's just the three of us.

"Here's the Haring exhibit." She beams proudly.

Along the left wall, flat-screen TVs run a loop of

Haring's video art. Most are videos of him painting or doing performance art. The right wall sports an assortment of silk-screen paintings.

"Take your time; look around," Oxana says. "I have another appointment so you'll excuse me."

Erik and Oxana exchange hugs; I shake her hand and thank her for her time. A moment later, Erik and I are alone. He slips his hand into mine and we walk the gallery.

"So, how did it go?" From the DictionErik: cracked, high-pitched voice—*Evan, you're upset; I can tell. That makes me nervous.*

I stare into the first flat-screen—a video of Haring drawing a design on the floor until he's literally painted himself into a corner. The irony is not lost on me.

"It was . . . great," I mutter.

Erik grins. "Isn't she amazing? I love Oxana. She's so smart, really knows her stuff."

"Yeah." I nod, my eyes never leaving the flat-screen. "Yeah. She pretty much told me I was a hack."

I try to stroll ahead to the next TV, but Erik hasn't budged and, still tethered at the hand, I yo-yo back. He tries a smile. "I'm sure it wasn't that bad."

I want to focus on the compliments, but it's the criticisms that thunder in my head. Maybe it's because this is the first time anyone has viewed my work critically.

Or maybe I suspect she said the nice things because I'm Erik's boyfriend. But even if the praise was sincere, it doesn't change that I'm unnecessary.

"She said I'm a decent painter," I concede, "but I won't be any good until I find my own style."

For a long time, Erik says nothing. Then he says, "Okay, then. What are you going to do about that?"

I unlace my fingers and retract my hand. "What do you mean?"

He points to the nearby dolly with my art. "Gauguin said, 'Art is either plagiarism or revolution.' You've got the first part down. What are you going to do about the second?"

Something electric sets the hair on my arms on end, clenches my jaw. Something I've never genuinely felt toward Erik until now: anger.

"Erik, did you know what she was going to say to me?"

In that instant, our roles reverse and I see him employ my own evasion tactics. A laugh to lower defenses. A smile to throw me off guard. Doesn't he know I invented these maneuvers?

"What I know is that I have a supertalented boyfriend who is going to go all shock and awe on the art world some day—"

"Did you know what she'd say?"

His face falls. "Evan, I want to see you grow as an artist. You're sitting on a powder keg of potential—"

"I don't believe this!" My shout comes back tinny as it ricochets off the gallery walls. "How could you put me through that? Why parade me in front of someone of Oxana Fedorov's stature so she can tear me down? If you thought I was a copycat, why couldn't you be a man and tell me yourself?"

The unthinkable, unfathomable, indefensible happens. My anger finds the chink in Erik's armor of infinite patience. Every pass he's given me—his tolerance and understanding—disappears. Now everything he's held back finally finds its voice.

"Why bring you here?" he asks, bitterness cracking his thunderous tone. "Why couldn't I tell you myself? If you really need to ask me, then you haven't been paying attention for the last year. I've been pushing you and pushing you because I think you've got talent, but there's nothing I can say or do to get you to go to the next level."

"You should have said something, instead of subjecting me to—"

"It wouldn't have done any good, Evan!"

We're shouting. I can't believe we're shouting.

Veins pop out of his forearms as he clenches his fists. "You're scared. I have no idea what you're scared of, but you're terrified. Maybe it has to do with keeping me out of that part of your life that involves your friends or anything else remotely personal. Did you think we could get this close and I wouldn't see the fear?

"Well, I see it." He reaches out suddenly, grabbing my hand and pressing it tight to his chest. "I can feel it every time we touch. I can hear it when I mention Davis and you change the subject. I put you through this today because you're never gonna get anywhere and be your own person unless somebody shoves you in the right direction. So, tell me, Evan, why are you putting *me* through this? Is it because you're scared Oxana's right?"

I'm used to fights with Shan where we go to last man standing. Those battles were a cornerstone of growing up. But none of that prepared me for this. I wasn't prepared to wound Erik by questioning him. To be the reason he loses his temper. To see him look away, his wild eyes yielding to pain. The anger continues to course through my body but the urge to fight drains from me when he turns his back.

On the drive over, I pictured our return to Nolan and Anna's. I pictured lying out on their deck, eating burgers off the grill, and cuddling with Erik under a blanket as fireworks lit the sky over Lake Michigan. I got different fireworks than I bargained for. I know I won't enjoy any of that, the way I'm feeling now. Angry. Betrayed. Sickened.

"Can you take me to the bus station?" I ask, when I

know I can speak without trembling. "You should stay with Nolan and Anna. But I think . . . I think I need to go home. Process all this."

Even now, there's a small part of me that wants him to say, *No, I'm sorry, you're right, I'm wrong, let's stay and work this out.* That little part reels to hear him acquiesce in a very different way.

"I'm not putting you on a bus. I'll take you home. I don't feel much like being in Milwaukee anymore."

Silently, we leave the gallery, load up the paintings, and begin the trek back to Madison. Erik gets on his cell to let Nolan and Anna know we've had a change of plans.

"It's not gonna work out," he says soberly into the phone. He means our visit. Not the relationship.

I repeat that all the way back to Madison: *He means our visit. . . . He means our visit. . . .*

stonewall

An hour and a half later, when Erik turns onto my street, I ask to be let out two blocks from home.

"Oh, right," he mutters, his first words since we left Milwaukee. "Wouldn't want to stop being a secret, would I?"

When we stop at the curb, I grab my bag and look at Erik. He didn't even look at me the entire drive back. His hands remain on the wheel, gripping it with white-knuckled ferocity. I'm angry but I won't leave it like this, so I lean over and kiss him on the cheek. I hear the breath he's been holding exit his lungs posthaste. He finally looks at me, eyes shiny in the dusk, and says, "Do you see why I thought you needed time to think about San Diego? Welcome to our first fight."

I promise I'll call, and he drives off. I go to my room. The paintings on the wall only remind me what a loser I am. I take each one down and shove them under my bed. When there's no room left beneath the box spring,

I take the tackle box where I keep my paints and shove it in the back of my closet. My brushes, too. Even though Oxana told me to, I don't want to paint my Haring. Not anymore.

For the first time in a very, very long time, I cry myself to sleep.

Two weeks pass as Erik and I dance around each other. Work dominates Erik's life, so we can't talk about the fight in Milwaukee. We trade text messages, mimic real conversation in brief phone calls. Sometimes it feels like we've forgotten everything it took us a year to build.

This is foreign territory for us and I'm not sure how to proceed. But time dulls my rage and I'm left wondering if I overreacted. Maybe this fight is nothing. I need some sort of Richter scale to tell me how bad things were. Are. Will be.

Shan and I are back to working together, but she refuses to talk about anything that went down at Erik's. And I don't force the issue. There's a part of me that wonders if she's right to worry about my relationship with Erik. I wanted to prove her wrong. I'm no longer sure I can.

Davis finally deigns to make a guest appearance in my life. I should be angry, give him the silent treatment for ignoring me as long as he has. But when he shows up with a bag of leftover Szechuan chicken and wontons, I grab at comfort while I can get it and we head up to my room.

For one glorious hour, I get something good back in my life. It's like when Erik and I drove to Milwaukee; we compete to see who can talk the fastest and listen the hardest. We just want to talk and get caught up as quickly as possible.

It's just as I'm polishing off the last of the fried wontons when he drops:

"What if I said I don't want to go to Chicago?"

Davis's voice is scratchy; I can only guess this comes from hours of smoking weed with Sable. I shove the wonton deep into my mouth to stop the first spurious comment from reaching my lips. Half the conversation has been *Sable this, Sable that, Sable can walk on fucking water.* Now, apparently, Davis has found something better than Chicago. And I hate knowing I wouldn't react this way if I knew that San Diego with Erik was still a sure thing. One possibility I'd never considered: losing them both.

"Dude," I say instead, mouth brimming with gooey wonton, "you've already sent in a deposit." I go for where he's vulnerable. Now that he's supporting himself, Davis can't afford to throw money away. Seeing how he reacts to the reminder that he's locked money into a dorm room and tuition will help me gauge how serious he is.

Davis rolls his eyes. "If. I said *if*. It's just something I'm thinking about. Besides, deposits are refundable."

Orange alert. He's already made sure he can get a refund. I chew more wonton. "What would you do otherwise? You hate Madison."

He leans back against my bed. "I hated the way people in Madison made me feel. I guess I'm just not feeling that way anymore. Without the trogs around, I almost feel human. And I'm not even saying I'd stay in Madison."

What strikes me most about this is the "I" and the "me." Every post–high school discussion we'd ever had was about us. Not us, a couple, but us, trying to find a place in the world. Cheesy, stupid—yes. I hate how fast it's gone from we to me, us to I.

But I can't say anything. I've secretly been part of a different us for a year now.

Two weeks ago, this would have been my out. If we'd had this conversation then, I would have told Erik that, yes, I was ready to move to San Diego. And I could have done it guilt-free. But now I find myself playing both sides to meet the middle. I don't want Davis making plans that don't involve me any more than I want to give up on Erik. I still want both of these futures because I don't know which has the best shot of working out. It's selfish but it's all I have.

Davis reaches over and touches my wrist. When I meet his eyes, I see something I haven't seen in a long time. Gentle, smiling, a little bit goofy. I see Davis.

"Hey"—his voice loses the rough texture and he actually sounds like himself—"don't be a tardmonkey. We can talk about this some more. It's just that I've got some new ideas. And I think you're gonna like 'em."

There's a *bleet* from my computer. Only two people send me e-mail. One of them is sitting across from me. I hop up to shrink the window and hide what I assume is a note from Erik.

But it's not.

"It's from Sable," I report. "It just says 'Meet us in front of the Darkroom tonight at nine thirty.'" The Darkroom's a gay bar on the southwest side of town. "We'll never get in there. They card everyone. And what does he mean by 'us'?"

Davis checks his watch. "Shit, I gotta go. Just do what it says. Meet us—"

"Hang on. *You're* 'us'?"

"Us. The Chasers. Everybody. Meet in front of the Darkroom and whatever you do, don't be late."

A second later, he's out the door.

At nine thirty, I pace back and forth in front of the ramshackle bar with the tinted windows. The music's so loud I can feel the sidewalk vibrate under my sandals. Couples go in and out; each one eyes me suspiciously. The street-lights hum and I check my watch. The Darkroom isn't exactly in a bad part of town, but it does attract an element I'm not too wild about.

I'm about to call Davis on my cell when I hear shouts and joyful chants from down the block. The Chasers, sans Ross, turn the corner, fists in the air. Sable stands in the middle as though they're his disciples. Their pace is brisk and they descend upon me, clapping me on the back and smiling. Sable winks at me.

"Thanks for coming, guy!"

And they all thank me. There's something warm in the greeting. People—other than Davis and Erik—glad to see me. I belong. It seems genuine and I can't help but smile. With everything that's happened lately, I need to feel wanted somewhere.

Davis steps from the back of the crowd, holding a baseball bat that glitters as though embedded with diamonds.

"Evan, it was awesome!" Davis roars, showcasing a couple powerful swings of the bat off to the side.

"What's going on?" I ask, looking from Davis to Sable for answers.

But it's Mark, with his backward Brewers cap, who says, "We trashed their cars. *Smash!*" Soon, everyone is mimicking the sound of shattering glass.

"I don't get it—"

I can't finish my sentence because Pete rounds the same corner where the Chasers just came from. Shoulders back, fists clenched: He's in fight mode. When he spots us, he calls out and in an instant, Kenny and the other trogs are at Pete's side. Kenny, the only trog bigger than Pete both in height and muscle, is cracking his knuckles. They charge, shouting obscenities.

Micah, the smallest Chaser, makes to dart inside the bar, but Sable orders him to stay put.

"Wait for it . . . ," he whispers as the army of hate closes in. And then, just as they're within a few yards, Sable mutters, "Go!"

As one, we turn and pile into the bar. The blast of the music almost sends me backward, but I know what's behind me and I'd rather face the lethal bass beat and whatever's inside. I grab on to Davis as my eyes adjust to the darkness. "Davis, what the fuck—"

A burly bearded guy on a stool just inside the door stands in our way. "C'mon, kids, get out. You know you're too young—"

"You gotta help us." Will, looking as pathetic as he can muster, pleads with the bouncer. "These guys. They're gonna beat the crap out of us." It sounds rehearsed.

We charge deeper into the bar, which is packed with shirtless dancers and guys downing beer by the pitcher as Pete and the trogs burst through the door. The bouncer moves to intercept but he's actually smaller than Kenny, who pushes him aside. We back farther into the bar. The trogs follow.

"You faggots totaled our cars!" Pete screams.

The F-bomb stirs the bar's occupants. All eyes converge on us.

Then, strangely, Sable steps forward calmly, hands raised as though surrendering. "You must be mistaken—"

There's a crack as Pete's right hook catches Sable on the chin, sending our fearless leader facedown onto the nearby bar.

And there's a stampede of people.

Bent at the waist, Mark charges, driving his shoulder into Kenny and sending them both into the nearby wall. Micah and Del jump in swinging, double-teaming Neil Perkins, one of the smaller trogs. Danny throws an elbow at Leo Austin, who handily grabs Danny, forces him into a full nelson, and allows Brent McGrath to work over Danny's stomach. A second later, Sable's back in the game, raining a hailstorm of punches down on Pete, who gives as good as he gets.

Then, the entire bar joins in. As the trogs continue to scream "Faggots!" they are suddenly on the receiving end of a lot of violence. Danny is tossed aside as a small gang of buff bar patrons begins to pummel Brent and Leo. I see that Kenny has wrestled Mark to the floor and has him in a sleeper hold. Knowing I can't turn back at this point, I lash out and kick Kenny in the kidney twice. Each time my foot connects, Kenny lets out a grunt. And something inside me tingles.

I've played my part; Mark is able to snake out of the hold. The bouncer is on Kenny, trying to twist Kenny's arm behind his back.

I catch sight of Davis, swinging his baseball bat furiously, attacking the knees and ribs of whatever trog he can get near. When he sees Pete and Sable going at it, Davis suddenly turns and swings the bat upward. It catches Pete full on the temple and sends the wrestler to the ground with a sickening thump that I can somehow hear over the chaos. There's blood. Davis stands over Pete's inert form—fire behind his pupils—and raises the bat over his head. I jump forward, putting myself between him and Pete, catching the bat before he can bring it down.

Our eyes meet and I'm sure that for just a moment, Davis thinks of me as the enemy. All of the anger he's pent up for years is now directed at me. It has to go somewhere. It can't stay inside anymore.

But I'll never know what would have happened next.

"Go! Go! Go!" It's Sable and in the midst of the battle, the Chasers start dodging and ducking and bolting for the door. Davis hovers over Pete for just a moment before following Sable. A nanosecond later, I'm out the door too.

The Chasers, led by Davis with his fist in the air, shouting war whoops, barrel down the street. I fight to catch up. Behind us, someone from the bar yells, "Hey!" and we change course, darting down an alley. As I get closer to the head of the pack, I see Davis clutching dog tags in his hand.

And we run. My feet pound, my thighs ache as I charge to keep up. Side streets, alleys, driveways—the surrounding neighborhood becomes a mosaic, shattered tiles of shadow and light with no connection to anything I understand. Sirens grow louder, then distant, and I refuse to look over my shoulder. We tear through the blackness perforated by sickly orange streetlights, not knowing if we'll ever see safety again.

liberation

Like a jump cut in a dream: We're running, lungs heaving. I don't remember when we stop. I only remember wishing we didn't have to. The farther from the Darkroom, the less real it becomes and that's fine with me.

And then, we're on the cool grass outside Washburn Observatory, atop the hill on the UW campus. The moon peeks out from behind a cloud. It's late enough that there's no one else around. Davis and Mark are lying on their backs a few yards away, passing a joint back and forth. A light breeze carries the secondhand smoke to me, and I blame my giddiness on it. Sable lies to my left, hands behind his head, grinning up at the stars. I have no idea where Will, Danny, Del, and Micah are.

We lie there for a long time. At some point, Davis crawls over to me on all fours, grinning madly. He holds up his dog-tag trophy and shakes it. Then he removes one of the tags from the broken chain and hands it to me.

"The perfect present. Happy graddy-ation!" He laughs and then scurries back to Mark, taking another hit on the joint. I slip the dog tag into my pocket and rest my head on the dewy lawn.

"So," Sable says, "do you get it now?"

Davis and Mark giggle uncontrollably at each other. He's talking to me.

"What do you mean?"

"When we were there in the thick of the fight . . . what did you feel?"

I swallow and say the first thing that comes to mind. "Scared shitless." It's true, but not as true as what I want to say.

Sable guffaws, his eyes fixed on the shiny decimal points that dot the night sky. "What else?"

I know what he's getting at, but admitting it makes me someone I don't want to be.

"Think about it," he goads. "Think about Pete when he and his jerk-ass friends came charging around the corner. Coming at you like a Category-5 prickstorm. Think about ducking into the bar. Think about the looks on those asswipes' faces when they saw what they were up against. What did you feel?"

I remember my terror; it's a visceral reaction to Pete. When Sable mentions it, I remember Pete's hazel eyes. Scattershot glances in every direction and that unmistakable drop of the jaw that said, *I'm in over my head.*

And I remember how it felt to pull back my leg and kick Kenny Dugan. Two kicks to his back. I wish I could have done more damage. I wanted to kick *through* him. Inside, I'm losing the battle to hide what I felt; the word wants out.

"Powerful."

Sable slaps me on the shoulder, hard and firm. "Damn straight. And don't tell me that didn't feel good."

"It felt great." I don't want the words to be mine. I don't say stuff like this. I don't kick people. I don't enjoy it.

Guess I do now.

"You're all right, guy." The compliment bleeds slowly from his gray teeth. "You're all right. I'll be honest. I didn't think you had it in you. I had you pegged as a wuss. But Little Dude, he vouched for you. Said you'd come through. And you did."

"Little Dude" and Mark are quieter. I think they've fallen asleep until a shooting star gets Davis all excited and makes Mark giggle all over again.

"Now you know how they felt during Stonewall," Sable says, propping himself up on his elbows. I follow suit. "You know what it feels like to say, 'Fuck this shit. I'm sick of it!' You know what it feels like to totally stick it to the people who've been sticking it to you forever. And it feels *great!*"

He shouts the last word and it echoes off the concrete courtyard in front of the observatory. It did feel great. So how can I feel great and still feel like shit? Doesn't this make me the same as the guys who beat the crap out of Cory Tanner in Reid Park? That's the reason Erik's making his *Angels* sculpture: to speak out against violence.

Erik. As I think about kicking Kenny and relive the surge, I can't help but think that Erik's right in a way he doesn't even understand. He said I'm hiding who I am from him. But even I didn't know this was me.

I didn't know I could be in a bar fight. I didn't know I could kick Kenny. And enjoy it. So, what else am I capable of? Maybe, in a way, I owe it to Erik to dig a bit further. Owe it to myself. Oxana said I need to infuse my paintings with my life, my perceptions. Don't I need to know what I've been hiding from myself before I can share that with Erik? Fly off to California? If that's even what I want anymore.

Or what he wants.

"So, does that mean I'm finally part of the inner sanctum?" I know Sable will respect the snide tone in my voice so I toss a sneer his way too. "No more of this keeping-me-out-of-the-loop bullshit. I proved myself tonight, right?"

Sable considers, tossing his head back and forth in an internal argument. Finally, he says, "Done."

Someone retches and I turn to find Mark puking his

guts on the lawn. Davis is passed out, I think; he doesn't react to the barf shooting from the guy right next to him. Sable laughs long and hard and I join in. Mark grins, wiping his mouth with the back of his hand, and gets to his feet.

"I'm outta here, guys," he mumbles, staggering first toward us, then down the hill.

"Later." Sable nods and we watch Mark disappear onto the dark street.

"So, what's up next?" I ask.

Sable tics off the next three words with a raised finger for each. "Revolution. Liberation. Identification. You can sum up everything you need to know about gay history in three time periods. The Sixties, Seventies, and Eighties. Tonight, you found out what it meant to be part of the Sixties—Stonewall. The revolution that started it all. Next up: the Seventies. Liberation."

Liberation. Perfect way to release all the other Evans inside I didn't know were there. Come out, come out, wherever you are.

I think the secondhand pot is getting to me.

Sable nods at the inert Davis. "You and Little Dude . . . ever do it?"

I grimace. "No!"

Sable holds up a hand. "Relax, guy. No harm meant. Just asking." He waits three, maybe four seconds. "So why not?"

"We're friends. That's it."

He rolls over on his stomach and lays sphinxlike, arms stretched out. "Where do you see yourself in ten years? No, let me guess: House. Yard. Wearing some stud's 'commitment ring.' Going out for cocktails with your coupled gay friends, talking about how great it is to be monogamous and happy and shit."

I laugh but his gaze tells me he's serious.

"Okay." I recline on the dewy grass. "Sure. I could do that. What's wrong with it?"

"What's wrong with it," Sable seethes, leaning in close so that I can feel his hot, beer-soaked breath on my cheek, "is that you have been bullshitted by society into thinking that's what you *should* want. You see Mommy and Daddy all happy—"

He doesn't know my parents.

"—with their house and their kids and they're a loving couple and you think, 'Yeah, that's the way it's supposed to be. So that's what I want too.'"

And then I feel it. His hand on my crotch—a subtle squeeze . . . then he rubs, slowly. And, God help me, I do what any guy would do: I get hard. I move to brush his hand away but he's firmly in place, massaging me gently. In spite of myself, I let out a staggered breath.

"Don't do that," I whisper but it sounds like a whimper.

"Are you attracted to me?" Our noses touch, our eyes are locked, and nothing Pete or the trogs has ever done to me has made me as terrified as I am in this moment. I don't know what I'll do if he tries to kiss me.

"Are you *attracted* to me?" he repeats, a threat in his tone.

"No!" I grunt and manage to pry his hand off me. I sit up quickly, nearly knocking our heads together. Fast as when he took down Danny, Sable swings his legs around and crouches next to me on the balls of his feet, ready to pounce.

"If you're not attracted to me, why did you get a boner?"

I glance at Davis, still unconscious. Sable grabs my chin and forces me to look back at him.

"I don't know!" I spit, teeth gritted. "It was a knee-jerk reaction. You touch a guy like that and he'll . . . Same thing would happen to you. Are *you* attracted to *me*?"

He doesn't answer the question but he's got that scare-crow of a grin back. "A knee-jerk reaction? Try a natural reaction. Your woody was your brain responding to a stimulus. Chemicals fusing with chemicals, starting a chain reaction from your brain to your junk. All it takes is the right kind of touch to set it off.

"That's all that 'love' is, guy." Sable is still crouched, pantherlike, and I'm still afraid to be near him. "All the straight people, they want you to think it's some bullshit about a man and a woman pledging fidelity and living out their lives together. Look at the papers. The divorce rate is out of control. Why? Because one half of the 'happy couple' can't keep what's in their pants to themselves.

"We're animals. We can build skyscrapers and program computers but when you fucking boil it all down, we're governed by the laws of nature. We have natural reactions. Monogamy is not natural. Hell, you just proved that. Got it up for a guy you probably think's a raving nutball."

To prove his point, he goes for my crotch again. I'm fast this time and shove his hand away before he makes contact. His eyes narrow. "It's all about control. The straights want to control us. They point to their Bibles and tell us that what we feel is unnatural. They're the ones who are unnatural. They're the ones denying what they really want. They want to be able to do it with anyone. They were raised since birth to think that monogamy is the way things should be. Paint a picture of wedded bliss and then they spend their lives suppressing their true nature. Everything they see reinforces it. But everything they do—cheating on each other, jerking off—should be telling them that they've got it all wrong. All wrong."

Sable rocks back and sits, hugging his knees to his chest. I look over at Davis. I imagine Sable has already given him this line. I can't think straight. I don't know if it makes sense or not. Sable can do that: make you doubt what you think you know. But everything else he said was right. At least about how I reacted to the fight at the Darkroom. I wish I could say I'm doing this to become a better artist, to figure out who I am so I don't have to lie to Erik anymore.

Truth is that I don't know where things stand with Erik. It's all about me now. I can't go back.

"So," I repeat with my best "all-in" voice, "what's up next?"

And Sable repeats:

"Liberation."

TITLE: *Lockdown*

IMAGE:

A snakelike chain shackled to a bike in
James Madison Park

INSPIRATION:

Dali's *The Persistence of Memory*

PALETTE:

Rusty bike rack = rust
Bike wheel = mercury
Spokes = battleship
Bike chain = verdigris
Background = sand

The details are sparse. The bike wheel is
warped, as though withering. The bike
chain has reptilian scales. The bike rack is
jagged and lethal.

*August 12. Last year. Summer was waning early in Madison—
cooler days mingling with the warm—so Erik and I vowed to
soak up every last minute of sun that we could before surrendering to fall.*

We'd been dating for almost three months and Saturdays

had become Question Days. We'd meet at James Madison Park just after noon—I'd paint, he'd practice yoga—and we'd ask each other question after question. I still remember that rush of excitement, when I couldn't learn enough about him. And the rush of fear that he'd want to learn too much about me.

On this particular Saturday, I lugged THE CLAW down to the park. Erik—at my request—brought his bike and chained it to a rack near the big oak on the park's west side. I aimed the octagon at the bike as he began his exercises. I was laying down a coat of sand-colored paint on one of the octagon's panels. Erik stood perfectly straight, hands above his head, palms together like a prayer. I heard him breathe deeply through his nose as his arms dipped to either side. He bent at the waist and swan dove to touch his toes. The first question of Question Day came just as he reached the ground.

"Why don't you paint people?"

Explaining this has always been difficult.

"When you paint somebody," I said slowly, "you suspend them in a single moment. I guess I'm waiting for the right moment. That defining instant that changes everything. So the image in the picture is the last time you'll ever see that version of that person again. Cut me some slack. I'm seventeen. It hasn't happened yet."

Erik continued his Sun Salutation: moving into a push-up

position, then back into Downward-Facing Dog. He exhaled. "Fair enough."

My question, sadly, wasn't nearly as probing. "What's your most embarrassing moment?"

Erik groaned, gliding into Upward-Facing Dog. "When I hit on Tyler."

I couldn't help it. I laughed. "I bet that went over well."

"Oh, he clocked me a good one. We were fifteen and didn't speak for a month. Then his mother told him he had two gay uncles, which he didn't know, and suddenly everything was cool with us again. Inseparable ever since."

I smiled. At least Davis hadn't slugged me when I tried to kiss him.

Erik got to his feet and slid into Warrior One pose. Closing his eyes, he asked, "Are you worried that telling Davis and your family about me will completely change your life?"

I felt winded. I set my brush down and took a breath to regroup. In an instant, Erik was at my side.

"Hey," he said over the wail of a late summer wind. "Hey, I didn't mean to hit a nerve. You can . . . you can talk to me about it, you know."

He stepped back and held both arms over his head to mime John Cusack holding up his boom box in Say Anything. It'd come to mean simply: Talk to me. He uses it when I get distant, wondering why this great guy loves me. I use it when he's at his Studio, getting broody as Gregory Douglass sings in the background.

"We'll talk about it," I assured him, not meeting his eyes. "Just . . . you know. Later."

He smiled, as he always did when he didn't want to push me. He stepped into tree pose. "Okay, do-over. I get the idea behind the octagon. Little scenes that mark moments in your friendship with Davis. What does the bike lock signify?"

I half laughed. "Would you believe me if I told you I don't know?"

He nodded, closing his eyes and breathing deeply. "Yes, I would believe that. It's totally you."

"How so?"

"You're a spaz."

I pulled a handful of grass from the ground and tossed it at him. Erik rarely breaks concentration when he's doing yoga, but he laughed and I resumed painting.

"It's like . . . ," I said, "it's like remembering the punch line but not the joke. Saying the punch line is still funny but you can't remember what led up to it that made it funny. Davis and I have been joking about a bike lock that looks like a snake for years. At one point, it was truly hilarious. But a couple years ago, we tried to remember why it was funny . . . and we couldn't figure it out. But we still joke about it. Weird, huh?"

Erik crouched down, made a tripod with his head and hands, and slowly lifted himself up into a headstand. "Not that weird. Ever read Shirley Jackson's 'The Lottery'? It's about *a bunch of people who perform a ritual year after year and nobody remembers why they do it. I guess sometimes, we all do things even after we've lost sight of why we started doing them in the first place."*

Erik leaned forward and effortlessly fell out of the head-stand and into Lotus position. I marveled.

"I can't get over you," I confessed as he sat there, unmoving and tranquil. "You do yoga. You're a great cook. You kick ass at volleyball. You sculpt. I just don't get it."

Erik's eyes remained closed but he arched his eyebrows. "What's not to get?"

I measured each word carefully. "I guess . . . all the jocks I know, they're kind of one note. Sports and that's it. But you've got all these different interests. I mean, I love it. I just don't know how you do it all."

Erik jumped up, joined me at THE CLAW, and slipped his arm around my waist. "I'm a dreamer, Evan. Sometimes I dream so hard I'm worried that I'll float right off the earth. All these things I do—the yoga, the sculpting—they give me something to come back to. They let me dream about finding the perfect guy and settling down, about getting a really awesome job, about taking a year off to travel the world. But I've got something to ground me too. I suppose I could just find one hobby and get really good at it. But different things interest me and that keeps me going and makes life seem . . . more real. Y'know? Or does that sound stupid?"

It didn't sound stupid at all. I looked over at my paints. What else did I have besides that? I wanted what he had. I wanted my life to be more real.

I stepped back and kicked off my sandals. "Show me."

Erik smiled. "Sorry?"

"Yoga. Teach me. I want to learn."

Erik surveyed my face; I was all business. He nodded, moved around behind me, and straightened my posture. He moved my feet together, then took my arms and, holding me from behind, moved my hands into a prayer position at my chest level.

"I love you," he whispered into my right ear.

I'd heard him tell Tyler at China Palace two weeks earlier, but this was the first time he said it to me. I thought I would stop breathing, my heart would stop beating. No, death couldn't come at a worse time. I wanted to keep going.

I turned to respond, but Erik pressed a finger to my lips. He explained the theory of the speed of stupid, saying he didn't want a response until I'd really thought it through.

He laid the palm of his hand against my cheek and we stood there, staring at each other, living off the vibe of a single word. He gently turned me so I faced away and adjusted my back, forcing me to stand up completely straight. He shook my arms so they hung loose at my sides.

"The most important thing about yoga"—his voice rippled through me—"is the breathing. Long, deep breaths. Through

your nose. Focus on your posture. Focus on your breathing."

It took me two more weeks of yoga lessons in the park to finish Lockdown. *It only took me two days of slow, intelligent thinking to tell him that I loved him too.*

namaste

A delivery of white hydrangeas signals a cease-fire. The attached card: "I was wrong. Forgive me?" Ross freaks when I leave him by himself in the store for the first time, but I duck into the cold case to call Erik.

"I really thought I was doing something good by taking you to Oxana," he says. "I could have handled everything better. Can we talk tonight?"

I hesitate. I'm terrified that he'll take one look in my eyes and know everything that happened at the Darkroom. How I helped lure the trogs into an ambush. How I kicked Kenny. How I enjoyed it.

How I reacted to Sable's touch.

But I'm the King of Evasions. By royal decree, Erik will never find out.

"Absolutely," I say, "I'm dying to see you." It feels good to admit that. Despite tinges of doubt, this is the longest conversation we've had in days and it puts me at ease.

"And I'm sorry too. I freaked out and I snapped and . . . Let's talk about it tonight."

We make plans to meet at the hospital after his shift. By the end of our conversation, things feel familiar and easy again.

"Miss me," he says, a smile in his voice.

You have no *idea.*

When the time comes that afternoon to meet Erik, I scramble to get to the bus stop and manage to hop on the one bus without AC. When I walk through the hospital doors, sweet, chilly air cools my sweaty bod and I take the familiar path to the all-purpose room on the second floor.

Once a week, Erik teaches a class called Yoga for People Living with HIV. It's a class he created for the hospital as part of his masters work. It started small, with just a couple people, but it's gotten so big that Erik was planning on starting a second session. I don't know what's going to happen to the class when he moves to San Diego.

We? When *we* move to San Diego?

Davis uses "I" instead of "we." I use "he" instead of "we." Where did all the "we"s go?

I peek in through the window of the door and see Mr. Benton, legs folded in lotus position, instructing the twenty or so people who fill the small room. His closed eyes flicker open for a moment and he winks at me. I open the door and Mr. Benton concludes the class by saying softly, "Thanks for coming, everyone. We'll see you all again next week. *Namaste*."

*Namaste*s echo from the students, who begin to roll up their mats. Mr. Benton gets to his feet and slaps me on the back. He looks even better than when we saw him at home. He's taking his meds. He knows better than to cross Super Nurse twice.

"Good to see you, Evan," Benton booms. "You missed Erik. He was with us, but he got called away to an emergency."

Benton slips on his shoes and we walk into the hall together.

"Erik tells me his sculpture is nearly done," Benton says. "He must be getting nervous. Isn't the unveiling coming up?"

I nod. On the drive to Milwaukee, Erik told me how he was dreading the unveiling ceremony in August. It was one thing for something he sculpted to be in Oxana's lobby. It was different for his work to be out in a big public space with a dedication plaque. Erik's not comfortable being the center of attention.

"Can't wait to see it. It'll really brighten up that park." Benton beams. Then he lowers his voice like a secret agent. "You know, back in the Seventies, Reid Park used to be the gay cruising spot. There was this concrete bench that faced a little bed of marigolds. If you sat there, it meant you were looking for action. That's where I met my first hookup. I was a stupid high school punk looking to get laid. Place went to hell in the Eighties. Got so you couldn't go down there without getting the crap beat out of you. I heard about those poor kids last year. I hope they can turn it around."

A thought hits me. "Mr. Benton, do you remember Stonewall?"

He shakes his hand in a "so-so" kinda way. "The riots? I was just a kid. I kind of remember them. Didn't really make a splash in the news around here. It's more something I learned about after the fact."

"But you lived a lot of gay history, right?"

Benton stares at me in that "open mouth, insert foot" way and I race to cover my slipup.

"Not that you're old! I just mean that there've been a lot of, you know, changes . . . advances in gay rights and . . . and stuff. In recent years. And you've seen it."

Good save, Weiss. No point in taking a diversion. This time I really do want to die.

Benton grips the strap around his yoga mat. He stares just over my shoulder, wearing the blank expression I remember from when he told me about his days as a publisher. "Sure. Sure, I've seen lots of changes. Some good, others not so good. Why do you ask?"

"Just curious. I have a . . . friend who's teaching me about gay history. He said that Stonewall really united the gay community, made it easier for gays to feel free in the Seventies. That it mobilized people like an army and—"

"Whoa!" Benton scowls and shakes his head. "You make it sound like a military maneuver, like it's something that was planned. No one sat down and decided to riot. It wasn't calculated. It happened spontaneously. People were getting tired of being pushed around, so they pushed back."

As I listen to Benton describe what he knows of that night, my mind pinpoints the key difference between what happened in New York and what happened at the Darkroom: premeditation. Sable and the others smashed the trogs' cars and lured them to the Darkroom. The real Stonewall wasn't an ambush. Suddenly, I'm less confident that Sable's "revolution" is on the up and up.

"Evan!"

Benton and I glance down the hall. Erik, his scrubs soiled, his eyes baggy, jogs toward us. Benton pats me on the shoulder, waves at Erik, and disappears around the corner. Erik kisses me—it's quite possibly the best kiss ever—and I forget all about the Darkroom.

"Listen, things are a mess here." He sighs, his face burdened with tired. "Twelve-car pile-up on I-94. I've been suturing wounds for the last hour and they need me a while longer. Rain check? I promise: lots of talking and making up later. Lots of it." He smiles and gives my butt a pat.

God, I don't want him to go. Even if there's more difficult talking ahead, I want him here. It means I don't have to think about other things. Things like, What the hell do I do about Chasers now?

"Go," I command, bravely as I can. "Be Super Nurse. I'll be here when you're done."

He frowns. "I'll feel guilty if you wait. I don't know how long I'll be. After we get the accident sorted, I have to check on my patients from last night. That's an even bigger mess."

"What happened?"

"You know that gay bar, the Darkroom? Huge brawl. I was here till two a.m. stitching guys up."

I hope that, as I lean on the wall, it looks cool and not like I'm trying not to collapse.

"Anybody . . . seriously hurt?" I can barely enunciate.

My stomach falls when he nods. "One guy—some kid just out of high school—is in a coma."

It could be anyone. But my gut tells me who.

Erik brushes my cheek with his hand. It should be comforting to be touched by him. I'm too sick to my stomach to enjoy it.

"Go home," he says softly. "I promise we'll talk soon."

I nod. He leans in for another kiss, one hand at the nape of my neck, pulling me in.

"I've really missed you," he whispers, poking my nose with his finger. A quick kiss, then he's racing off down the hall. I stumble out of the hospital and catch the bus home.

A single word repeats and repeats and repeats.

Coma.

Back home, I duck into my room unnoticed. I slip off my shoes and start the yoga routine that Erik and I have done together at least once a week since that first yoga lesson. I've never done it alone.

My hands lift up over my head, palms together. Eyes close. Breathe in through the nose. Slowly.

Namaste. *I respect the divine in you.*

Right now, I'm not feeling very divine at all.

shan

My meditation crumbles when I hear shouts and squeals from the living room. I plod down the hallway to find Mom pulling Shan into a bear hug as Dad struggles to pull himself up to standing with a cane. Once he's balancing on his good foot, he's part of the hug too.

Mom spots me and beams. It's unsettling.

"Your sister is having a baby!"

My eyes dart to Shan, whose smile fades only enough to remind me I'm not supposed to know this. Though I dropped out of drama club, I give a Tony-worthy performance, whooping and hugging my sister. I even slap Dad a high five. Maybe that's a bit much.

What follows is what I expected. They sit in the living room and talk about baby names, buying Shan a crib. I watch them from the kitchen where I lean against the wall, nursing a glass of milk as they all talk a mile a minute.

"Why didn't you tell us sooner?" Mom finally asks, shaking a finger at Shan.

Shan looks across the room to me. "Because Spud just graduated. You should be congratulating *him*."

Dad waves his hand. "Yeah, yeah. We did."

They didn't.

"Did you?"

I blink as Shan enters virgin—excuse the phrase, in light of the circumstances—territory. She's never challenged our parents.

Shan shakes her head. "I saw the camera. You took one picture of him at commencement. One. That's pathetic."

Suddenly, both Mom and Dad are looking at me. Like I put her up to this. I look away.

Shan throws down the gauntlet. "What did you get him for graduation?"

Mom looks stunned. "We've been . . . busy. Your father . . ."

Dad nods at his cast. "My hip . . ."

"He's leaving in a month!" Shan says, pointing at me. I wait for her to mention Erik, mention San Diego. She doesn't. "And if he's got any sense, he won't come back. You might want to think about that."

My parents have never done contrite. They don't quite manage it now, but they're certainly flirting with shame.

Mom and Dad make awkward excuses. It's getting

late. Time for bed. Then they're gone to their bedroom. But Shan's new energy, complete with an iron pair, revs up. She joins me in the kitchen and rummages through the drawers, pulling out an arsenal of barber's shears and placing them on the table. I slowly get up but she stops me with a look and a word: "Sit."

She just went Angry Oprah on our parents and now she's got sharp things. Like I'm gonna say no.

I take a seat and she puts a bath towel around me like a giant bib, then starts running her fingers through my hair. Growing up, Shan always cut my hair. We haven't done this in a while. I can only assume it's some sort of healing ritual. Or I'm about to lose an ear.

"Whoever's been cutting your hair since I moved out should be brought up on war crimes charges. You look ridiculous."

"Ladies and gentlemen, this year's winner of our Most Likely to Become 'M' Contest . . . ," I mutter but she silences me with a snip of the scissors close to my nose.

She starts cutting and we're silent for a long time.

"Tomorrow," she says . . . finally. "I'm going with M to the hospital to get D out of his cast. He's going to be a bear for a few weeks while he recovers."

"I'll try to imagine what that will be like."

"Then I'm catching a late flight home. Sorry I won't be around for the unveiling of Erik's sculpture."

215

That's probably a good thing. Erik will be nervous enough as it is without Shan giving him the hairy eyeball.

She runs a comb through my hair. "And I was thinking . . . Have you ever considered going to art school in New York?"

I had. Briefly, when I found out that's where Keith Haring went to art school. But by then, Davis and I had settled on Chicago. New York was no longer an option. I know her question has nothing to do with her concern for my education, though.

I catch her scissoring wrist so I can turn to face her. "Do you really hate Erik that much, that you're trying to get me away from him?"

She frowns and takes the chair across from me, putting her hands on my knees. "I don't hate Erik, Spud. You two really work well together." Her voice bears a small grudge but I'm glad she admits this.

"And that's why you attacked us that night at dinner?"

She sighs. "On the weekends, Brett volunteers at a free clinic in Brooklyn doing pro-bono accounting. He never works with the patients but he overhears things. He tells me how he sees these gay kids come in, some of them younger than you, wanting blood tests, half of them not even knowing what their diagnosis means. They think it can all be fixed with some pills. They can't tell you the first name of whoever they had sex with last night but they can rattle off the names of the pills they want. These kids are getting sick because they're stupid."

Her eyes well up. "When you sat there with Erik, I kept thinking, 'It could be Evan at that free clinic.' I didn't want to think you were . . ."

Shooting pains pierce my gut. She must see the hurt in my eyes because she quickly grabs my hands.

"And then I got home and went, 'Shannon Marie Reynolds, you are the biggest moron on the planet.' I've been regretting everything I said since that night. It's taken me this long to say anything because I was too embarrassed about my behavior. I had a panic attack. That's all. You're smart enough to make your own decisions. I need to respect that."

I squeeze her hands in return, thankful that I might actually get my sister back. "Next up, Shan Reynolds singing 'I'm Bringing Stupid Back.'"

She laughs and swipes me upside the head.

"Now," she says, marking a course correction, "I'm still not wild about you running off to California with Erik. When you finally drop this on M and D and they ask my opinion, I'm going to tell them what I think."

"Which is?"

Her jaw shifts left, then right, and she admits, "I'll let you know when I figure that out."

"Okay," I say. "Good to know."

She gets up and resumes the haircut. "So . . . how are you?"

The question is loaded.

"Fine. Why?"

She snips near the top of my left ear, then tilts my head for a better angle. "I know I haven't seen you much lately but you haven't left the house. Not spending time with Erik? Or Davis?"

I almost tell her about Milwaukee. Almost ask for advice on how to fix things after a fight. But admitting my relationship problems now would only fuel her misgivings about Erik. I change tack.

"I'm hanging in there. I've . . . I've been thinking about talking with M and D. I just don't think it's going to happen. Does it really even need to? I mean, I'm eighteen. If I want to move to California—"

She sucks on her teeth and runs her fingers through my hair. "Can I ask you something?"

Has anything good ever followed that question? "Sure."

"You've been dating Hottie McBubblebutt for a year. And you haven't told anyone? Not even Davis?"

"Right." She noticed his butt?

"And Erik's letting you get away with that?"

Yes, because I take advantage of his trust. But instead I say, "It's kind of complicated. He doesn't want to push me."

"Push you into, what, admitting he exists to the people

who know you best? I'm sorry, Spud, but that's lame. If this guy makes you happy, so happy that you're ready to follow him to California, why aren't you telling the world?"

Erik can zero in on my every mood swing, every evasion, in a way I never thought possible. But it's Shan who can nail my every insecurity to the wall. She brushes my cheek. Apparently, I'm crying.

"Because . . . I keep waiting for it to end." I don't recognize my own whisper. It's wan, colorless. "Every time I want to tell someone about Erik, I look at my paintings. No two people look at a painting the same way. Everybody brings their own perspective. If I tell someone about Erik, I'll see me through their eyes. And if I see them doubting that someone like Erik could love me, I'll see it too. And I'll know it's true. Then I'll blow it. I'll completely wreck things with Erik and everyone will be right. But keeping Erik from Mom and Dad and Davis means I get to protect who I am when I'm with Erik."

Shan pulls the towel from around my shoulders, shakes off the excess hair, and dabs at my moist cheeks.

"Wow," she whispers back. "Really? Being embarrassed that you love someone is worse than losing Erik? If that idea is worse for you than the actual loss itself, you need to seriously reexamine your feelings. *Do* you want to move to San Diego?"

Shan starts to pack up the shears into a small gray

pouch. She's doing her very best not to look at me. *C'mon, Shan—right now, more than ever, I need sage advice. What do I do?*

But the wisdom never comes. I think she's about to speak but there's a knock at the door. We both look at the clock. Too late for visitors. I answer it to find a tall, lean police officer, notebook in hand.

"Excuse me." He nods respectfully, glancing at the notebook. "I'm looking for Evan Weiss."

He's in the house. His uniform is black. We sit. Shan's hand rests on my shoulder.

Incident at the Darkroom. Brawl. Boy in hospital. Classmate.

"Do you know Pete Isaacson?" Baseball bat. Brown wood.

Details sketchy. Someone said I was on the scene helping. Was I on the scene?

Shan eyes the hallway. Summon Mom and Dad? Keep them at bay?

I think of Erik. I want Erik here. No. No, I don't.

Where was I the night of the fight?

Baseball bat.

Shan speaks up. Whoever said I was there was mistaken. I was at home. Painting in my room. When the fight happened.

If I wasn't there, do I know who was? Lots of red, crimson, carmine.

Baseball bat.

He gives me a card. Call if I remember anything. Call if I hear anything.

I can't look at Shan as I close the door behind Officer Brogan. I rest my head against the door.

"I just lied to a cop, didn't I?" she whispers. "You were there."

"I was . . ." I don't know how to finish. ". . . looking out for Davis."

"Shit," Shan mutters. "How'd I know COD was mixed up with this?"

I turn. My face feels like it's caving in. "Shan, it's not like that. He was . . . in over his head. Pete threw the first punch. Davis just . . ."

Again, Shan's eyes dart to the hallway. This time, I know she wants to wake up Mom and Dad, get them involved. I grab her arm, squeezing desperately.

"Please," I beg, "let me handle this. It doesn't sound like they know who—"

"Jesus, Evan, there's a guy in the hospital. You can't just pretend this didn't happen."

"I won't. I'll . . . try to get the guys who did this to see reason." It's a hollow promise. Sable won't take reason.

221

"It got out of control, that's all. It was a mistake."

"It was more than just you and Davis. Who else was there?"

"Please, Shan. I know what I'm doing. I promise . . . nothing stupid like that will happen again. Trust me."

And in that moment, her face reminds me of Erik. That look he got when he gave me my graduation gifts and asked, "I've been a good boyfriend, haven't I?" That look that says, *This isn't what I signed up for. Who are you, anyway?* Both then and now, the look is justified. I'm ashamed of this.

Shan glances one more time at the back hallway and then fixes me with the most potent stare I've ever seen. "No more violence or Mom and Dad find out, got it? I'm not covering for you again."

I put my hand to my heart, my eyes welling with wet. "I promise. I swear, oh God, I swear."

She squints. "Was Erik—?"

"No!" I almost shout, then I gulp down a huge breath and shake my head. "No, Erik doesn't know anything about it. Please don't—"

"I got you out of trouble with the cops," she says, pulling away, "but you have to decide what to do about your boyfriend."

And she's gone to her room. I have to decide what to do about my boyfriend. But I can't. I don't know what's wrong with me, but all I can think about is my best friend. I picture Davis, or, at least, how I remember him. Not who he is now. A Chaser. A Chaser wannabe. Does he know any of this? Does he know what happened to Pete?

The old instincts kick in. I have to hope that Erik will understand. Because everything I've ever known screams at me: Protect Davis. And right now, that means getting closer to him. Getting closer to the Chasers.

lies

"Smile!"

An incandescent flash punctures my vision. The Chasers mill around Sable's room. Mark and Del hunch over Sable's laptop. Will and Davis graze on the motley assortment of chips and snacks everyone brought. When I arrived at sundown, I was greeted with smiles, claps on the back, friendship. Like when they saw me at the Darkroom. I should feel like I belong here. But tonight, belonging doesn't matter. Protecting Davis does.

We're two fewer tonight; Danny and Micah must have been spooked by the fight.

Sable checks the picture he just took of me on Mark's digital camera. He nods, then says, "Okay, lose the shirt."

Everyone else has just gone through this, so I don't hesitate to doff my polo. Sable raises an eyebrow and whistles. "Nice. Would never have guessed you had that much tone."

Wolf whistles all around and I flush. Yoga's been very good to me. Even Davis can't hide his surprise. I growl, "Just take the damn picture."

Another flash and then Sable commandeers the laptop, uploading the photos.

"Why are we doing this?" This from Will, whose skeletal shirtless photo rivals Davis for Scrawniest Guy in the Room. I'm surprised Will is still with us. He asks this at least once every meeting.

"It's like paying dues in a club," Sable says. He logs on to a website: MadCityEscorts.com. He starts by posting Mark's photos—two very cheesy torso shots, biceps flexed, bare-chested—and creating a profile. Mark's the only one of us who can really claim having a "bod." I'm betting that his ad gets the first reply. "This is how you're contributing to our operating expenses."

Nobody asks, and I suspect I'm the only one curious, what operating expenses we have.

"It's also," Sable continues, typing away, "how we're learning about the next stage in gay history: the Seventies, or, as I like to call it, the liberation movement. Before Stonewall, the gay community was cowering, hiding in the shadows. But once we stood up for ourselves, we realized just how much we'd been oppressed. Then, we knew we could have sex with whoever we wanted, whenever we wanted."

"Sex?" Will can't hide his alarm anymore. "I thought we were just being, you know, escorts. Taking guys out for dinner or whatever."

Sable shoots Mark and Del a look and all three laugh. Davis joins them. Sable turns and says with forced innocence, "That's right, Will. Because paying for sex would be prostitution. And that's illegal. But what these guys are paying for isn't sex. Your time is valuable, right? They're paying for your time. That's all."

A few keystrokes later and we all have profiles on Mad City Escorts. None of us looks like the other guys on the site, who are all ripped, seductive. But Sable assures us that, by the end of the week, someone will have put in a request to spend time with each of us at two hundred dollars an hour. We split it fifty-fifty; we each keep one hundred and Sable gets the rest for the "operating expenses."

We split up for the night. Davis and I disappear into his room. Once the door is closed, he throws a couple playful punches at my gut.

"So when did you get so buff?" he asks, a wicked glint in his eye.

"Shan," I say quickly. "She's teaching me yoga. It's nothing."

Davis plops down on his bed. "Yoga, huh? Maybe you could teach me. Gotta turn these pipe cleaners into pipes." He flexes his right arm and absolutely nothing happens.

"Hey, listen." I lower my voice and cast a quick look at the door. "The police came to my house the other night. Asking questions about the Darkroom. And Pete."

The Davis I grew up with would be terrified at the mention of cops. This Davis, with a posse of new friends, this Davis is angry.

"Son of a bitch. Big Pete's a badass when he's picking on the fags, but turn the tables on him and he runs to the cops—"

I shake my head. "He didn't run anywhere. He's in a coma."

I want—need—him to react. Shock. Fear.

No go.

Davis mulls this over; he's unconsciously pounding the mattress with his fist. "So it must have been one of the other trogs who talked to the cops. We gotta figure out who—"

"Does it matter? Don't you think . . . we're in over our heads here? Sable is—"

"This isn't Cicada's fault!" The force in his voice is startling. "He's looking out for us. Nobody else is doing that. Cicada's giving us what we always wanted. We're not scared little kids anymore. I wish we'd known Cicada a long time ago. Pete would have gotten what was coming to him a lot sooner."

I raise up my hands defensively. "Okay, I'm not saying

anything about Sable. We just don't have a lot of experience picking fights. Or following through."

Now Davis is excited. It's like he's come from a revival meeting, full of joy and the Word. "There's so much we didn't have experience with. Until Cicada came along. Can't you feel it? How great it feels to walk down the street with your head up?"

I've been doing that for a while. Ever since Erik.

Davis is just getting started. "Okay, I wasn't sure about this escort service thing at first either. But it's part of our heritage. I want to be just like the guys who lived through Stonewall. And came into their own. Those guys don't take shit from anyone. They live out loud and proud. I didn't realize any of that until Cicada. For Christ's sake, isn't this what we always talked about?"

It's exactly what we always talked about. Fitting in. But fitting in never involved putting people in comas.

We sit quietly for a few more minutes as Davis comes off his buzz. Then he says, "So . . . what did you say to the cops?"

I groan. "Shan vouched for me. Said I was at home with her that night."

Davis, who I thought would be relieved, frowns. "Evan, that could seriously screw us up. The whole reason we didn't tell you about this beforehand was that you were supposed to be our alibi. We needed someone who wasn't there when we smashed up those cars to say we'd been with him the entire time."

I bite back my anger at being used that way. I need to reason with Davis. "Sorry. I'm new to this covering-for-guys-with-baseball-bats thing you've got going." I avoid anger. I'm okay with sarcasm.

Davis is on his feet. "We have to tell Cicada."

"Look," I say, standing between him and the door, "I'm the only one they talked to. If they suspected anyone else, they'd have stopped by here. Or Mark's house. Or Del's or . . ." I'm struck by my own words as the implication kicks me in the stomach. How did the police know to come to me? Why was I singled out for questions? Why do they think I helped with all this?

"I think you're in the clear," I assure him, although I question how assuring I sound. "Just . . . lie low. Don't get in any more fights for a while. It'll blow over."

Davis keeps eyeing the door but, for now, he sits back on his bed. "I dunno," he says. "Whatever. I'm kinda tired."

"Sure thing. G'night." And I'm out the door. Before I hit the bottom of the stairs, I hear a door open, a knock, another door open, and Sable's unmistakable "Hey."

Erik, in his purple yoga pants and glistening with a patina of fresh sweat, is surprised when I drop by unannounced. Surprised, but pleased.

"I'd hug you but—" He indicates the sweat. But I grab him anyway and hold him tight. Tighter and longer than I maybe should.

"Something up, babe?" The question is soft, inviting.

We move to the love seat and he stays close, never losing contact, making sure I have an anchor. We're quiet for a long time and then Erik throws his arms up into the air, holding that invisible boom box. I smile and rest my head on his shoulder.

"I'm happy to sit here all night," he whispers, rubbing my leg. "But if there's something on your mind . . ."

All at once, I know it was a mistake to have come here. We still need to talk about Milwaukee. That should be my reason for being here. But I'm too scared to talk about that. And I can't say anything that's on my mind without unraveling everything I've worked so hard to hide for the past year.

"Davis?"

The name jolts me. Because Erik seldom mentions Davis, it's like the report of a cannon when he does.

I look into his eyes, and his square-egg-shaped face is oddly expressionless.

"Evan, I know I've got my broody moments. And you get me through those. But there are times when you get all distant and I can't do anything about it. And I suspect— though I can't prove—that it's about Davis." Then he sighs, bracing himself. "I gotta ask: Are you sleeping with him?"

Sleeping with Davis? I was felt up by Sable and got a woody. I just went live as a paid escort. But sleep with Davis? Hell, no.

I don't know whether to laugh, be insulted, or beg him to understand how much he means to me. I settle for taking his hand in both of mine and looking him directly in the eye.

"There is nothing going on between me and Davis. Never has been. Never will be."

Before Milwaukee, that would have been enough. This is after Milwaukee.

"Well, there's something there. I know it, Ev. I don't know what it is because you won't tell me. He's your 'best friend.' That's all you ever say. That is, until you figured out it was making me uncomfortable to hear about him and then you never mentioned Davis again . . . I'm guessing so I wouldn't insist on meeting him."

Volley after volley finds its mark and I can sense everything rending apart. How long have I thought I was getting away with things I was never getting away with? How many omissions were really admissions? And then, the killing blow.

"Does he even know we're dating?"

It takes all I have to steel myself for this.

"What are you talking about? You're the best thing

that's ever happened to me, Erik. Of course he knows about you. In fact . . . he was just ragging on me, too. Going on about how all I talk about is this 'Erik guy' and 'when do I get to meet him.'" I change my tone, trying to make it funny. Please let it be funny. "I suppose I've kept you to myself for too long. So, yeah, let's get together with him. I mean, it can't go worse than dinner with Shan, right?"

I remember the look on Erik's face when we fought in Milwaukee, when he finally gave in to all the suspicions he'd accumulated over a year and confronted me. That look is back. I can feel time running out.

"No, really, we just have to coordinate our schedules. Davis is totally psyched. He can't wait to meet you."

I smile but my stomach lurches. In our year together, these are my only outright lies to Erik. I've always placated myself, thinking my omissions were innocent. A lie was a deliberate, articulated untruth. But these half truths, my evasions, have become as poisonous as the lie I just spoke.

Arranging dinner with Shan gave me a Get Out of Jail Free card once. The pressure to learn about my life stopped for a while. Will the mere promise of meeting Davis be enough to satisfy him? Nothing he says or does right now will let me in on his thoughts. The DictionErik is a bust.

All that follows are tepid agreements that we'll arrange a meeting soon. Erik is clearly drained; I can't tell what he hates more—being suspicious or that he feels I've given him reasons to be. Well, I have. And it sickens me. I keep my eyes on the cool, gray cement on the walk home. I don't deserve the colors that State Street affords.

I don't deserve Erik.

More, he doesn't deserve me.

escort

Dad, newly freed from his cast, insists on driving to the airport when we drop off Shan. In the backseat, Shan and I regress to children again, screaming "We're gonna die!" every time Dad charges through a yellow/red light.

"Next person who says 'We're gonna die' gets thrown out," Dad snarls, looking at us in the rearview mirror with an almost playful look.

Through the next yellow/red, Shan and I look at each other and yell, "We're gonna pass away!"

Mom shakes her head.

Casual observers of our family wouldn't think anything had changed since Shan's Great M and D Smackdown. Mom still rides my ass about doing cold-case inventory. Dad still nods when I talk and asks me what I said once I'm done. For the most part, casual observers would be right. Nothing's really changed.

Much. You'd have to be a Weiss to see the difference.

We don't have family game nights or talk about how our days went at the dinner table. But there's a hint of global warming going on; a few ice caps have dissolved. With any luck, I'll be far from Madison before things get too touchy-feely. Not sure I could handle that.

At the airport, Mom is at her Momest. "I want updates," she insists to Shan. "Regular baby updates. Sonograms, checkups . . . Tell me everything."

Dad goes on about how he's too young to be a grandfather but hints that maybe now there's an heir to his great grocery store empire. He wouldn't be Dad unless he reminded both Shan and me what disappointments we are for not picking up that particular torch.

"Help me with my bags, Spud?"

I grab her luggage and after an assault of parental hugs and kisses, I walk her to the baggage check.

"There's a spare room in New York," she says. "It's the size of your bedroom closet, but it's free."

"I'll remember that."

We hug.

"Say good-bye to Erik," she says, and I'm paranoid enough to wonder if there's double meaning. Then she gets really serious and says, "Stay out of trouble."

Of course, we both know it's too late for that. She gives a wave before disappearing in the security line.

Back in the car, the parental détente takes an uncomfortable turn.

"When do you and Davis move away again?"

"Move-in is Labor Day weekend," I say. It's not a lie. I just don't confirm that's still what I'm doing.

"Chicago, right?"

She says it slowly. I know she knows it's Chicago. She's fishing for something.

"Chicago," I confirm.

She doesn't say anything else, doesn't look back at me.

Dad grunts. "Christ, Joan. Even *I* know it's Chicago."

Almost a week after Sable first created our online profiles, I get an e-mail from Davis: *Saddle up. We've got dates tonight.* I close my eyes and focus.

I don't know how to love my boyfriend and protect my best friend at the same time. I have to pick one. The choice seems simple: Davis is in danger. Erik is not. I think of Erik's *Fierce Angels*—going where no one else dare go—and know what I have to do.

Erik's right. Giving a shit is hard.

It's raining so I take the bus to the RYC. I pass under Erik's window on the way. It's dark up there; he's out with Tyler and their friends. He'd invited me to join them but I said I had to work. Apparently, now that I've started, I can't stop outright lying to Erik.

Davis is already in Sable's room, wearing a tight black T-shirt, ripped jeans, and flip-flops. I think he thinks it's sexy. I feel overdressed in my button-down shirt and slacks. I thought we were going on dates. Mark's also there, working on Sable's laptop. Davis keeps scalding Mark with dirty looks. He's not happy with how close Mark has become to Sable.

"Here's the deal," Sable says. "I told these guys you'd meet them outside Hüsnü's. It's not like a double date or anything, so don't hang out together. That might creep them out. You're Andy"—he points to Davis—"and you're Charlie." He points to me.

"Sorry?"

That anemic smirk spreads across his face. "Give me some credit, guy. I made up names for you to protect your privacy. You don't want these guys getting clingy. Stalking you."

That had never occurred to me.

"Get the money up front. Be charming. Remember, these guys want to have a good time. You're providing a service: hospitality. Be hospitable. Always let them make the first move."

"Why?" Davis asks for both of us.

Mark chimes in with his "well, duh" tone. "In case

they're undercover cops. It's entrapment if they make the first move."

I turn to Mark. "What about you? Got a date?"

His eyes never leave the laptop screen. He just grins. "Oh yeah."

Davis and I leave the RYC and walk the length of State Street to Hüsnü's, this Turkish restaurant near the UW campus.

"I told Sable to put our dates at the same restaurant," Davis informs me with an elbow to my side. "I figured you might be kinda nervous. So even if we can't be at the same table, you'll know I'm near. Look at me if you get lost and don't know what to do."

I nod, trying not to laugh. I picture how tongue-tied he gets any time he's near a guy he likes. It's a good thing Davis is getting the money up front. He may not last the night.

"So what did Sable say? About the cops?" Why hide that I know what I know?

If Davis is surprised that I know he talked to Sable about the cops, he hides it. "He's not too worried. He was pissed at first that it kills our alibi. But he figures that if they haven't questioned anyone else by now, they won't."

Davis takes position in front of the restaurant. I duck under an awning across the street. A tall guy—maybe forty, lean, wearing a business suit—approaches Davis.

I expect Davis to cave on first contact. But he flashes a smile, totally cool. They shake hands and disappear into the restaurant.

"Charlie?"

A second later, I remember I'm Charlie. I turn to see a guy, slightly shorter than me. Unshaven, dumpy, and I'm pretty sure that sauerkraut smell is coming from him. And he's a bazillion years old. Davis gets the business suit, I get a Hawaiian shirt two sizes too small with mustard stains down the front. God, I hope that's mustard. How did I not see this coming?

Dexter (as he introduces himself) and I go into the restaurant and he's finding every excuse he can to touch me—his hand at the small of my back, guiding me to the table, a brush of the shoulder as he pushes my chair in. The lighting is dim, candles dot every table.

"So," he says, his eyes smiling over the top of his raised menu, "your profile says you play lots of sports. How do you like to stay fit?"

"Hockey," I lie, not sure why that's the first to come to my mind. "I play hockey during the winter. When it's warmer out, volleyball and . . . track."

"You ever wrestle?"

I don't like the breathy quality to his voice when he says, "wrestle."

"No," I say, not too quickly. "Never wrestled."

He lays the menu down and hits me with a viscous smile. "Really? You're built like a wrestler. Very lean. Muscled."

Then I feel them, fingers settling on my knee. Not rubbing, not gripping. Just there, immobile, like three disgusting sausages.

I dig into the complimentary naan, shoving fistfuls into my mouth as Dexter orders for us both. I look around and spot Davis at a corner table. He's smiling and laughing, touching the forearm of his date with every guffaw. How did this happen? When did we switch roles?

"So what else are you into?" Dexter probably thinks he sounds sincere. He doesn't.

I can't think of any reason to lie, and maybe it will bore the hell out of him, so I say, "I paint. A lot. I paint pictures."

The bread is gone—devoured—so I start downing my water as fast as I can and flag the waiter down for a refill. I'm hoping that if Dexter sees me with my mouth full, he won't ask more questions. But he doesn't stop: What do I look for in a guy? Do I like to masturbate? Would I ever let anyone watch?

And then, those fingers snake their way up my inner thigh. The muscles in my back seize as a spasm shakes my leg. I can feel the heat of his fingers through my pants as he strokes up and down. I can't help it; another spasm. He must think I'm enjoying the attention because he smiles even more. I close my eyes and try to pretend it's Erik.

Mistake. Summoning Erik's gentle touch makes my stomach lurch and the bread and water tell me they want out.

"I'm sorry." I jump up. "I—I can't do this."

I'm too loud. He looks around to see if anyone's watching. No one is. Yet.

He motions me to sit and lowers his voice. "Look, it's my fault. I know, you need the money up front. I just didn't want to be obvious about it. It seemed tacky. Sit down. I'll pass it to you under—"

"No," I say. This time, lots of people look. Including Davis, who has stopped enjoying his date's company and is now glaring at me like he's the one being embarrassed. Dexter looks away, disavowing that we're together. I take advantage of his refusal to look at me and charge out of the restaurant.

I run blindly away from State Street, down an alley to University Avenue, stomping in puddles and never looking back. My stomach still threatens to rebel, and all I can feel are those three heavy fingers, weighing on my knee with phantom force. I don't even realize I'm crying until I barrel headfirst into a crowd of people and fall down. And then I want to die.

"Evan?"

Erik is crouched next to me, kneeling on the wet pavement. Above him, Tyler and the others huddle around, all staring down at me like I'm the Elephant Man.

"Evan, what's wrong? I thought you were working tonight."

But I'm sobbing uncontrollably now and demi-words come out as choked gasps. The city, the people—a smear of clotted color. I feel his strong hands on my shoulders, massaging gently, and all I can think about is how he'll never be able to get the stain out of the knees of his pants.

He throws a look over his shoulder. "Go. We'll catch up."

We'll. Oh, God. He said "we'll." I lied to him, I went on a date with an old troll, and I still belong to him. I'm still a "we." I can't stop it anymore. I turn my head and give the naan and water their freedom.

Erik doesn't miss a beat. He wipes my lips with his fingers and helps me to my feet. He gently guides me under an awning to keep me out of the rain. I lean against the building. I'm shaking so hard my muscles ache. My sobs become violent wheezes.

Erik holds me and the tears start all over again as I feel his hard body against mine. This is how he calms me. He assures me he's close. I relive our last night in bed. I relive our first night in bed. I relive ten seconds ago: "We'll catch up." I keep thinking, *We, we, we, we, we, we, we . . .*

And it's there. His hand cupped around my left cheek,

that familiar thumb rubbing softly, slowly, just below my eye. From the DictionErik: *Calm down. I'm here. Calm down.*

And it happens. The wheezing stops. The shuddering stops. The blurry colors focus and there's Erik, his hair that sexy shade of wet and tousled, his eyes squinting with concern. (Or fear? That's fear.) I'm as normal as I can be right now.

"Better?" he asks. There's pain and concern in his voice.

Erik's hurting. He let Oxana tell me I'm a follower because it would have hurt too much to tell me himself. I didn't pay attention and then I made the same mistake all over again: I started following Sable. Now he's hurting again. I may not be a genius like Haring or Picasso but even I can see the pattern. Even as the rain blurs my vision, things become a lot clearer.

I pull him in and kiss his cheek. I whisper in his ear, "I have to do something. Go catch up with the gang. I'll talk to you later."

And before he can protest, I vanish into the shadows.

I'm at the RYC, banging on Sable's door. A minute later, it flies open. Sable stands there wearing a jockstrap, the thick hair on his chest just shy of an actual sweater. Past him, I can see Mark lounging on the bed in his boxers. They're both sweaty.

"Dude," Sable grunts, "what the hell?"

"That's what I should be asking you!" I'm up on my toes to meet his eyes.

His powerful fingers lock around my shoulder as he yanks me into the room and closes the door. He pushes me up against the wall.

"You need to calm down." His voice is low, dangerous. I should be afraid; I have no doubt he could do serious damage to me. I really don't care right now.

"Monogamy is just the straights trying to keep us in line.'" I spit his mantra back at him. "We can sleep with anyone we want. We don't have to be stuck with one person, right? Is that really what being gay means to you? Sleeping with anyone? My 'date' was this kinky old perv who couldn't keep his hands off me." From the bed, Mark laughs. I duck past Sable and stand over Mark. "Did you know about this?"

Mark's on his feet. He's only an inch taller than me but he's muscular and, from what I saw at the Darkroom, he has a lot more experience fighting. I see a hint of Pete in his eyes and I know he's seconds away from launching into me. Let him. I took shit from Pete for years. There's no way I'm submitting to this asshole.

Sable steers me to a chair and sits me down. He nods at Mark, who sits back on the bed, then he squats next to me so we're eye level.

"I never said this was gonna be pretty, guy," Sable says. I'm sure he thinks it's a soothing voice, but it's the audio equivalent of chewing tin foil. "Those 'kinky old pervs' might not be much to look at, but they're your ticket to liberation. Remember? That's what we're learning about now. The Seventies. Being part of the community. Doing what everyone does."

"Everyone does *not* do this!"

He ignores me. "If you want to get past this phase in the training, you gotta escort for a full month and take as many dates as come up. You want that freedom, don't you? You don't want straight people telling you who to fuck, saying you can only ever be with one person. Shit, if it were up to them, they wouldn't even let you do that. It's all about liberation. You can't back out now. You're so close to being a true Chaser."

I can't stand looking at Sable and his bloodshot eyes anymore so I turn away. Nearby, his laptop is open. The website on the screen shows two naked men wearing leather restraints having anal sex. A big banner at the top of the page screams, "Bareback Bugchasing Party!" It lists a date in early August, but before I can see more, Sable reaches past me and snaps the lid shut.

"Getting ahead of yourself," he says, forced calm to his tone. "Identification's phase three. You're not done with phase two yet."

I head for the door. "I'm out. And Davis is out too."

Sable stops me with a laugh. "You can't be out if you were never in, guy. And I don't think you can speak for Little Dude. He's in a lot more than you ever will be."

I slam the door, leaving Mark and Sable to their laughter.

I walk around in the rain for hours. When I finally go home, it's three a.m. I should collapse in bed and pray I get enough sleep to be coherent when I face Erik tomorrow. But I switch on the computer instead, trying to remember the URL for the site on Sable's computer.

Failing, I go to Google and try the word I saw on the screen: "bugchasers."

Eighty thousand hits come up. I'm still visiting links two hours later, my skin crawling with every click. The sun rises. Morning light fills my room. I finally understand what Chasers has really been about from day one. I know how dangerous Sable is.

But I've no clue what I do next.

bugchasers

Instinct tells me to do what I always do when I have a problem: go to Erik.

But when he's there in front of me, what the hell do I say?

Did you know there are nutjobs called bugchasers who try to contract HIV and Davis is one of them? Telling him about Sable and the bugchasers opens the door to a thousand other questions I'm not ready to face. Plus, I already have plenty to answer for with him. And answers will take time and I just don't feel like I have any now. Time *or* answers. If Sable's "identification" means having unprotected sex with someone infected with HIV, I don't have long to stop Davis.

When Erik's cell goes to voicemail for the fifth time, I give up and start biking around Madison, hitting his studio, the hospital, his apartment, and any other space he's been in the past few weeks.

Dammit, Erik, I've never needed you this badly. Where are you?

Running out of options, I head over to Mr. Benton's apartment, hoping Erik's there doing an impromptu checkup. I reach for the doorbell but see the front door ajar. I push it in and find Mr. Benton curled up on the floor, shivering.

He's a complete one-eighty from the last time I saw him. His cheeks are hollow. A thin, crimson ring surrounds each puffy eye. He's staring out into nothing. His skin is splotchy and he's swallowing constantly. I've seen him during his "bad" periods before, but this is the worst I've ever seen him.

I kneel at his side and recoil as I touch his hand. He's burning up.

"Mr. Benton?" I ask, feeling his sweaty forehead. "Can you hear me? It's Evan Weiss. Can you hear me?"

He swallows a few more times and holds out a hand, taking mine. A limp smile seizes his lips. "Evan? You're so cold."

"What are you doing on the floor?"

He looks around, barely able to pivot his head. His eyes cross, as if he hadn't realized he was on the floor. "I was . . . I wasn't feeling so good. I thought I'd go to the hospital. I got as far as the door and . . ." He shakes.

I take out my cell. "I'm calling an ambulance."

He moans. "No. Please. Don't need another bill from the meat wagon. My keys are on the kitchen table. Can you take me? Please?"

The next ten minutes blur. I grab the keys and get him to University Hospital. The emergency room staff takes him away to a room as I talk to the admitting nurse, who knows me.

"Can you page Erik?" I ask. "He'll want to know about this." She agrees and I head to Benton's room.

An hour later, I'm still sitting at Benton's bedside. Surrounded by numerous beeping machines and IV stands, I page through his scrapbook. I grabbed it on the way out, knowing he'd want it here.

I hold it open, staring at the picture of the White Satyr Collective. *By the Eighties*, Mr. Benton had said, *most of the Collective was gone.* I look at Mr. Benton, ashen and sweaty. Did the Collective choose this? Did he?

Sometime later, Mr. Benton's fever breaks and color returns to his face.

"You scared me," I scold. "You think Erik was mad when you missed your checkup? Imagine what'll happen if you're too sick to attend the unveiling of the *Angels*."

"It'd be easier to wrestle the Grim Reaper than deal with your boyfriend when he's pissed," Benton rasps before sipping from a cup of ice water. "Thanks for the assist. You're a prince and a gentleman."

I chide gently. "You stopped taking your meds again, didn't you?"

Mr. Benton holds up three fingers and lifts his chin. "Scout's honor. I'm taking them every day. But sometimes the virus puts up a good fight. Just gotta ride this out."

I think about everything I read online last night about HIV and bugchasing and my curiosity gets the better of me.

"Mr. Benton, can I ask you about . . . your disease?"

Benton raises an eyebrow. "AIDS, Evan. If you don't say it, you're only giving it power. And, yes, ask me anything you want."

I take a deep breath. "Did you try to get it?"

His glare tells me I couldn't have asked anything more insulting. He lifts his hands and points around the room. "Yes," he says dryly, "because all I've ever wanted out of life is an unending supply of heart monitors and glucose bags and medication that leaves me dehydrated. Oh, and the constant diarrhea is a treat."

I quickly try to explain. "I was reading online last night. About these guys. Bugchasers. They don't care if they catch HIV. In fact, they want to. It's like a status symbol to them. So they have unprotected sex—"

Benton holds up a hand and I stop. His breathing staggers. "First. To answer your question. No, I did not *try* to contract HIV. I got HIV because I was young and reckless and I didn't care who I had sex with. And I had a lot of sex. I don't know who gave it to me. I also don't know how many men I may have infected before I found out."

His eyes well, a mix of anger and sadness, and he continues. "Second. I've heard about these bugchasers. They call HIV 'the gift.' It's an obscenity. They think that because they're young and weren't alive when the epidemic was at its height, that they've missed out on an important part of the 'gay experience.' They think it makes them *unique*." He hits that last word with disgust, his lips curling in a snarl.

"Third . . ." He fixes me with his most serious gaze and says, "Why are you asking me this, Evan?"

"No," I respond fast, "no, it's not like that. I'm not . . . I don't want . . . I'm not stupid enough to contract—"

The hole I'm digging gets deeper as I realize I'm only insulting him with every syllable. But Benton lets me off the hook with a smile and a wave of his hand.

"It's okay. You're responding exactly the way you're supposed to. It's insidious." He sighs, folding his hands neatly in his lap. "Not just the disease but the way we treat it. It's the only disease in the world that forces us to talk out of both sides of our mouth. We're constantly telling the people who are infected there's nothing to be ashamed of and we're scaring the shit out of everyone else, saying 'You don't want to get that' and thrusting condoms in their hands. It's okay to *have* it but not to *contract* it. It's a mixed message. And that's what's insidious. There's no better way to respond."

Mr. Benton takes his scrapbook and holds up the picture of the White Satyr Collective. He begins pointing them out one by one. "Dennis Parr . . . brilliant playwright. He coulda been the next Edward Albee. Dead: August fourteenth, 1985. . . . Albert Dean. Actor. Poet. Composer. Got offered a part in *A Chorus Line* and moved to New York but never made it onstage. Dead: April thirtieth, 1985. . . . Marshall Whitman. Has two sculptures at the Museum of Modern Art. Could have had more. Dead: June twenty-first, 1985. . . ."

He catalogs the others in the picture but I can hardly hear him. I can't believe he remembers all of these dates. Then I realize how close together they were. That's the sort of memory you don't shake, when your closest friends die within months of one another. When he said the Collective fell apart, I'd assumed the members had moved on to other things. I hadn't imagined this kind of loss.

He turns a page and I see a small Polaroid of Mr. Benton and a withered man in a wheelchair, whom I recognize as Arthur, Mr. Benton's partner. They're holding what looks like a quilt between them. On the front of the quilt, in a mosaic of multicolored fabric, is the image of a sailboat.

"Arthur loved sailing. This was taken a week before he died," Mr. Benton whispers. "We made that square for the AIDS Memorial Quilt. The quilt was supposed to be a remembrance so no one would ever forget what happened: the senseless loss. Apparently, these bugchasers never got the message."

Or they're creating their own message, I think. After hearing Mr. Benton's version, Sable's take on the Eighties doesn't ring true. "I have a friend," I say slowly, "I think . . . I think he's mixed up with these guys."

"Has he been exposed to the virus?" The real question is: *Has he had unprotected sex?*

"I don't know. I don't think so."

Mr. Benton closes his eyes and exhales through his nose, making a quiet rattling sound. When his eyes open, they are the very definition of serious.

"I think you know what you have to do." He closes his eyes again. "I'm sorry. I'm really drained. I need to rest. Give my best to Erik when you see him. And thanks again."

I pat his hand and exit into the cool, white hallway. Still no Erik. I wander the corridors of the hospital and find myself in the ICU. I glance occasionally into the rooms at the people hooked up to machines.

That's when I see Pete Isaacson through a window. His head bandaged, his eyes shut. A thin bar of fluorescent light casts harsh shadows down his swollen face. Someone, his back turned to me, sits hunched at his bedside. I step into the doorway.

The figure turns and, as he does, I can see past him. Pete's inert hand lies on top of the thin seafoam green blanket. His visitor's hand is on top of Pete's. Not just on top. His fingers are interlaced with Pete's. Tightly. I feel heat in my chest as I stare into Kenny Dugan's eyes.

When Kenny recognizes me, he's on his feet and in my face.

"Don't you—You fucking—Get the hell out—" He's sputtering and quivering and trying to be the same tough guy who broke my arm a year and a half ago. But I don't buy it. I can't. Because every syllable, every sound has a color of its own, from a palette I know intimately. The color of fear, of reprisal, of denial, but mostly of sheer terror. He didn't want me—or anyone—to see him holding Pete's hand.

Kenny's shoulders pull back and I know that he wants to cream me but good. He wouldn't dare—not here, not now. We stand toe to toe.

I ask calmly, "Is he going to be okay?"

Kenny's nostrils pulse. He's close to hyperventilating. I'd like to think there's something in my rational tone that calms him down because, even though it takes a moment, he begins to deflate.

"He came out of the coma yesterday. Now he's doped up on pain meds."

I can't ever remember hearing Kenny's voice without that angry edge. Even answering questions in class, he was full of attitude and defiance. As he talks about Pete, the arrogance is gone. He's vulnerable.

I can't shake the image of Kenny holding tightly to Pete's hand. When I look back to Pete, Kenny jabs a finger in my face. "Listen, fag, you don't know what you saw. You think you know but you . . ."

I know, Kenny. I know.

"You're a fucking coward, Kenny," I say. "Davis and I took your shit all the time and we never once squealed on you guys. Not fucking once. You get a little of your own back at the Darkroom and you go to the cops and turn us in."

Kenny's jaw sets and I'm pretty sure he no longer cares about the trouble he'll get in for starting a fight in the hospital. He raises himself up to his full height, a good three inches over me, and draws back his shoulders. But instead of hitting me, he says, "I didn't tell the cops about your friends. I only told them what you did."

"What I did?" I must be totally insane because now I'm in his face like a kamikaze gnat. "You're pissed because I kicked you? You broke my arm, you asshole. And you're pissed—"

And there it is. His eyes soften and Kenny turns his back. He sits next to Pete again. I can be pretty stupid sometimes but you have to cut me slack for not putting it all together, given the history we share. Officer Brogan's exact words: *Someone said you were on the scene helping.* Not helping trash the cars. Kenny had seen me step between Davis and Pete. He had told the police I wasn't involved, that I was trying to help. I don't even need to ask why. I just picture his hand in Pete's.

Kenny stares at Pete. "You protected Pete. I protected you. But I can't stay quiet about the rest much longer. Pete's parents know I know something. They've got the police pushing me to tell them who did this. You and me? We're even. I owe nothing to nobody else."

The meaning is clear. Kenny has no idea who Sable and the others are. He couldn't turn them in if he wanted to. And he wants to. The only person he can still rat out is Davis.

He turns like he just wants me to leave so he can return his attention to his friend. Attention Pete can't appreciate, doped up as he is. Attention Pete probably doesn't even—

"Does Pete know—"

He whirls. "If you fucking say anything to him or to anyone else—"

I take out my wallet and remove the dog tag that Davis gave me at the observatory. I toss it to Kenny. "I'm not saying a word. But—and listen to me, Kenny—if I hear you've beat up or even glared at another gay guy again, I'm gonna come down on you like the fucking wrath of God."

I walk away, my breath even, my thoughts clear. So this is what life is like when you throw out the rules.

Erik and I almost collide as I return to the nurse's station outside Mr. Benton's room. He grabs me into a tight hug. "I'm sorry. My cell battery's dead, I lost my pager, it's been the day from hell. I've been looking for you everywhere. I just clocked in and they told me you brought Mr. Benton. What's going on?"

It's funny. We both spent the day racing around trying to find each other. It's funny but I can't laugh.

I catch him up about Mr. Benton. His face falls and he gives me another tight squeeze. It's all I can do not to cry.

Erik leads me into an echoey stairwell, away from the clamor of the nurse's station, and strokes my cheek. "I was worried about you last night. You can't just break down like that and run off. I even went to the store looking for you. Some guy named Ross said he hadn't seen you. What's going on?"

I swallow. "Have you ever been in a situation where you cared a lot about someone and you had to do something—something that you meant to be helpful but would hurt them in the process? And you might even lose them?"

Erik stiffens. An overhead page requests his presence in radiology. He nods and says, "I guess so. People who live at the speed of stupid dig themselves holes. The smart people who love them help them dig out. But I think we can only do that for so long. I think at some point, you have to learn to cut your losses and move on. Even if it means getting hurt. Even if it means hurting them. Sometimes you let people live as fast as they want and you look out for number one. You know?"

He's paged again. Erik leans in and kisses me. Not a quick "we're in public so let's be polite" peck. A long, slow kiss that instantly catapults me back to the last night we spent together in bed. The last time I felt nothing could ever come between us.

Erik whispers, "I'm off work at nine. Any chance I'll see you at my place later?" The double meaning is clear: *I need answers.* I nod and he says with a wink, "Miss me."

It's not until after he's gone that it occurs to me: Erik thought I was talking about us.

I think about the Gregory Douglass song Erik plays when he broods:

> *I'll miss you hard enough to hide it,*
> *I need you hard enough to try,*
> *I love you hard enough to move on . . .*

I can fix that. I know I can. I can make sure he understands that will never apply to us. But later. What I have to do now, I'm less sure about.

I go looking for Davis.

TITLE: *Forward*

IMAGE:
A stack of lead bars, as seen on the
Wisconsin state flag

INSPIRATION:
Matisse's *Le bonheur de vivre*
(*The Joy of Life*)

PALETTE:
Background = sapphire
Lead bars = topaz
Shadows = ruby

An explosion of color in wide, unpol-
ished strokes. The trapezoid lead bars
have rounded edges, hugging one another
tightly. The background matches the
vibrant blue of Wisconsin's state flag.

Once—once—*I tried to control the Boing.*
In my defense, I was twelve and hadn't really come to
understand the full scope of Davis's obsessions. How powerful
they were at the start. Or how quickly they gave up the ghost.
After being dragged to Boy Scouts and stamp collecting

and soccer lessons—none of which lasted more than a week—I announced to Davis that I was going to teach him how to paint.

"What for?" he asked. "How will that help us fit in?"

That's what it was always about. Fitting in.

"Think of it as something to do until we find a new club to join," I said.

I still can't believe he said yes.

So we spent the next few weeks doing rudimentary lessons—how to draw basic shapes, how to visualize the final product in your mind's eye. One day, we caught a bus to the UW Arboretum. I brought THE CLAW and a window shaped like a cross that I got from an old church. We set up in a marsh near Lake Wingra and I started work on a landscape in the style of Gauguin. Davis just wanted to watch me paint. After about ten minutes, he started making little grunts and shaking his head.

Finally, I said, "What?"

He pointed to the bottom of the window. "What's that?"

"It's grass."

"Uh-huh," he said, looking out into my field of vision with exaggerated effort. "Yeah, I don't see any red grass out there. What the hell? You're always doing things like this. Painting with colors that you don't really see."

"It's called artistic interpretation."

We'd had some variation of this conversation at least twice a year since we met. I would try to explain . . . well, art. It never ended well.

He plopped down in the grass next to me, sitting cross-legged with a look of feigned exasperation on his face. "Yeah, yeah, you've said that. Why can't you just let colors mean what they mean?"

I laid down my brush and folded my arms, ready for battle. "Oh. Well, what do colors mean?"

"Well, like, red. Red should mean love. But when you paint hearts or other lovey stuff, you paint them purple and blue and white and . . . It's just weird."

"Okay," I said slowly, "well, isn't red also the color of danger? Isn't that the color of a stop sign? There it means to pay attention. Am I supposed to love a stop sign?"

Davis looked lost.

"There's no universal meaning attached to color. When you try to tie color to a single meaning, you're limiting what you can say. That doesn't mean you can't use a color to represent a feeling or an idea. But you need to keep your mind open to all possibilities. That's how you make art."

For a moment, Davis's eyes flared with appetite. I'd finally found the right words and he got it. I'd witnessed the birth of a Boing, one I could get excited about too. I was so worked up, I ignored the fact that I knew the ultimate fate of each and every Davis Boing. This was going to be different. I knew it.

The lessons continued. Davis stopped watching me and began experimenting on his own. He started with small picture frames as his canvas. Mainly, he played with color and light, *getting the feel of it all. He even went to the store and got his own set of paints and brushes. When I sensed he was getting anxious to actually paint a picture, I found two small windows and we took THE CLAW to the State Capitol down in the center of Madison.*

It was a quiet Sunday afternoon with no one around. The Capitol building looks very much like the Capitol in Washington, DC, shaped like an upright, oblong pill. Near the information desk on the first floor is a huge Wisconsin state flag. The flag's crest is fairly simple: a miner, a sailor, a stack of lead bars, a badger . . . But Davis freaked when he saw it.

"No way can I do that."

I began contorting THE CLAW so it would hold both windows, aiming them directly at the flag. "Don't worry about painting the whole thing. Pick a part of it. The badger. The bars of lead. Use your imagination. It doesn't have to be a perfect representation."

Once THE CLAW was in place, we each began mixing colors. I started right in, focusing on the cornucopia in the lower left of the crest. Davis stood there for a long time, just staring up as if hoping for divine inspiration. Then he poked at some silvery paint and began dabbing in the shape of a trapezoid. We painted for about an hour. A Cubist cornucopia filled my window while Davis had managed a very realistic replica of the stack of lead bars.

"See?" I said, elbowing him. "That's amazing for your first

painting." But as we wiped our brushes clean, he frowned and shook his head.

"It's not as good as yours."

His tone might as well have been a dirge, signaling the premature death of another Boing. Not this time, I remember thinking. Give me 40,000 volts, stat.

Clear!

"I've been doing this longer. If you stick with it, each one will get better." I tried to sound supportive, but desperation colored my voice. The patient was fading fast. Silently, I pleaded: Don't give up, don't give up. "You should see my first paintings. Not half as good as yours."

But that was the last time we went painting together. A few days later, I suggested we take THE CLAW out so I could teach him about negative volume. Davis flipped the page of the manga he was reading and yawned. "That's okay. I don't think painting's for me."

Of everything I'd seen Davis take up and drop—Boy Scouts, drama club, stamp collecting, band, choir—his dismissal of painting felt personal. Like he wasn't just dismissing painting but our friendship. Or maybe because I thought—I hoped—it would give him the discipline to follow through on something. Anything. I know now that it was arrogant to think I could teach that to Davis. At the time, I just wanted him to know what painting had taught me.

Every work of art—painting, novel, song—anything you

work really hard to achieve comes with a point of no return attached. A moment of evaluation: Is this worth continuing?

You're forced to think things through. You enter into a relationship with each new painting. It's intimate and intense. Giving up is like breaking up.

When I start a painting, I put a lot of thought into deciding if it will be worth the journey. But that's a painting. Something I'm totally at ease with. Bigger things, like relationships with other people?

I crash and burn.

ultimatum

Storm clouds darken the sky. Another front moves in, sending winds that bend the trees and toss whitecaps across the surface of Lake Mendota. My legs throb as I pump my bike's pedals, determined to outrace the imminent downpour.

I make it to the RYC seconds ahead of the thunderclap that summons rain so thick it makes everything outside gray. Inside, Davis shoots pool with Will. He swaggers around with his cue, holding it over his shoulder like a caveman wielding a club.

"Will, I need to talk to Davis."

Davis singes me with a glare, obviously still angry about last night. Will looks to Davis, who nods, giving him permission to leave. Davis turns back to the game and shakes his head. "What the hell happened to you last night?"

"Did you sleep with that guy?" I demand, a little louder than necessary.

Davis laughs. "Nah. We went back to his place, messed around a bit—"

"Messed around?"

He rolls his eyes. "Just a lot of grab-ass. Anyway, he got totally wasted and passed out before we could get to the good stuff. S'okay, I didn't want to fuck him anyway."

I lean in so our noses nearly touch. "Was he HIV positive?"

I've caught him off guard. Davis's eyes narrow and he takes a step back. He knows I know. He brushes it off with a head toss, then turns back to the pool table and lines up a shot. "I don't know. It never came up. Probably not. That's not how I wanna get the gift anyway. I wanna wait."

The gift.

Click, click. The six ball caroms off the side and lands in the corner pocket. The cue ball spirals back toward Davis, who's waiting, ready, with his cue.

My skin crawls, growing cold. "Davis, you don't know what you're doing."

Davis grins. *Click, click, click.* The nine ball stops just shy of its pocket. Davis rotates to set up his next shot. "Look, Cicada's pretty pissed about that stunt you pulled last night but I think I can talk him down from it. You can still be a Chaser."

I snatch the cue ball and shove it into the nearest

pocket. He sets his cue on the table slowly and puts his hands on his hips. I stare him down. "No, I can't. I've seen what HIV can do to someone. You can't go through with this."

Our raised voices earn sideways glances from people across the room. Davis grabs my elbow and ushers me into a side hall. He's smiling but his eyes are hard and distant, like he's trapped between remembering who I am and who he is.

"The final initiation," he says in a low, seductive murmur, "is gonna be awesome. We're getting together with a bunch of guys who've been living with the gift for years. Sable's going to tell them everything we've done to earn our right to be called Chasers. And then they're each going to pick one of us to pass the gift on to." He stops, throws a conspiratorial look over his shoulder, then smiles. "Except me. Cicada said he would take care of me personally."

This isn't my Davis. The color has gone from his face and his eyes are filled with dreams we never talked about. The journey we started together when we were nine— toward belonging—is apparently something he's will-ing to continue alone. Acceptance, his voice tells me, is finally within his grasp.

He gently pulls me down and we sit cross-legged on the floor. It's like we're back in my bedroom, chewing down egg foo yung and finding our lives in fortune cookies. It could be that. It's not.

"Everything you think you know about HIV is wrong," he assures me with a pat on my knee. "You know how Cicada told us that the heteros want us to think that it's not natural to sleep with any guys we want? Well, this is the same thing. They want us to think HIV is this horrible stigma, that only 'bad' people get it. But it's not. It's a badge of honor. That's why it affected the gay community first. It's like . . . a mark from nature, something to make us special. They called us queer to ridicule us. Well, we took that word back and used it with pride. They tried to make us feel shame about getting AIDS. Well, we're taking that back too. We own that. You can't be ashamed of something that makes you belong."

I can pick out each of Sable's half truths, the ones clogging Davis's logic. "Davis, it's a killer. There is no cure."

He scoffs with a smile that reminds me too much of his new mentor. "More hetero propaganda. HIV doesn't have to be a death sentence. Not these days. There are medications you can take and you can live a normal life. So you take a few pills every day. Small price to pay to be somebody.

"Once you get the gift, it's a sign of power. The fear is gone. You have nothing to worry about anymore. You're finally in control of your own destiny."

Every time I've lost Davis, when he's become so con-
sumed by his own thoughts and misery that he loses
touch with the world, I've always been able to get him
back. I've been able to get him to realize that he's not
alone. Sometimes it took jokes, sometimes it took yelling.
But I always won. Right now, I don't feel like I'll ever win
again.

"Davis," I whisper, because my throat is too dry to do
otherwise, "I want you to drop out of Chasers. I want you
to tell Sable that you're finished and move out of the RYC.
If Malaika knew what Sable was doing—"

"Don't say a word!" I can't tell if Davis is afraid of
Sable being exposed or afraid of what Malaika would
think of him.

"I won't," I say, secretly knowing that if that's what it
takes to stop this, I'm ready to do just that. "She doesn't
have to know about Sable, the Darkroom, or anything.
Just move out of here and . . . and . . ." I punt. "Move
in with my family. I don't know how I'll get my parents
to agree to it but they will. Then . . ." I have no idea
how I'll explain any of this to Erik. "We'll figure the rest
out."

He studies my face. After nine years of friendship, he
can read my every look, and this one says: *I'm not messing
around.* I wait for him to back down, to respect everything
we've been through and admit I'm right. But his expres-

sion is one I can't read anymore and he says, "Not gonna happen."

I think of Mr. Benton and the nights Erik spent with him, waiting for his fever to break. I wonder: If Davis keeps this up, who will be there for him, waiting for his fever to break? He's about to stand when I catch his arm. "Davis, I can't let you do this. If you don't drop out of Chasers . . ." He's past the point where telling Malaika would mean anything. Fortunately, I can hit harder than that. "I'm going to the police with what I know about the Darkroom."

Davis freezes. "You'd never do that."

I play my last card. "Maybe. Maybe not. If I don't, Kenny Dugan will."

He has to believe that.

"If he does, then you go down too," Davis sneers, each word blistering as it comes out. "You were as much a part of it as the rest of us. Plus, you lied to the cops about knowing—"

"I'll take the heat," I promise him, not budging. "If they send us all to jail, then I'll go. I can't let you throw away—"

Davis yanks his arm back. He throws one more taser-like glare before walking away. And I let him go. It would hurt too much to follow. Even though it seems impossible for things to hurt worse. We've had fights where we didn't talk for two, three days. We always made up. I used to think we always would.

Always isn't as long as it used to be.

My drenched clothes are draped over the radiator in Erik's living room, though it won't produce heat for another four months. I'm finally dry. His jeans and Badgers hoodie hang loosely from my body. I'm rolled up in a ball in the papasan chair when the door clicks open and Erik enters with a bag of groceries.

I've lit a few candles and he seems more surprised by that than to find me huddling in the growing darkness. He abandons the groceries in the kitchen and then kneels next to the chair. My cheeks are flushed, raw, and damp. My nose, I can only imagine, is red and caked with vile things. He offers me a Kleenex and I blow.

His hand rests on my knee. That calming touch sends any tears I had left into hiding. And he waits. Patiently. He knows I'll talk. He knows me.

I wrap my arms around his neck. He pulls me in and runs his hands through my hair. I'm safe. I'm welcome. I'm home. We move to the love seat; Erik lies on his back, I lie on top of him, my head resting on his chest. His heartbeat, strong and rapid, coaxes my own to match his.

"It's time," he says softly, "for you to tell me what's going on. Why you were crying the other night. Why you ran from me. Why you're crying now. Because, Evan, it's starting to freak me out." He takes a deep breath. "I dated guys who had these . . . mood swings. Meant they were dealing with a guilty conscience. They started to lose track of all the lies they'd told. Get flustered and angry and sad and then clingy and . . ."

His arms lift into the air. *Talk to me.* I reach up and draw his arms back down, forcing him to hold me. I press my ear firmly against his chest and his heartbeat pounds a tattoo within. It fills every inch of me.

"There's so much I want to tell you," I say, tracing a vein on his bare forearm with my finger. "So much I'm *going* to tell you. But just trust me one more time. Trust that I'll explain once we're in San Diego."

With my ear to his chest, my voice reverberates in my head and I hear a thousand distorted echoes of these words. A thousand affirmations. I've made my choice.

He lifts my chin and turns my head so I can look him in the eyes. His chest stops rising; he holds his breath. "Do you mean that?"

He shouldn't trust me. He should say, *Evan, I need to know what's going on because it could affect our future and I can't commit to bringing you to San Diego if you aren't totally open with me.* But he doesn't. Yet again, he trusts that I'll provide all the answers once we're away from here.

Once more, love overrides.

I scoot forward and kiss him, then return to position my head near that comforting heartbeat. "Once we're in San Diego, I'll tell you everything you ever wanted to know."

unveiled

"They're gonna hate it. They're gonna boo me off the stage, tear it down, and sell it for scrap metal."

Erik is currently a jigger of top-shelf crazy. In just over an hour, *Fierce Angels* will make its debut in Reid Park. He's pacing his apartment, spouting off every worst-case scenario he can imagine. To say he's nervous is to submit the winning application for Understatement of the Year.

The last week has been spent talking about Milwaukee—apologies and tears from both sides—and working toward becoming who we were. It's been about planning for San Diego and the future. In this moment, though, none of that matters. We're inching closer to the unveiling ceremony, which Erik has been dreading.

And if it wasn't bad enough that Erik is somewhat attention-phobic, two days ago he found out he's expected to say something at the unveiling. He's been Basket Case Erik ever since. Apparently, public speaking is not his friend.

We go over the notes for his speech. As he practices to his audience of one, his voice is effete and melancholy. To keep him focused, I crack jokes. I walk him through relaxing sun salutations. I stand him in front of the antique mirror leaning against the wall in his living room so I can straighten his tie. It's like our fight never happened.

When he's as calm as he can be, we climb into the Jeep and head for the park. Erik's hand rests on my knee. He's stopped asking about my family. All the queries fell prey to my promise to join him in San Diego. Instead, he's been pressuring me about my painting.

"If there's anything else you want to paint in Madison before we leave, you better snap to," he says, reminding me that we leave in just a week. "I haven't seen you pick up a brush . . . in ages."

He means to say, *Since Milwaukee*. And it's true. I can't shake what Oxana said. I've even stopped studying Haring's work. I've thought about it: What does it mean to be my own artist? There is an answer to this question. The answer eludes me.

At the park, there's a stage set up near the picnic shelter. Next to the stage, a huge white sheet keeps the *Angels* from prying eyes. There are about fifty white plastic folding chairs arranged for the audience, but I'm surprised to see that the attendance is at least four times that number. Some kids are already milling around the refreshments table, sneaking bites before volunteers shoo them away.

Near the stage, Malaika greets us both with a hug and introduces us to Madison's mayor, who will give the keynote. She also introduces us to Cory Tanner, the kid who was in the hospital for months after getting beaten here. He's in a wheelchair, looking from face to face as if struggling to remember if he knows us. Malaika says that she'll speak, then Erik, and then, together, all the speakers will unveil the *Angels*.

As we get ready to start, I bear-hug Erik and say, "Good luck." The seats are all taken but as I move to join the SRO crowd, Malaika takes my arm and leads me to the stage and a reserved chair next to Erik's. I smile, sit, and grasp Erik's hand. TV news crews line up along the front of the stage. Erik spots them and I can feel his hand grow clammy in mine.

"Just do it like we practiced," I whisper, giving his fingers a squeeze.

"We practiced," he reminds me out of the corner of his mouth, "in our underwear. Are you willing to strip to keep me calm?"

I poke him in the ribs. "Whatever it takes."

A police officer steps from the crowd, approaches the mayor, and they talk with concerned looks. The cop looks familiar, like maybe he's spoken at school or the

RYC. He and the mayor survey the gathered horde, the officer occasionally pointing out people. He then hands the mayor a slip of paper and walks back to his post. The mayor joins us onstage.

"Anything wrong, Gabe?" Malaika asks quietly.

"I don't think so," the mayor replies. "We thought there were some protestors here—we'd heard rumors people from that church in Kansas were making a trip up here to spread their hate. But it's just some kids handing out flyers. I think they're pro-gay. I'm not worried."

He hands the flyer to Malaika, who scans it and nods. I look past Erik and read it myself. It's handwritten, poorly photocopied.

STAND UP AND TAKE PRIDE IN BEING GAY!

Be a CHASER

Meeting tonight after the ceremony Meet by the new statue at 8 p.m.

Panicking, I look into the audience. I easily spot Sable, handing out flyers like an usher at the opera. My scan picks up Mark, then Del, then Will, and finally Davis, who's not far from the edge of the stage. I can't tell if he's seen me. Several moments pass before I realize I've pulled my hand out of Erik's.

The Monona High School pep band strikes up "We Are the Champions" and the crowd erupts in applause. The mayor takes the podium. He speaks, but I can't hear him. I can only focus on Davis, who has stopped handing out flyers and has taken point near the front row. He's listening to the mayor. If he'd seen me, I'm sure he'd be staring. Like I am at him.

Has Sable "inducted" him yet? How long will it be? It's only then that I place the cop talking with the mayor as the same cop who came to my house. Officer Brogan. He's standing not three feet from Davis.

Malaika's speaking now. "A tide is turning," she says. "We as a city have to unite and send a clear message: There can be no room for hatred. We will brook no intolerance. We bring the fight to the intolerant, using their own hatred against them." I think about Pete in the hospital and sickness wells in my stomach. I think about Kenny, so fucked up with feelings he hates having. I count the days until I'm in California and can start over, tabula rasa, and none of that will matter.

"And now," Malaika says, her warm voice warbling slightly through the cheap sound system, "I'd like to introduce the artist who designed and built the sculpture we're about to unveil. Mr. Erik Goodhue."

Whistles and hoots punctuate the applause. Erik squeezes my knee and steps up to the podium, holding his note card. "Thank you. It was an honor to be selected to create the work you're about to see . . ." He stops, staring intently at the card. I prompt him in my mind.

After six months of work . . . After six months of work . . .

Then he turns the card facedown on the podium and swallows. "Listen, I'm terrified to talk in front of people." A chuckle ripples through the crowd. "I thought writing my thoughts down would help me through this but it's not. So I'm just gonna punt. The fact is, I made this statue because I could have been Cory Tanner. I got the snot kicked out of me almost every day when I was in middle school."

I never knew this. Erik? With those muscles, with that confidence? Beat up?

"My mom—she passed away when I was nine—she used to tell me about angels. She said we all had angels to protect us. I don't know where Cory's angels were when those thugs were taking a baseball bat to him. But his angels are here now, with us today. His angels will stand here as a permanent reminder that there is grace all around us. And it's through that grace that we'll persevere. It's a grace we find through unity. It's a grace that comes from loving and being loved."

He stops, mouth poised to speak, like he thinks he should say more. But he glances at me and I nod. There's nothing more to say. He nods back. "I'd like to show you the *Angels* now."

All of the speakers move to the covered statue. Erik turns and holds out his hand to me. I watch as Davis, who'd been staring at Erik with rapt attention during his speech, follows Erik's outstretched hand and our eyes meet. I can feel the crosshairs home in.

I stand and face Erik, smile on my face. I cross the stage and take his hand. The other speakers, Erik, and I take the rope and as the crowd counts to three, we yank, sending the cloak fluttering to the grass.

A shaft of pure sunlight hits the polished wings, washing the first few rows of spectators in radiance. The crowd can't decide whether to "oooh" or scream in appreciation so they choose both, competing with the wild applause for decibel supremacy.

Erik leans in to kiss me, his soft brown eyes dancing. I know that look. It's the one I keep inside whenever he's not around. It's the one I would have cried for, remembering in Chicago. Only I don't have to remember now. I've chosen California. And I can have that look with me every day.

I don't want to know the look I'm getting from Davis.

At the reception, Erik is the man. Everyone is shaking his hand, complimenting the statue. People ask to get their picture taken with him next to the *Angels*. He gets business cards. Hot guys hand him slips of paper with their phone numbers. Erik hands me the numbers to tear up. I smile, the proud boyfriend, but my chest is tight. I don't know where the Chasers are and that scares me.

Then I spot Kenny. He's standing near the picnic shelter with a husky man; from the resemblance, I'm guessing it's Pete's dad. He and Kenny are speaking to Officer Brogan.

Kenny caved. He's squealing on Davis.

Not now. Not in front of Erik.

Erik pokes me in the ribs, our prearranged signal that the accolades are making him uncomfortable. We say our good-byes, he takes my hand, and we head out. We get close to the edge of the park when I see Sable and the Chasers, huddled near the *Angels*. Mark and the rest are talking to kids holding the flyers they got during the ceremony. New recruits. Sable's got an eye on Officer Brogan.

Davis breaks from the group and charges over. Instinctively, I try to remove my hand from Erik's but he won't let go.

He knows.

"So, uh . . . this is your statue?" Davis asks Erik, while he glares at me.

"Yep. Did it myself." Erik beams. He releases my hand, only to slip his arm around my waist and pull me into his side. He holds out his free hand. "I don't know if you remember, but we met once. Last year, after my volleyball game. You're Davis, right?"

I'm sure Erik feels me stiffen. *Please don't do this.*

Davis shakes his head. "You know me? I don't know who the hell you are."

I look past Davis. The new recruits can't take their eyes off Sable, whose flailing arms tell me he's started his sales pitch. I want lightning to strike him. He's the last person who should be anywhere near that statue and what it represents.

"I'm Evan's boyfriend. I'm Erik." He's still holding out his hand but Davis regards it with disgust.

"Boyfriend?" Davis throws back his head and laughs. "Oh, man, are you in for a trip. Good luck. I really mean that. Maybe he won't drag you down like he does everybody else in his life. Maybe he'll be honest with you. He is honest with you, right? He's told you everything about him? Like how he's obsessed with artists. Like how he can only relate to his paints. Like how he tries to help but only makes things worse. Hope you know what you're in for."

He's lashing out. Making shit up just to hurt me. That's what I tell myself. If I think for a second that Davis really believes what he's saying, it means the last nine years have been a lie.

Across the park, I hear Sable's booming voice: "Move!"

Suddenly, the Chasers scatter as half a dozen cops, led by Officer Brogan, descend on their meeting.

Erik's arm drops from around my back. Davis throws me one more searing glance before bolting to catch up with Sable. I can't care. I have bigger problems.

I reach for Erik and he recoils. His face is sapped of color. I stand in front of him and I'm reminded of every time I've lost Davis. Erik's brooding was never like losing Davis. Now they look identical and I've never had to reclaim Erik before. I don't know where to begin.

"Erik," I say firmly, fighting to hide the quiver in my tone. "Don't listen to him. Okay? Just . . . just listen to me."

"You said," he whispers in an even, measured tone, "that he knew about me. That he wanted to meet me. You. Lied."

"You don't understand what's been going on. I really thought I was protecting him. Erik, he's really screwed up right now—"

"Him? Or you? What have I told you from the start? I can deal with just about anything. But not lies."

The sounds of the nearby celebration evaporate into the heat of the summer sun and the only thing I hear is Erik's every word quietly ripping through me. I find myself wishing for the yelling we did in Milwaukee. It hurt less. But that's because this time, I have no defense.

Finally, he turns to look me directly in the eyes with that expression he reserves for regretting the past and hating himself for all the trust he put in past boyfriends.

"I can't deal with this, Evan."

I want to reach out. I don't. I want to smile reassuringly. I don't. I want to say, *I love you and your yoga and your square-egg-shaped head and your lopsided smile and that's what matters.*

But I don't.

Nothing—no fight with Davis, no argument with Shan or my parents—has prepared me for a situation where I stand to lose everything. There are a million things I want to do but I don't know that any of them will set this right. Apologies, excuses, stories . . . Something tells me this goes beyond anything they could achieve. So instead I do the stupidest thing of all: nothing. "Are we . . . breaking up?"

His jaw drops. Erik doesn't end things in anger. Instead, he shakes his head. "I don't know what we are. And I don't think you do either."

For just a second, thunder bursts in my chest. *We're not done. We're not done.* But then he adds, "We need to rethink San Diego."

He walks away. My vision goes out of focus as the park distorts and blurs like a child's watercolor painting.

LOCAL TEEN DIES OF HEARTBREAK

No. No more diversions.

Two blocks down, Erik turns the corner, disappearing from sight. Too little, too late, I thrust both arms up over my head and hold them there higher than John Cusack could ever manage. *Turn around, Erik. Just look at me.* I pray he'll pop back around the corner, see my arms raised, and obey our private signal.

He doesn't.

I turn to the sky. I feel like it should be raining. Isn't it usually raining in these situations? That would be better. I summon my palette. I imagine a black sky, streets that glow red. Darkness. Despair.

Instead, I'm forced to deal with a brightly lit, warm day that's anathema to everything I feel.

When it hurts this bad, shouldn't it at least rain?

With Erik now halfway back to his Jeep, I realize I have to finish the conversation by myself. I summon Erik in my mind. He's not mad. He still wants me to move with him to San Diego. He smirks and gives me a single playful command.

Miss me.

More than ever.

missing

Space. I'm convinced Erik needs space, so I give it to him. I let three days pass. I corral every urge to call, write, or use semaphore. I picture a hundred different ways to apologize. I think about painting him something. I imagine throwing myself at his feet and begging for forgiveness. I picture romantic symbolism, getting an actual boom box and standing outside his windows blasting "In Your Eyes" at full volume.

But in the end, I don't have the courage. I've screwed up beyond belief. I'm dying to apologize but he has to make the first move. I've proven that, if it's left to me, I'll slaughter it.

Friday nights at the store bustle during the school year, but with the fall semester still a few weeks away, it's pretty quiet. With Shan gone, I'm working most of my shifts with Ross. He's not such a bad guy. He picked up the job pretty fast. Even figured out how to get on Mom's good side (no small task). We never talk about Chasers. Until tonight.

"So, you still hanging around that Davis guy?" he asks, scraping a wad of gum off the floor.

I dodge a real answer with, "He's really busy with Chasers. You still see Del?"

Ross shakes his head. "Won't even give me the time of day. To hell with him. If he's willing to give up on years of friendship just 'cause some wacko moves to town . . . Who needs friends like that? Right?"

Silently, I hope. I hope I can still get through to Davis. I hope to fix things with Erik. But I'm not about to share that with Ross, so I keep my hope quiet.

"To hell with him," I concur, raising a can of beets in a mock toast.

The bell over the door tinkles and we both look up to find Mrs. Grayson crossing soundlessly over the threshold. She moves like a husk, empty and light. She's in a pale tan frock that hangs loosely from her brittle frame. Her haunted eyes seem more dazed than usual, if that's even possible. Ross, who's never met Davis's mom before, picks up on this too. I extend my arm, like I've watched Davis do a thousand times before. Mrs. Grayson's fingers chill me as she takes my elbow.

"Mrs. Grayson, are you all right?"

"I can't find my Davis." Her voice cracks and she

swallows repeatedly. "I can't find my Davis and I'm so, so thirsty."

I snap my fingers at Ross and point at the giant fridge. Not missing a beat, he grabs a water bottle and offers it to her. She downs half of it immediately. I turn, placing my body as a sound barrier between her and Ross.

"Get my mother."

And he's gone up the stairs.

"Do you need to sit down?" I lead her to a nearby step stool.

Mrs. Grayson sinks like a stringless puppet onto the seat, her head weaving slowly around as though still not entirely sure where she is. "Yes. That would be nice."

I turn the sign to CLOSED and lock the door. Mom and Ross arrive on the scene as Mrs. Grayson fishes in her pocket, pulling out a small pill bottle. She takes out two small yellow pills and they disappear with the rest of the water.

Mom crouches near Mrs. Grayson. "Clara, should you be out on your own like this? Does your husband know you're here?"

Mr. Grayson, I can assure my mom, does not know she's here.

"I can't find my Davis," is all she says. It becomes an eerie, unsyncopated chant.

And I realize: It's the second Sunday of the month. Davis was supposed to pick her up at Mendota and didn't.

(Christ, did she walk here from Mendota? It must have taken her hours.) And where was Davis? Did the police catch him? Is he hiding with the other Chasers?

Listening to Mrs. Grayson babble, I finally know a way to get through to Davis. When he opens his door at the RYC and I'm there with his mom, he'll figure it out. He'll remember he forgot to pick her up. He'll remember all the years he spent taking care of her. Any thoughts of Sable or catching HIV will be gone.

"Mom," I say, snatching the keys for the truck from behind the counter, "I'm going to take Mrs. Grayson to Davis. He's probably just really busy." The silence that's been the cornerstone of our relationship serves us now. I only need a glance: *Something is wrong with Davis.* She responds with a nod: *Do what you have to.*

I take Mrs. Grayson's arm and we move to the back door. "C'mon, Mrs. Grayson. I can take you to Davis."

"They left yesterday morning."

I'm glad Mrs. Grayson is slouching in the antiquated high-backed chair in the next room because I really don't need her to hear Malaika.

"They?" I ask, glancing over at the room keys behind her. The keys for both Rooms Three and Four hang on their pegs. "Davis *and* Sable? Do you know where they went?"

"Sorry, no." Malaika sighs. "I wasn't here when they

left. I only know they dropped off their keys. Davis left most of his belongings. Mr. Sable didn't have much to begin with."

It feels like I've been slammed against a wall. Like stupidity has finally achieved escape velocity.

I look over at Mrs. Grayson. She's curling her fingers around a frayed strip of cloth on the arm of the chair. She's singing softly to herself. I can't be the one to tell her that her only child has disappeared.

Malaika folds her arms. "Shortly after they left, the police came, looking for Davis. Now, you know I don't tolerate anything that would bring the police here, Evan. What's going on?"

The best answer I have is the truth. "I don't know anymore."

Malaika reaches under the counter and produces a large sheet of paper, the size of a small poster. "The police dropped this off yesterday."

At the top of the poster, in huge, red block letters, it says MISSING. Below is a large photo, a school portrait of a guy with neatly trimmed hair and a clean school uniform. It takes me a moment to recognize the devil's smile. I glance at the information below—when he went missing, his stats, his distinguishing features—but I can concentrate only on his name.

Todd Sable.

"He's a runaway? But how . . . ? Wait, he's seventeen?" We always assumed he was older.

"He told me he was twenty-two." Malaika nods. "It's not the first time I've been lied to, I suppose."

At the bottom of the poster, it says: IF YOU HAVE ANY INFORMATION ABOUT TODD SABLE'S WHEREABOUTS, CALL 212-555-8615 OR THE NEW YORK POLICE DEPARTMENT AT 212-555-9800.

"If the second number is the police," I think aloud, "who's the first number?"

Malaika glances at the poster. "Possibly a direct line to the parents."

I glance over at Mrs. Grayson, who picks gently at her sleeves. I have no idea what to tell her.

Malaika reaches under the counter. "I believe Davis left this behind."

She places a small octagonal window on the counter. Backlit by a desk lamp, each picture glows with muted, ethereal hues. She pats it gently and smiles. "This is one of yours, isn't it?"

I know it intimately but my eyes still dart from scene to scene, memory to memory. An acrylic patchwork meant to celebrate a friendship, now a memorial to its passing. No colors or words can explain what brought us here.

When I don't reach out for the window, Malaika says, "I've been looking for some new art for around here. Brighten up the place. May I buy it?"

"It's yours," I whisper, curling up the poster. "Can I hold on to this?"

Malaika doesn't ask why. She smiles. "Good luck."

I gather Mrs. Grayson and we go back to my house.

My mother decides that Mrs. Grayson will spend the night at our house. As she settles Davis's mom in Shan's empty room, I fire up my computer. It's now when I'm most grateful for knowing Davis as well as I do. I go to Yahoo to access his e-mail account. Even if he's changed his password, it won't be hard to figure out the new one. He's nothing if not logical.

Or so I've always thought.

The password's the same: tardmonkey. I check the last few e-mails, the ones sent from Sable to the Chasers, and it all becomes clear.

> We don't have time to find out who squealed
> to the cops. We leave for NYC tomorrow.
> That's where we'll do the final initiation and
> you can call yourselves Chasers.

It's dated two days ago. The day after the unveiling of the *Angels*. The last time I thought I knew my future.

When Davis was still in town, I could reason with him. I would have waited, hoping to talk him out of sex with Sable or anyone willing to infect him with HIV. That's not an option now. I can't protect him if he's not here. I can only think of one thing to do.

I take the poster that Malaika gave me and flip open my cell phone. I dial, holding my breath, not sure what to say.

"Hi . . . Sorry to wake you. I . . . think I know your son."

letter

Dear Erik,

I love you but I don't know what to do. I want to see you or call you but I know you need space. I guess I'm settling for shoving this letter under your door.

Something big has come up. Davis has skipped town and I think he's in trouble. I've traded in the plane ticket you gave me for a flight to New York tomorrow. I'm sorry. I'll pay you back for it.

For the past year, all I wanted was to be what I thought you wanted me to be. But I can't be that guy. I've only ever been the outsider. With you, I found a way to let my guard down. You have no idea how hard it is to suddenly belong with someone. I got overwhelmed. I fucked up.

I kept so much of who I was hidden. Because I didn't trust you to love me. That was a mistake and I'm sorry. I let fear tell me what to do and I made quick, stupid decisions that I regret. But I hope you know the one thing I don't regret is loving you. I never lied about loving you.

I'm sure you want me to choose between you and Davis, and this might seem like I'm choosing Davis. I'm not. I have to protect him, even if he doesn't want me to. I learned that from you. Maybe I can try to make you understand when I get back. Or maybe you'll just want the money back for the ticket.

I don't know how long I'll be gone. I'll call when I'm back in town.

I love you.
Evan

TITLE: *Squiggles*

IMAGE:
Three blue squiggles and two yellow
circles on a white background

INSPIRATION:
Jackson Pollock

PALETTE:
Squiggles = aqua
Circles = sunrise
Background = milk

The blue squiggles are jagged, rough-
hewn, like surgical lacerations performed
by a madman. The circles are misshapen,
barely circles. There is at once chaos and
order, symmetry and spontaneity.

*Davis was sitting next to me in art class the day our teacher,
Ms. Blake, raved about the* Mona Lisa *replica I'd painted.
"You'd make a killing selling forgeries," she said with a wink.
Ms. Blake was pretty and young and probably exactly the kind
of teacher most other ninth graders had crushes on. Me, I was
just glad for the attention.*

"What you should do," Davis said as the bell rang and we filed from class, "is take your paints down to State Street this summer and do portraits of people. Charcoal artists do it all the time. If you're as good as Ms. Blake says, you could make a bundle."

"I don't think I can work that fast," I explained. "That Mona Lisa took me almost two weeks of nonstop painting."

But Davis was already gone, lost in a Boing that he was convinced would solve all our problems. Until that point, my painting had been a weird hobby to him. Suddenly, he saw it as a source of limitless revenue. Exactly what we'd been looking for so our plan could succeed.

That was the year we'd decided to disappear: leave Madison and never look back. It was one of the worst years with Pete and the trogs. Everywhere we went, they were there to dole out some new humiliation: atomic wedgies, cherry ICEE showers, or just random pummelings. And every time we'd sit down for a late-night dinner of Chinese leftovers in my room, our discussion would always storm toward escape. San Francisco came up. New York. Miami. Toronto. And each daydream dissipated when we realized that we weren't going anywhere without money.

We tried to raise the money. But double shifts at our jobs and the occasional lawn-mowing gig wasn't cutting it. So when Ms. Blake suggested that my work was on par with a great painter, it was only natural that Davis would see this as our next great venture. I was skeptical.

Like most Boings, I assumed the steam would run out of this one pretty quickly. Or so I'd thought.

One Saturday afternoon I trekked across town to the Phillson Art Gallery, maybe my favorite place in all of Madison. They offer free monthly art history classes; I haven't missed one in years. That's where I get my inspiration to study certain painters. Mr. Phillson, the curator, admires all artists. I don't think there's anyone he doesn't like.

I was sitting on a bench in front of a sculpture of a silo when I heard the door to the gallery open behind me and Mr. Phillson say, "May I help you, young man?"

A squeaky voice answered. "Yeah . . . I, uh, wanted to sell some art."

I froze for a moment and when I glanced over my shoulder, sure enough, there was Davis, leaning up against the counter near the front of the gallery. He was holding a small square window—a painting I had given him for Christmas the previous year. Squatting down, I ducked behind a nearby wall.

Mr. Phillson regarded the painting and then looked around, perhaps looking for a hidden camera. But then he smiled broadly and said, "I see. Is it something you're sure you can part with?"

Davis's eyes traced each line of the painting. "Well, it's kind of important to me. But it's more important that I get it sold."

That was the first time I ever doubted Davis. Watching

him shift from foot to foot, like he does when he lies to his father, I thought the unthinkable: He was going to sell my gift to skip town without me.

Mr. Phillson studied the painting for a few seconds. "A touch of . . . Jackson Pollock about it?"

Davis nodded enthusiastically. "Yeah. Yeah, Pollock." I was just glad Davis wasn't trying to pass it off as an actual Pollock.

Mr. Phillson picked it up and held it to the light. "It's very interesting. By a local artist?"

Davis crossed his arms and leaned in, obviously thinking Phillson was falling for it. "Yeah. Friend of mine. One of the best. Our teacher said he's a prodigy. There's more where this came from. He paints a lot. I can bring more in if you're interested."

Phillson's face fell a bit. It was clear he now felt he was leading Davis on and that it was time to stop. "Yes, your friend is very talented. I'm just not sure it's . . . a good fit for our gallery."

Shock lit Davis's eyes. "But I really need to sell it. Couldn't you at least display it? You know, hang it up somewhere so that maybe somebody else could buy it?"

"Why is it so important to you?"

Davis shoved his hands in his pockets and I thought he just might shuffle out without another word. Instead, he mumbled, "My friend is really good. I want other people to know that. I think his art will help him get out of this town. I figure if one of us can get famous or something and get out of here, it should be him."

I never heard what Mr. Phillson said in response. My mind reeled to hear Davis tell somebody that he thought I was good enough to be famous. And that fame would get me away from Madison, from the trogs . . . even from him. He was willing to walk away from our friendship if he thought it would make things better for me. I had never considered that an option. Somehow, it just seemed that the only way for things to get better was to stick together.

That was how things were supposed to work.

I was torn. Part of me was touched: He was ready to end our friendship if it meant one of us—me—could be saved. But another part of me had to wonder: Was he capable of the same thing? Would he move on if he thought he'd do better without me?

Here and now, I have the answer.

flight

The Dane County Airport isn't exactly a major Midwest hub, so I can only score a ticket on a puddle-jumper to O'Hare where I'll connect with the flight to LaGuardia. I've never actually flown before. The tiny windows look like mini canvasses. I'd love to get my paints and sketch the skies on the glass. I have a feeling the airline people would disapprove.

Waiting on the tarmac, I count six of us on the flight to O'Hare and I start to worry when the robust flight attendant—magna cum laude of the *Lord of the Flies* Charm School—begins eyeing us up to determine our weight and rearranging us in our seats. How safe is this if sitting in the wrong seat can send us spiraling to our deaths?

I shove my backpack—the one piece of luggage quickly packed for the trip—under the seat and buckle up. I lean back and close my eyes, hoping that I'll figure out how to find Davis once I'm in New York. I only have one clue as to where to begin and it's a long shot.

The light through my eyelids dims and I open my eyes, expecting the flight attendant to harass me again because my inconceivably low body weight will place us in jeopardy unless I scoot a millimeter to starboard.

It's Erik. He has a battered camouflage duffel bag slung over his shoulder. My throat closes just when I need oxygen the most. I might not survive this much happy.

He stares down at me for a long time, unreadable. I miss my DictionErik. Since I last saw him, all definitions are defunct. Time to recatalog, redefine.

He glances at the empty seat next to me.

"You'll have to ask der Führer," I whisper, nodding at the flight attendant. "Sitting in the wrong seat could make us all die a lot."

I can't believe I'm fucking making jokes. I can't believe he's here.

Believing is something I need to do more of.

He shoves his bag under the seat next to me as a mechanical buzz shakes the plane. The propellers rev and I catch a pungent whiff of jet fuel. Erik slides into the seat, soundlessly but bursting with color.

"Mr. Benton says you've made some . . . interesting friends."

Once he's strapped in, I position my hand atop my

knee, like a lure. It takes a decade, or maybe it's a moment, but he entwines our fingers and gives me an encouraging squeeze.

We say nothing on the flight to Chicago; we just draw energy from being together again. Once we're on the 737 to New York, I rechannel that energy and break down. I cry. I sob. And I tell him everything. My parents. Davis. Pete. Sable. Chasers. And how much I love and don't want to lose him.

He lets me get all that off my chest and it takes almost the entire flight to paint the full picture of how terrible I am and how rotten I feel for treating him the way that I have. I'm sure once we touch ground, he'll want to turn around and go back to Madison and that will be the last time I ever lay eyes on him again.

The only sign I get of what's going on in his mind is when he says, "You might not have been talking about us when you asked about situations where you're forced to hurt someone you love. But I was definitely talking about us when I said that sometimes you have to cut your losses. You need to decide if you can be honest with me. Because it doesn't seem like there's been a lot of that. Otherwise, I'm going to have to take my own advice about moving on."

I don't speak as we descend. I don't have to. Because now he knows it all.

—————

I always ignored Shan when she complained about how expensive it is to live in New York City.

My bad.

The price of everything is obscene and I didn't plan well, grabbing just a handful of cash for what I assumed would be a quick trip. The cab from the airport to Shan's apartment building in Hell's Kitchen nearly wipes out my entire budget. Hopefully she can suggest a cheaper way back to the airport. That is, if she doesn't mind seeing us. I sort of forgot to mention we were coming.

So when we buzz her apartment and she comes down to greet us, it's with a mixture of happiness and confusion. I get a hug; Erik gets a nod that he returns with an equal amount of discomfort. She escorts us to the elevator and eyes our luggage. I give her the fifty-cent version of why we're here.

She rolls her eyes. "And M and D are . . . ?"

"I'm off work the next couple days," I explain. "We'll be back in Madison before they realize I'm gone. I hope."

Shan sighs heavily. "Let's catch this on the replay. You hopped on a plane to New York, didn't tell M and D you were leaving, didn't think about how you'd get around, didn't plan on a place to stay, and you're looking for Davis but have no clue where he is." She shoots Erik a blame-filled look.

He narrows his eyes and lowers his voice. "Hey, doll,

I'm just da musk-ell. Skeezix over dere, he's da brainz."

God, he's sexy when he's weird.

"*You* should know better," she snaps, again at Erik.

"Okay, the mad needs to stay over here," I pipe in, pointing both thumbs at my own chest. "Erik was—" I stop myself from saying, "Not supposed to come," and finish with "—a last-minute angel."

"And there's sort of a plan," Erik says. "We just need a base of operations—"

"Chez Big Sis." I smile.

"And someone who can tell us where to find . . ."

He jerks his thumb at me and I produce the slip of paper on which I've written Mrs. Sable's address. Shan takes it and whistles.

"Seriously? This guy lives on the Upper East Side?"

I retrieve the address. "Used to."

"Wow," she says. "Major dough in the family."

I'm still reeling an hour later after we've dropped our stuff off at Shan's and she's given us a subway map and instructions on how to get to Sable's address. Given his ratty clothes, I'd imagined Sable as a bum, living out of a cardboard box in an abandoned warehouse in Harlem. Not the beautifully manicured historic brownstone that matches up with the address Mrs. Sable gave me on the phone.

We ring the bell and I almost laugh when the door

opens. Mrs. Sable has the same long face as her son, sharp cheekbones but rosier cheeks. Her curly hair spills down to her shoulders. Her gold necklace shimmers in the sun. She's wearing a burgundy dress that stops just below the knees.

"Mrs. Sable?" I ask, even though I know there's no mistaking her. "We spoke on the phone. I'm Evan. This is Erik." I want to say "my boyfriend" but I take nothing for granted. "We were hoping to talk to you about Todd. Maybe get a look around his room? See if there's something that might tell us where he is?"

She smiles in a way that's more sincere than anything I ever saw from her son. "Of course, Evan. Won't you come in?"

She leads us into the house and up a winding staircase. The forest green wallpaper is laced with gold flecks. A bright silver chandelier twinkles like a fallen star over the entryway. She takes us down a short hall and into a bedroom. It's not quite the cardboard box I'd imagined but I can easily see Sable—Todd—living here.

Heavy-metal posters hang lopsided on the walls. Heaps of clothes litter the floor. A series of shelves near the window holds a ragtag collection of antiquated cameras. The bed, of course, is unmade. On a small desk in the corner sits a small pyramid made from translucent brown prescription bottles.

"I appreciated your phone call," Mrs. Sable says, her voice heavy and soft. "I've been desperate for news about Todd. I can't imagine how he ended up in Madison, but you think he's back in Manhattan?"

"Pretty sure," I say.

"And you came all this way to find him?" She's a little suspicious now, probably wondering if he's in trouble. She has no idea.

"We think he's traveling with a friend of ours," Erik says and the thought of Davis being Erik's friend too makes my hands go cold.

"You know," she continues, "not long after you called to tell me you thought Todd was back in New York, a friend of his showed up and said Todd couldn't make it, but he was hoping to get some things from his bedroom. He promised that Todd would be around soon. I didn't know what to do. I didn't want to say no and possibly send my son even further into hiding, so I let the young man take what he wanted. My main concern was that Todd wasn't getting his HIV medications. But his friend just took an address book and a camera."

"What did he look like?" Erik asks. "The friend who came for the address book?"

She describes him. Average height, blue eyes, blond hair. Davis isn't average height. It's probably Mark. I'm not sure how many Chasers came with Sable.

"Mrs. Sable," Erik asks, "do you know where your son might be? Did he have any usual hangouts?"

She shakes her head. "I checked most of them after he disappeared. No one's seen him."

Erik squints at a framed photo on the wall and I join him. It's a black-and-white shot of the New York skyline at night. A thin haze—smog—distorts the lights from the buildings and I instantly know why he took this shot: The haze effect makes the buildings look inverted, like it's all negative volume. A blue ribbon dangles from the frame—first place.

Erik asks, "But have you checked them since you knew he was back in town?"

Mrs. Sable smiles. She escorts us downstairs to a kitchen loaded with appliances and gadgets and copper pans hanging from a steel rack above an island. As she rifles through a Rolodex, jotting down addresses, I take a picture of Sable from the side of the fridge. Because he looks older than he is, it's hard to tell when the picture was taken. He's fast asleep and lying in a hospital bed.

"If you don't mind my asking," I say, "how long . . . how long has Sa—Todd been . . . positive?"

Mrs. Sable's face steels. "I should be used to talking about this by now, shouldn't I? Well . . . We thought that sending Todd to a boarding school when he was thirteen would be good for him. He was always a little rowdy. But he fell in with the worst element once he got there. Drug users. Six months after he started classes, he was infected by a dirty needle."

I look to Erik, who raises an eyebrow. Sable hadn't wanted to catch HIV at all. It was an accident.

Mrs. Sable stops writing, her eyes taking on that distant look I'd seen a dozen times before from Mrs. Grayson. "He . . . didn't take the diagnosis well. We tried to explain that there were medications and as long as he took care of himself . . . But he felt cheated. Angry. We had to pull him out of the school and have him tutored here at home."

"Why was that?" Erik asks.

Mrs. Sable looks down. "He became . . . violent. He would cut himself at school and shove his bloody arm at his classmates, telling them he would infect them. He kept saying that if he had to live this way, so should everyone else. We had a terrible fight in the spring. I wanted him to go to therapy to deal with his anger. That's when he ran away."

Mrs. Sable hands me a list with about eight places on it. Our fingers touch when I take the list. Hers are shaking.

Mrs. Sable sees us to the door. As we step over the threshold, she says, "I hope you find your friend. And if you see Todd . . . tell him he doesn't need to send his friends to pick things up. He's welcome here anytime. I really do want to see him."

I'm reading the list of addresses as we take the steps down to the sidewalk.

"Let's do this the smart way," Erik says, poking the list. "Let's go back to Shan's, get out a map, and plot out these places. We can save time if we've got a plan—"

Erik stops because I've stopped. Coming around the corner, head down, is Mark, wearing a sleeveless black shirt. He's hardly a yard away when he notices me. He shoots a look at the brownstone, then turns and bolts. I take off after him, Erik in tow. We chase him a block before Mark ducks between two buildings. As the alley dead-ends, he stops.

"Who's this?" Erik asks as we catch up. Before I can answer, Mark spins around, throwing a wild haymaker. There's a blur of arms. I flinch, then find Mark on his knees. Erik's hands grip Mark's wrist, now bent at what I can only guess is an uncomfortable angle.

I notice Mark sports a tattoo of a praying mantis near his wrist. The skin around the bug is pink and puffy, suggesting it's very new. It's hard to tell if he's grimacing at the way Erik's holding his arm or because Erik is also digging both his thumbs into the raw, freshly tattooed flesh.

Mark lets out a gasp as Erik gives his wrist a small jerk. He turns to me. "I'm guessing this is a Chaser?"

I nod. Mark tries squirming but falls limp with a little more pressure from Erik.

311

"Can we talk now?" Erik asks him.

"I thought you said you got beat up in middle school," I say.

"I did. Funny thing, the beatings stopped after my dad signed me up for jiujitsu."

"Yeah, I've heard that can happen."

"So." Erik returns his attention to Mark with another wrist twist. "Talk to me, Sparky. Where's Sable?"

hell

There's a reason so many gritty stories that take place in New York feature dimly lit streets with crumbling buildings. These streets really do exist. When the cab drops us off in some shadow-stained corner of the Bronx, a movie set unfolds. But there are no cameras or dollies reminding us it's fiction. This is all too real.

Most of the streetlights are out; the few that burn offer spots of murky white light that mark our path. The buildings seem to bow forward under the weight of their own misery. Or maybe they're under the influence of the midsummer heat that's making every breath a struggle. The distinct smell of urine saturates the air and there's garbage in the gutter. Erik holds up the address we got from Mark before he bolted, peering at it in the semidarkness. Then he points at the building dead ahead.

"That's the place."

The sidewalk vibrates with a thunderous trance beat and the basement windows, covered with newspaper, flash and flicker with magenta, aquamarine, and amber. A yellow sign on the building proclaims: CONDEMNED! A few chunky guys in tight T-shirts hang out on the front steps, making out. We step around them and descend the stairs to the basement.

Just before we open the door, Erik turns and holds my face in his hand. "We're going to get Davis and get out. If anything happens—if I tell you to run—you do it and you do it fast. I mean it, Evan. Run means run."

The door swings open, the sweet, earthy smell of pot hangs in the air with an iridescent luster. It's wall-to-wall guys. Party lights flash from each corner. The temperature goes up and my sweat glands go into overdrive.

Most of the guys are naked or wearing leather chaps. Some are in leather harnesses with silver spikes and studs. Tattoos paint almost every arm—a few insects but mostly plus signs and blood-red biohazard symbols. Everyone's moving to the pulsing beat, grabbing somebody else and going at it. Erik takes my hand as we navigate the sea of sex.

A lean, muscular guy in a bright yellow Speedo steps from the throng. His blond hair tumbles over his ears.

"Welcome, boys!" he shouts over the tumult. "Here to give or receive?"

The guy looks me up and down and Erik insinuates himself between us, looking up into the tall guy's face with a forced but friendly smile. "Looking for a friend. Name's Davis. Seen him?"

Blond Guy tries to steal another look at me and Erik sidesteps again to block his view. Blond Guy shrugs a shoulder. "You won't find a lot of names here. They don't matter much. If you just want a good time, check out the back rooms." He throws his thumb over his shoulder. "There's some fresh meat back there. Don't get too rough—I haven't had my shot yet."

Then he slithers off, pulling the first guy he sees into his arms. Erik leads me forward. I catch sight of a familiar face. Leaning up against a gutted fireplace, too stoned to stand on his own, is Del. He's got a drink in one hand and he's wearing only a pair of tighty-whiteys. I divert Erik to the fireplace and shake Del by the shoulders.

"Del!" I shout. He shoots me a goofy smile. "Del, are you okay?"

He gives me a big thumbs-up. "I'm next in line!" He raises a glass in celebration and takes a big swig. "Great party, huh, Rick?"

"I'm not Rick," I say, not knowing who the hell Rick is. "Is Davis here? Who all came from Madison?"

Del tries to concentrate. "Just me. Me and Mark. And

315

Davis. Me and Mark and Davis. With Cicada. Have you met Cicada? Cool guy."

I point to the back rooms. "What's going on back there?"

Del grabs his crotch and makes a grinding motion with his hips. "We're becoming Chasers! We're getting the gift!" Some guys overhear this and cheer in celebration.

A flash of strobe light, an errant glance, and I catch my reflection in a mirror on the wall. It's Shan staring back, disapproving, the frown she wore all summer. I wonder: *Is this scene what she conjures when she thinks about having a gay brother?* Would she believe me if I told her this sickens me? Yes. She knows better. She knows me. This place? Nothing I want.

"Come on!" Erik shouts in my ear, pulling me toward the back rooms. Del collapses against the fireplace rubble and laughs stupidly.

The hallway is dark and I can feel the floorboards beneath my feet give a little with each step. We pass by two rooms, each missing doors. Inside, two and sometimes more guys are rolling around on old mattresses, groping everywhere they can.

We get to the last room at the end of the hall. It's lit by a tiny lamp in the corner. The twin mattress on the floor is losing its stuffing. Alone, Davis lies on his back, a fading ember. His eyes are open, glazed. He doesn't move. I can see blood caked between his legs and on the mattress.

I kneel next to him, taking his head into my lap. His breathing is shallow. "Davis? Can you hear me?"

Erik does a quick checkup: pulse, breathing, pupils. He scowls. "We need to get him to a hospital." He rifles through a pile of clothes, finds the smallest pair of boxers, and slides them up Davis's legs. As he reaches the midsection, Davis flinches and cries out. I can't tell if it's pain or fear. Davis's eyes grow wild, looking around like he's just woken from a bad dream. "It's okay," I whisper, but he can't seem to hear me over the music.

"Help me," Erik says, throwing Davis's arm around his shoulders and hoisting him up. I grab Davis's other arm. He hangs limply between us, his head bobbing uselessly. Dazed, he manages small steps.

We mow our way through the labyrinth of writhing bodies and we're almost to the door when suddenly all of Davis's weight is on me. Erik has been yanked back into the room. Sable towers over him.

"What the fuck do you think you're doing?" Sable's bloodthirsty voice is the only thing loud enough to drown out the ear-splitting beat. He's in his black trench coat, his hair held back in a ponytail. I try to warn Erik but Davis slips from my grasp and I struggle to keep him from hitting the floor.

Erik holds up his hands. "The kid needs medical attention. I'm a nurse. We're just going to take him to the hospital."

And then, Mark is at Sable's side, burning hate at Erik with his eyes. Sable puts his arm around Mark's shoulders. "My friend says you weren't very nice to him. I don't think you're gonna be very nice to Little Dude. In fact, I don't think Little Dude wants to leave the party. Maybe you should just leave."

Erik nods. "Yeah, that's the plan. But Little Dude's coming with us."

Lightning fast, Sable reaches into his coat and brandishes a knife. Mark lurches forward but Erik demonstrates his prowess again, tossing Mark aside. Erik reaches up with both hands to wrest the knife from Sable. They struggle for control. In a moment, I lose sight of the knife as it disappears below their waistlines. I hear Erik yell, "Evan, get out! Get out now!"

I pull Davis tightly to me and I push our way out the door. I drag him to the street and lower him to the curb. I turn to go back for Erik when he plows into me. As I go to steady myself by holding him, my hands are bathed in a thick wetness, and we both collapse to the ground.

damage

If I could assign physical coordinates to a nightmare, it would be the corner of Eighth and Baker in the Bronx: St. Mary's Hospital. The familiar, odorous antiseptic sting yields to vomit and scarcely diluted ammonia. The walls hemorrhage three different shades of plaster and drywall. The floors are a collage of neglected stains and missing tiles.

I am not alone. Nearly two dozen others sit, waiting for medical attention. We are all presided over by a gum-chewing, rumpled-scrubs-wearing slackass at the admissions desk, paging through his newspaper. He doesn't care that some of these people are bleeding.

The blood.

First Davis, collapsing to the sidewalk. Then Erik and me.

Blood everywhere.

I remember hysterics, all me. Desperately yelling for

help. Flagging down one of the few cabs in the neighborhood. I can only imagine the driver's reaction to watching me shove two men, both of them bleeding, into the backseat, all the while screaming "Hospital! Hospital!" over and over, pressing my hands on Erik's wound.

When we arrived, they whisked Davis and Erik off quickly because, by that time, we were all soaked in blood. I only narrowly avoided an examination room myself.

No. I'm fine. Take them.

I stumbled my way through admissions—paperwork, questions—and talked to a cop who is apparently on duty at the hospital at all times.

No, officer, just an accident at home. That's why he's bleeding. Nothing to report.

I was dying to turn in Sable. But Davis is already in trouble with the law back in Madison. Getting the cops involved here will only complicate things. Sable's free for now.

Unless something happens to Erik.

Then I sat. I waited. I wait more.

I want my paints. My brushes. I want to stand outside on the sidewalk, peering in through the grimy window, ready to capture the moment when Erik comes out from behind the swinging door, good as new. Because he can't

die. Not over something stupid like this. He wasn't supposed to be here. He shouldn't pay for my mistakes. He's
going to come through that door. And I have to paint that
moment of emergence. I need to.

At one thirty a.m., Davis, in an oversized shirt and
pants that came from God knows where, is led into the
waiting room through a swinging brown door. The thin
doctor has a hand on Davis's shoulder. The doctor looks
tired. Davis still looks dazed. I wave and the doctor brings
Davis to me, guiding him to an adjacent chair.

The doctor must believe the "we're brothers" line I
put on the admissions form because he addresses us both
very frankly. Results of the STD screening will be available in two weeks. A tear in the anal wall, risk of infection, prescribing antibiotics as a precaution.

"We don't have PEP," the doctor says.

"What?"

"Post-exposure prophylaxis treatment. If there's a
chance he's been exposed to HIV, it needs to be treated
with the urgency you'd treat a gunshot wound. In other
words, immediately." He yawns. "We don't have PEP here
but he should get it and soon. The longer you wait, the
greater his chance of contracting HIV."

This is a hospital! Why don't you have it? I want to
scream. Then, instead of telling me where we can find it,
the doctor narrows his tired eyes.

"Your brother is not responsive so I'll ask you: Was this consensual?"

I don't know what to say so I nod.

The doctor brandishes a small pill bottle filled with antibiotics for the possible infection from the tear in Davis's skin. I must have taken it; it's in my hand. I'm only half there. I won't let my eyes leave the swinging brown door. The one keeping me from my boyfriend.

"Erik," I half shout, when the doctor tries to walk away, "the other guy I came in with. How is he?"

What lie had I told about Erik? Another brother? A friend? Or had I finally stopped telling lies about Erik?

Thin Doctor holds up his hands helplessly and I'm sure he thinks that look is sympathetic. But he really looks empty. He disappears behind the brown ER door. Swing, swing. I get two quick glimpses into the room beyond. No Erik.

Forty-five minutes pass. Davis's head droops and I can't tell if he's doped up on pain pills or just being a dick. I spare him a handful of glances at times when I'm not eyeballing the brown door.

"Why are you here?"

This might actually be the second or third time he's asked. Davis's voice is low, unrecognizable.

"We're waiting for Erik." My voice wavers when I say Erik's name. I can't believe he's asking.

"Why are *you* here?"

"I am here," I return in anger, "to stop you from making a stupid fucking mistake."

A serrated grin carves Davis's face. He giggles softly to himself. "Oh. Of course."

I stand and try to peer through the diamond-shaped window in the brown door. I only see a paper curtain. I wonder if Erik's behind it. I want to paint that window.

Turning back, Davis is staring at me. Or rather, through me.

"You know what we should do? You know what we should do, Ev? Find a tattoo parlor. This is New York. There's got to be a twenty-four-hour tattoo parlor." He rolls up his sleeve, exposing his skinny left wrist. "A big cricket. Right there. That's who I want to be. That's my bug. A cricket."

My stomach implodes. *He only thinks he got the bug,* I tell myself. He doesn't know for sure. There's still a chance he wasn't infected. Still a chance that nothing happened.

But something happened.

As Davis's laughter gets louder, the cop I talked to earlier steps into the room. He glares at Davis. I smile weakly. This sort of attention is the last thing we need. I grab Davis's face.

"Listen," I whisper, "I need you to just calm down. Okay? Erik will be out soon, we'll all go back to Shan's for the night, and tomorrow we'll head home."

"Home? What is that exactly? Home to Mommy and Daddy's store? Home to a secret boyfriend? Home to what, Ev?" he seethes.

I don't have an answer to this. I swallow. "We'll figure that out."

Davis guffaws loudly. The cop starts toward us and I shrug an apology to him. I hold up the bottle and give it a shake, hoping this says, *I just need to give him his meds.* Cop nods but doesn't take his eyes off Davis. I make like I'm opening the bottle.

"Oh, that's fucking great, Ev. *We* will figure it out. You, me, and . . . Erik? He into threesomes?"

"You and me," I reply evenly. "We will figure this—"

"Why? Why would I want to figure anything out? Especially with you? What is there to figure out, Ev? Better yet, just tell me what it is that you have to contribute?"

His hands ball, his breaths escape in howitzered bursts. As he shifts in his seat, he winces in pain, favoring his right side. *Tear in the anal wall. Risk of infection.*

"C'mon, Ev," he continues through bared teeth, "I want to know why you came here. What you thought you'd save me from."

"Sable—"

"*Sable* saved me!" he spits, cauterizing what remains of our friendship. "From Madison. From my dad. From you."

Just like that, I'm back at the Orpheum, in line for *Rocky Horror*, being rejected. Back then, it stung. Tonight, it decimates.

"Sable," Davis says, "gets me. He knows a lot and he's got a lot to say and you just never wanted to listen to him. He could have saved you too if you'd given him the chance. We could have come to New York together, you and me. But you had your little secret. *Erik.*"

Never say Erik's name with that tone again.

Davis leans forward. "I got saved. What did you get?"

"Sable is weapons-grade crazy!" I finally retort. "He hates the world. He's pissed off that he got HIV and all he wants to do is infect everybody he can."

I've given him what he wants. Davis eats my fury and regurgitates a smile. "God, I feel so stupid. You know, I stood up for you. Sable said you didn't understand HIV, what a gift it is."

"It is not a gift!" Cop shoots me a look when I shout. I'm shaking with rage. More softly, I say, "And deliberately infecting someone—"

"I wanted it!" Davis is calmer than ever now, as if some sedative has kicked in. "I asked for it, Ev. He didn't trick me into coming to New York. I asked for what you and I always wanted. Acceptance. And now I got it. Having HIV means I'm *somebody*."

He puts his hand on my knee. I nearly jerk away.

He whispers, "It's what we wanted, Ev. You can still have it."

I think about Mr. Benton, choking down countless pills, doing whatever it takes to fend off the virus. This was nothing Mr. Benton asked for. It was not a gift, a status symbol.

I make one more attempt to reach Davis. "Did we want the same thing? Did we really?"

Davis slinks down in his chair, shaking his head. "I can't believe I tried to tell Sable you'd come around. He read you better than I could. I told him you'd get it. But you don't. You won't. This is just like you."

He waves his hands in front of his face and makes an explosion sound.

"What are you talking about?" I ask.

He jerks his thumb toward the ER. "How soon before you screw things up with Lover Boy? Wanna take bets? I mean, if you haven't already. He didn't seem too happy back in the park in Madison."

"You don't know anything about Erik," I counter.

He holds up a hand. "But I know you, Evan. You're going to do what you always do. Hide behind your paintings, your windows. 'Look at me! I make pictures so I don't have to deal with real life! I copy other people's work and that makes me special.' Hell of a lot of good it did you. At the end of the day, you still don't belong. You're pathetic."

I can't respond because a short doctor pushes through the swinging brown door and surveys the room. He's gripping a clipboard. Dark stains mar the front of his purple scrubs.

"Evan Weiss?"

I go numb and I hear every TV medical drama I've ever seen play out in my head. *I'm sorry. We did everything we could. He lost too much blood.*

I stand, trembling. The doctor smiles and motions me over with a nod of his head. When I approach, he shakes my hand and for the first time in this hellhole, I feel reassured.

"I'm Dr. Munro," he says with a bass so potent I could swear it's James Earl Jones. "Sorry we kept you waiting so long. Erik begged me to come tell you he'd be out soon."

My lungs ache and I realize it's because I'd momentarily stopped breathing.

"He's okay?"

Munro nods. "He's got quite a deep gash. Took a lot of stitches to patch him up."

"He lost . . . a lot of blood."

Munro scrunches up his face in a "naaah" sort of way, which makes me love this man. "I'm not saying it wasn't a nasty wound but it looked a lot worse than it was. I'm sure it hurt like hell, though. But I'm supposed to tell you that he was very manly and didn't cry or anything." Then he mimes crying as if to say, *Erik bawled like a baby.*

I laugh and that's when I notice a set of rainbow-colored rings on a chain around the doctor's neck. He gives my elbow a squeeze and says, "Give us about ten more minutes and I'll have your boyfriend back where he belongs."

At the end of the day, you still don't belong.

Goosebumps prickle my skin and the color seems to spring back into the room. I plop down in a chair across from Davis, relieved and exhausted.

"When we get home," I say softly, "you should go see your mom. She panicked when you didn't pick her up at Mendota. She misses you."

An aborted retort catches in his throat. It's possibly the only bull's-eye I'll score tonight.

As promised, Erik emerges from the emergency room minutes later, walking stiffly and wearing an ugly plaid shirt I've never seen before. But he's got a tired smile on his face. I march up to him and say the only thing I can think of.

"You suck at jiujitsu."

He shrugs. "Yeah, I'm thinking there's a reason I never brought it up. Couldn't have you thinking I was less than perfect, right?"

I glare at the hideous shirt, yellow and green intersecting like a thousand crosshairs around his chest. It's completely clean but I'm convinced that if I stare long enough, I'll see the blood again. Erik's blood. Sable's blood?

Erik models the shirt with a labored runway twirl. "You like? They gave it to me to replace my old shirt. It's the newest from Milan. The pinnacle of hospital lost-and-found-box haute couture."

"Did he . . . ?" *Bleed on you.* I can't even say it.

I don't have to. Erik gives my shoulder a weak squeeze. "I don't think so. I don't even know if he got cut. But I'll get HIV tests for a while, just to be sure."

I throw my arms wide. He points at his wounded side.

"Evan, I love you, but hugging me now is grounds for—"

"Breaking up?"

"Vivisection."

He hands me his cell phone.

"There are, like, thirty messages from Shan. I would have answered but I'm on pain meds and might have accidentally told her what I think of her. Didn't you call to tell her where we are?"

No. No, I didn't. When we get back to Shan's place, we're boned.

The three of us catch a cab. My eyes never leave Erik, who winces every time he shifts to get more comfortable. Davis doesn't say anything the rest of the night. We make it back to Shan and Brett's around two in the morning. After a tongue-lashing from Shan, we bivouac down. Erik gets the spare bed to himself. My tossing and turning would aggravate his wound. Davis and I get sleeping bags on the living room floor. Davis is out cold when his head hits the pillow. I flash back to any number of nights we did this in my bedroom. I wonder if he's dreaming the same thing.

No. He's not.

As I drift to sleep, I keep hearing Davis tell me that I'm going to blow things with Erik. *Like you always do.*

I think about Oxana. *Where are you, Mr. Weiss? Where are you?* Everything she said shoots through me. I'm a prism, each word splintering out in a spectrum of colors I alone can see. All this time I've been following. Painters. Chasers. I never stopped to think where it all led. Now it finally makes sense.

At the end of the day, I can sweep my brush across the glass and capture a moment, but I'm stupid to think I'm in control. In shaping my art, I'm the one who's shaped. In distilling what I know and what I want to be, I'm forming a path. To art. To yoga. To Erik.

At the end of the day, the picture creates me.

TITLE: *You Are Here*

IMAGE:
A street map of Madison with a large star
labeled YOU ARE HERE

INSPIRATION:
Picasso's *Composition with Skull*

PALETTE:
Background = dun
Street lines = helio blue
Street names = raw umber
Star/YOU ARE HERE = magenta

From early in Picasso's Cubist period, the
street blocks are deliberately misshapen,
crooked and angled. By contrast, the
streets themselves are almost unerringly
straight. The star's girth is exaggerated, the
words are slanted and harshly sketched.

When I was nine years old, I met Davis George Grayson.
   *Not like we should have: in a class or on a playground. But
in a gutter. Where he found me crying.*
   I had run away. My one true rite of passage: the patient

*zero of childhood clichés. An impulsive decision over some-
thing Shan and I had fought about. Who knows what it was
anymore? At the time, it was world ending. Mom sided with
Shan so I stuffed a backpack with clothes and left.*

*Tears in my eyes, I marched off into the August heat wave.
I zigzagged down side streets and alleys, trying to lose anyone
who might follow me. Not that anyone would, but I had an
active imagination.*

*Then I lost myself. In a strange neighborhood and getting
hungrier by the minute. I tried to head home, but I had no clue
where I was.*

*Exhausted, I sat on a curb and cried, hoping someone
would take pity on me, tell me to click my heels three times,
and this would all be over. Then, a small shadow fell over me.*

"Hey," said a squeaky voice.

*I looked up and caught my first sight of Davis. His hair, a
farrago of sandy curls, fell down into his eyes. He hid his small
frame under a bright lemon-colored San Francisco T-shirt. His
jean shorts and sandals did little to mask his willow-branch
legs. I wouldn't have guessed he was my age—he was short
back then, too. But he was talking to me and that was all that
mattered.*

"Anything to do around here?"

*I expected taunts. "Crybaby!" "Whiner!" He didn't seem
to care that I was obviously bawling my eyes out. Already, he
was special.*

I sniffed back more tears and said, "What?"

He sat down next to me and jerked his thumb over his shoulder to where a teal moving truck was backed up to a beautiful house.

"We just moved here and I'm bored out of my skull. If we were still back in California, I'd go to the Boys and Girls Club or something. But I don't know what there is to do around here. They won't let me help unload the truck and I'm going apeshit."

It wasn't the first time I'd heard someone my age curse but it was the coolest swear I'd ever heard. Apeshit? Awesome.

I smeared my tears with the heel of my hand and gave it a thought. "There's a Chuck E. Cheese over by East Towne Mall," I suggested.

He nodded. "That's cool. I rock at air hockey. Is East Towne far?"

I had to admit: "I have no clue where I am. I . . . took a wrong turn."

Davis didn't even blink. Instead, he pulled a neatly folded brochure from his back pocket, opening it to reveal a Madison street map. "Mom's terrified I'll get lost so she makes me carry this," he explained, pointing to the map. "She even marked our house on it." A lopsided star, crudely drawn in red marker, branded a spot on Wells Drive. He tapped it with his finger and said in a mock deep, authoritarian voice, "You . . . are . . . here."

I traced the streets and found Pinckney and Gamble, the corner of our store. It was embarrassingly close, only a few blocks. I must have spent the better part of the afternoon going around in circles. I thought I'd gone an incredible distance, only to realize I was practically back where I'd started.

"Come on," Davis announced, standing. "It looks pretty easy."

"I can find it." I stood, securing my backpack to my shoulder. "You don't have to—"

But he was already walking down the sidewalk, holding the map out in front of him like he was following a compass. As I scrambled to catch up, we were stopped by a high, wavering voice. "Davis?"

Mrs. Grayson hasn't changed much since I met her. She was barely real, even back then.

Mrs. Grayson moved with tentative steps to the edge of the driveway, eyes darting nervously for unseen predators.

"It's okay, Mom," *Davis called, then whispered to me.* "What's your name?"

"Evan," *I whispered back.*

"Ev here is just showing me around the neighborhood."

Mrs. Grayson's eyes raked over me but I'm not sure she actually saw me. I must have passed inspection because she nodded absently and said, "Don't go far."

Davis smiled, and there was something gentle and reassur-

ing in the gesture. Just about to start third grade and already taking care of Mom. "We won't."

We turned and made our way up the sidewalk. Davis heaved a sigh. "She's getting better. Her therapist got on her case to give me a little more space. Back in California, I practically wore a leash."

And it all came out during the walk back to my house. Everything. His life in San Francisco. His mother's emotional descent mirroring his father's growing distance from the family. I can't imagine that kind of candor now; I have no idea how Davis managed it at nine. But I also couldn't shake the feeling that he needed to share all this. And he'd decided I could be trusted. Me. I never told him but that's when I first felt love for Davis.

When we got back to the store, I invited him in.

"You live over a grocery store?" Davis asked, grinning. "That is so cool. It's like your own personal buffet." In fact, it wasn't like that at all. Anything we wanted from the stock was taken out of our allowance. But why explain and ruin my newly instated coolness?

Dad was at the register reading the paper. He looked up long enough to see it was me before going back to his reading. I grabbed us each a Dr Pepper from the cold case and we sat outside on the steps of the store.

I don't know how long we talked. He told me about living in California and I tried to indoctrinate him into the concept of cheese and brats, two staples he was going to need to embrace to make it in Wisconsin. I told him about Grant School, where we'd both be starting third grade in a few weeks. When it looked like it might be getting dark, Davis got up to leave.

"So, I guess I'll see you in school?" I asked.

Davis scrunched up his face. Here it was at last. The admission that he didn't want to be caught dead with me, like everyone else. But then he said, "What's wrong with tomorrow? I have some unpacking to do in the morning. We should do something when I'm done. There's supposed to be a lake around here, right?"

Davis had a lot to learn about the isthmus city.

"You can show me that."

We agreed where and when to meet. Then Davis walked home.

Sometimes I imagine an alternate life for Davis. A life where we didn't meet that stiflingly hot August day. A life where Davis just showed up as the new kid in school, an unknown quantity with bright eyes and an infectious smile. I wonder if we still would have ended up as friends. Did I doom him to a stagnant social life because he showed up to school with me, the class joke?

In that alternate life I picture, Davis made friends with everyone who ever ignored me. He instantly received everything he wanted: recognition, belonging. He never got beat up. He never went to extremes to fit in.

But that's my imagination. In reality, I have no reason to believe Davis would have been popular even if we hadn't met. But I also never thought I could be loved by someone like Erik. That alone tells me anything is possible. And if there was a chance Davis could have been someone else without me. . . .

I don't have many regrets. But I told myself years ago that if Davis, even unknowingly, sacrificed another life to be my friend, I owed it to him to be the best friend I could. To always stand by him. To make sure he never once regretted helping some dumb, lost kid find his way back home.

Back then, getting home was the answer. Today, nothing's that simple.

gone

The next morning, Davis is gone.

I'm the first to notice. When I wake up, his sleeping bag is empty. I'm not surprised. But I don't raise the alarm. I sit cross-legged in the middle of the floor for a long time, just staring at the vacant bag. Something in me wants to be angry. But I'm too numb to respond.

Shan and Brett stumble out to the kitchen, followed shortly thereafter by Erik, wincing and clutching his side. It only takes a moment for them to register exactly what has happened.

This is the point where anyone else would give up. We'd done our best. We got him back. Time for things to be over. But that's not what happens. These people who have every reason to be angry with me for countless lies and evasions, these people who should turn their backs on me—these people mobilize.

Brett spreads out a map of the city. "I was in the

kitchen about an hour ago for a glass of water. He was still here then. He didn't have any money so he can't have gone far."

Shan grabs the cordless phone. "He'll go looking for Sable. It's a long shot but maybe his mom can help us with other ideas. Find Sable, find Davis. What's her number?"

I turn to Erik, who is paging through the address book on his cell phone. "I'll call and get us a later flight."

"No."

I say this to everyone. It's not loud, but it's forceful. "It's time to go home."

We say our good-byes to Shan and Brett. Shan's hug, even though hampered by baby belly, is crippling, and she cries. She throws a one-armed hug around Erik, who smiles. As Brett talks Erik through how to catch the bus to the airport, Shan takes me aside.

"So?" she asks, a glance at Erik. She no longer looks disapproving.

"If he'll have me," I say. We hug.

"If he won't," she whispers in my ear, "he doesn't deserve you."

On the bus, I call Mrs. Sable. I let her know we weren't able to find her son. This is one lie Erik approves of. She thanks us, but her voice is hollow. I think she knows it's time to move on too.

An overhead chime assures us it's now safe to use electronic devices. Bullshit. If it's so dangerous to listen to my iPod during takeoff, why is it suddenly safe at 30,000 feet? I'd rather listen to the plane's engines than think I was responsible for crashing us into a cornfield by plugging into a podcast.

"So," Erik says, "does this crap with Davis have anything to do with why you haven't touched your paints in a month?"

The days of Erik letting me get away with stuff are gone. The King of Evasions is dead. Long live the king.

I relay the story Oxana told me about Picasso and his blue period. "All the time I spent studying painters . . . I only ever looked at their work. I never learned about their lives and understood *why* they painted. That's why my stuff sucks."

"Your stuff doesn't suck," Erik says. "Evan, everybody learns by imitating what they know. You just never figured out how to stop. Quit feeling sorry for yourself, pick up your brushes, and take the next step."

But I shake my head. "I'm done painting. I need to find something new to do with my life."

Before he can question me, I pull out Oxana's copy of Haring's journal and show him the passage that said every painting I've ever done is unnecessary. He scans it, then stares at me blankly.

"Did you read the *whole* thing?"

He points at the sentence just past the underlined text I read in Milwaukee.

> *If they are exploring in an "individual way" with "different ideas" the idea of another Individual, they are making a worthy contribution, but as soon as they call themselves followers or accept the truth they have not explored as truths, they are defeating the purpose of art as an individual expression—Art as art.*

I spent the last month feeling like Haring had called me out. Now he's vindicating me. Talk about a mixed message.

"Are you calling yourself a follower?"

I shake my head.

"Do you plan on exploring a little truth?"

I nod my head.

"Then I think you might have a shot at this whole 'finding your own voice' thing after all. I think that's what Oxana was trying to pound into that stubborn head of yours."

I gently close the book and slide it into my backpack. I'm not sure my stubborn head can take much more pounding. "Is he still working? Haring, I mean. Is he still painting?"

Erik's shoulders press back against the seat. "I thought you knew," he says quietly. "He died of AIDS."

Oh.

Erik turns to me and asks, "Do you want to move to San Diego?"

I whisper, "Do you still want me to move to San Diego?"

Erik slips his hand into mine; our fingers mesh together. This is the closest thing we have to an answer right now.

When I walk through the door back home with Erik at my side, I expect the world to spin out of control, faster and faster until centrifugal force pastes me against the wall. But, no. For once, I make an intelligent decision. One that took me a year to think about. Standing in my parents' kitchen, things slow down to a sane speed for a change.

"Mom. Dad. This is Erik. He's my boyfriend."

Mom blinks as she looks Erik in the eyes. "Do you live in San Diego?"

Dad squints as he looks Erik up and down. "Your head looks like a square egg."

It's Mom who suggests we visit Mrs. Grayson at Mendota. "She needs closure."

Don't we all?

We clip visitor badges to our shirts as a nurse escorts us down a pale white hall.

"Will she even understand what we tell her?" I ask as we approach Mrs. Grayson's room.

"She'll know," Mom says. "Mothers always know."

Mrs. Grayson's eyes are glassy. Her head bobs from side to side, a childlike smile on her face. Mom starts with small talk, which is sadly limited to how well the store is doing.

"Have you seen my Davis?" Mrs. Grayson asks. Her voice is oddly strong. Like she's fighting to be lucid.

I don't know what to tell her. Mom offers assurances so I don't have to.

"We'll keep an eye out for him, Clara. Let him know you miss him."

Mrs. Grayson nods sadly. For a second, I think she gets it. *Really* gets it. She knows she'll probably never see her son again. Then a nurse stops by and feeds Mrs. Grayson her evening meds. Soon, her head is swaying again. Any epiphany she may have had disappears. She doesn't have to worry about Davis now.

"So that's closure?" I ask as we stand to leave.

"Only for the lucky ones," Mom says.

———————

Later, at home, I find a set of really nice luggage in the living room with a bow tied to it. My graduation present.

I ask Mom, "If you knew about the ticket to San Diego, why didn't you say something?"

She's honest. "If I'd said anything, would it have made a difference?"

No. It wouldn't.

She heads down the hall toward her bedroom and says, "Next time, *you* can feel free to say something."

It's an invite. Not sarcasm. I'm not sure I'd know how to say something. But I like knowing I can.

Before bed, I write to Mr. Grayson, explaining that Davis is gone but not saying why. I hope he gets that he has to help his wife now. But I'm not holding my breath.

pentimento

My bare chest is pressed tightly to Erik's back, my arms scooped up under his arms, my knees nestled into the backs of his. I slide my face closer to his left ear. His breaths escape in furious bursts. I glance at the clock. Two in the morning. Time for restlessness to prowl.

The bedroom is stark. We spent the morning at my parents' house, loading up the U-Haul with everything I own. It was sad; I didn't even take up a quarter of the truck. Dad watched us from the store; he's still adjusting to the idea that I have a boyfriend. Mom kept busy in the kitchen, occasionally offering us lemonade or doling out odd bits of household advice. *Be sure to immediately wrap and refrigerate any leftovers. Never turn the thermostat over sixty-eight in the winter.* In the time it took to move my bed, my dresser, my paintings, and a gross of boxes, she gave me more advice than she had in eighteen years. But at least she tried. I stopped in the store before we left, telling Dad I'd be in for my shift tomorrow afternoon. He nodded but never took his eyes off his ledger.

We unloaded my stuff into the State Street apartment, took a break, and then began the much longer task of loading Erik's stuff back into the truck. He's leaving tomorrow for San Diego.

I'm not.

The plan is simple, so simple it's hardly a plan. Even though Mom and Dad have Ross now, I'll be working at the store until at least mid-December. I have income. And savings. To prevent Erik from paying a huge fee for breaking his lease, I'm going to sublet his apartment until December when the lease expires. After that . . .

We have to be sure, Evan. Maybe we just need to do a little more thinking. You have to know that you can handle my suspicions and neuroses and I have to know that I can trust you.

I de-spoon myself, moving to the edge of the bed where I stand and look down. Erik lies naked, undisturbed, on the bedsheets. I resist the urge to reach out and touch his shoulder. Instead, I take the plane ticket from my nightstand. It's the second one I've been given in as many months. This one is dated December 15.

There's e-mail. There's the phone. Hell, I'll even fly back a couple times as my schedule allows. I'm not giving up on us, Evan, and you shouldn't either. But let's slow down just a bit, take some time.

And I had to ask.

No. I won't be dating anyone. I'll be honest and say that I hope you won't either. But that's part of what this time apart is about. If you decide you need to see other people, all I ask is that you tell me about it. But I won't be dating anyone.

I step out of the bedroom. The living room's cerulean darkness is mottled with half-open boxes. I've attempted to spread my few possessions around to make it look homey. It's like trying to put rouge on an elephant. The hardwood cools my soles and I close my eyes and sway, remembering the times Erik and I spent dancing barefoot in this very room. We danced once more tonight. We made love—and it was magenta and taupe and sapphire—and when we were done, he held me gently as I cried. When I was cried out, I held him; it was his turn.

I won't lie to you. We both have some big decisions to make. And you'd better be doing some thinking because I sure will be. You might decide you're better off in Wisconsin or Chicago. I might decide I'm in no rush for a long-term commitment. Or maybe we'll both decide that the fifteenth of December is the start of Evan and Erik, Part Two. Whatever we decide, we have to make the right choice. Promise me you'll do some serious thinking over the next few months. Promise me.

I promise.

Propped up in the corner sits the antique oak mirror, orphaned so that I might have a lighter easel. My reflection as I approach is dark and nebulous, the streetlights spilling away from the mirror's base. I realize it's been two days since I last thought about Davis, worried about him. He would have found the mirror gaudy. He wouldn't have seen what I see. One big canvas.

So do it, Oxana coaxes me. *Paint your own Haring. Let it stand as a testament that it's time to move on and find out what Evan Weiss has to say.* I unpack my paints; it feels good to hold them again. I spread them out in the faint patches of light, squinting to read the labels. I begin mixing in the semidarkness, squeezing from tubes, picturing the hues and tints in my memory and hoping the dim light doesn't taint my perceptions. It'll be interesting to see what shades I've come up with, once the sun is up. I study the reflection, tall and lean, settled and unsettled, and begin to paint.

UNTITLED SELF PORTRAIT

INSPIRATION:
Keith Haring's *Radiant Baby*

PALETTE:
Background = too many colors to name
Body outline = black
Body fill = white

The background consists of jigsaw puzzle pieces, exaggerated in size, crooked and twisted. Each piece, bordered by thick black lines, alternates with a variety of hues of my own creation.

In the foreground, I am a faceless, featureless infant outline, squatting as though attempting to stand for the first time. Black lines—my radiance—surge out in every direction from my form. The interior of the body is painted in white.

But the portrait is unfinished. I have until December to mix the perfect color to fill in the last, unpainted portion of mirror. In the center of the chest, where the heart should be, is a silver, reflective hole.

A small, square-egg-shaped hole.

afterword

A daunting presence since the seventies, HIV and AIDS continue to exist as a global epidemic, affecting both LGBT and straight communities. More than 56,000 new cases of infection are diagnosed every year in the United States alone. One in five people infected with HIV is unaware that they carry the virus. This year AIDS will kill more than 18,000 people in the United States.

For more information, please visit the following websites:

http://www.avert.org/

http://www.cdc.gov/hiv/default.htm

acknowledgments

Endless thanks to the trifecta who made this happen: my agent, Robert Guinsler, and my editors, Anica Rissi and Annette Pollert.

Thanks to the following beta readers whose feedback was in-freaking-valuable in getting through all this: Charlotte Sullivan, Swati Avasthi, Nicholas Hupton, Susan Power, Brett Fechheimer, Mark Schroeder, Pamela Jo Pape Schroeder, Michele Campbell, J. Quinn Malott, Joel Anderson, and Trisha Speed Shaskan.

And my thesis committee: Lawrence Sutin and Mary Logue. I couldn't have asked for two wiser guides along my path.

Aaron Black, wherever you are, thanks for sparking the idea!

And, of course, all my love and thanks to Benji—my very own Erik—whose faith means the world to me.

about the author

To get to where he is today, Brian Farrey's path took this route: student, stock boy, waiter, college TV program director, local TV news promotions producer, community theater executive director, bookseller, community relations manager, and publicist. He'll leave you to guess which were willing choices and which were not. He currently acquires young adult novels for Flux. He holds an MFA in creative writing from Hamline University and lives in St. Paul, Minnesota, with his husband. He has an almost obsessive love of *Doctor Who* (both old-school *Who* and the recent reboot). You might find him skulking about www.brianfarreybooks.com.

Great reads from Lambda Literary Award winner
ALEX SANCHEZ!

Boyfriends with Girlfriends

Bait

The God Box

Getting It

Rainbow Boys

Rainbow High

Rainbow Road

NEED
A DISTRACTION?

READ ON THE EDGE WITH SIMON PULSE.

BRIAN FARREY

JASON MYERS

TODD STRASSER

LYAH B. LeFLORE

HANNAH MOSKOWITZ

ALBERT BORRIS

PETER LERANGIS

ROBERT MUCHAMORE